THE PRINCESS
AND
THE THIEVES
OF THE RED SEA

By

OMAR DINI

First Published in Great Britain in 2021 by Maple Publishers.

A CIP Catalogue record for this book is available from the British Library

First format ISBN978-1-915164-40-7
Second format ISBN 978-1-7395982-2-8
Ebook ISBN 978-1-7395982-4-2

ACKNOWLEDGEMENT

I learnt from my experience that writing a novel in a language you are still learning is really a daunting task. I started writing this book once I was less confident in my English language proficiency and was afraid of failing to complete it. However, with the help of some great individuals, I eventually did it and now feel proud of it. The extraordinary individuals who stepped to my rescue and injected life into my book are Simon J. Groombridge and Awad Dini. Without them, I would have never produced this book, and I am grateful to both.

I am particularly indebted to Simon J Groombridge, who edited my book to his best and filled the gaps in my English language. He came to my rescue once I gave up hope of publishing the book, and I abandoned it on my laptop. I would take advantage of this opportunity to express my deepest gratitude to Simon for his limitless and unconditional help.

Similarly, I am so grateful to Awad Dini, who hugely contributed to the book's marketing strategies and cover design and who was always ready to shore me up whenever I succumbed to the pressures of difficult times. Apart from his fantastic contribution to this book, Awad has built my website where this book and my other books can be found.

ABOUT THE AUTHOR

The author of **The Princess and the Thieves of the Red Sea,** Omar Dini, is an interpreter, writer, and educationist who lives and works in the United Kingdom of Great Britain. He was born and grew up in Somalia, and before he travelled to the UK, he worked in Mogadishu, the capital of Somalia as a journalist and was the founder of Qaran, a once widely read local newspaper. He obtained a BA degree in Creative Media Writing and Journalism with Communication Studies from Middlesex University, and later, he underwent a Post Graduate Certificate in Education (PGCE) course at Birmingham City University. Mr Dini is the author of Shabashaba and The Careless Elephant and the Rude Worm.

1

CHAPTER

A long time ago, in the beautiful back garden of a white palace perched on a hill overlooking a white sand beach from the west, mother Hibo, overjoyed to see her precious nine-month-old little girl taking her first steps, crooned 'Daa-Dah… Daa-Dah Daa-Dah,' which in her language means one step after another. Under the orange glare of the evening sun sinking behind trees and the west wall of this Palace's compound, Hibo holding her daughter's tiny hands and taking slow steps backwards kept repeating 'Daa-Dah … Daa-Dah' whenever the baby shuffled clumsily towards her. The mother and her daughter continued shuffling one after another until their journey ended at a nearby bench. Tears of happiness welling up in her eyes, because of her little girl's efforts, Hibo sat on the bench. She put her child on her lap, kissed her on the forehead and hummed:

My special one, the blessing of my eyes

As the morning sun warmth on earth

You warmed my heart from a chilling despair

You saved me from being a barren mother

You are a light which shone on me

The only heiress, the star of this kingdom

My dear daughter, be a good queen

And the beloved leader of this nation

After your father retires from power

The little girl's father, King Erek, was watching the interaction between the mother and her daughter from the steps of a back door of the building that opened to the garden. Overjoyed to see his little daughter starting to take her first steps and having heard the mother's song, he walked towards them. He approached them, his face flashing with happiness, and he sang out:

My special one, the blessing of my eyes

You heard what your mother said

Now it's my turn, Dhudi; listen to me.

Grow to be a gracious, beautiful girl

Be the wife of a respected husband

A charming prince and the brave

Be the mother of the prettiest girls

And of gallant boys, who lead the army

Be the future Queen of my kingdom

The rest of what I would say to you

Is in the secret yellow scroll

The wise man is keeping for you

God bless you, Dhudi, my baby girl.

Dhudi, the girl in the songs of the singing parents, was the only daughter of King Erek, the King of Zaila and the Thorny Land, and of his wife, Queen Hibo. Her parents sang for her so joyfully this evening because she brought unimaginable happiness into their lives. She was born after they'd been married for twenty-five years, once her mother was forty-nine and her father was sixty-five years old. Both parents believed Dhudi was a miracle sent to them by God, who decided to save them from being childless parents with no offspring to inherit their wealth and the kingdom. Queen Hibo and King Erek were a special couple, who shared a true love, and now they'd got a child to share that love with them. They fed her together to their best, and at nights before she fell to sleep, they heaped praises on her and told her she was the best. After she fell asleep, they prayed to God to keep her safe and hung a talisman they believed would protect her from evil spirits on the frame of her bed.

On her first birthday, they invited the most influential people in the kingdom and folklore dancers to a lavish party held on the beach to introduce her to the public as the princess of Zaila and The Thorny Land. At the beginning of the party, Hibo carrying her daughter put her down and set her free on the beach, then the little princess taking tottering steps, ran into a crowd of men dressed in white sheets, Asian shawls and embroidered caps, and women had on long garments with colourful fringes, pearl beads and beautiful sashes strapped across their chests.

The crowd looked at her admiringly and gave her way as she passed them, running around aimlessly. She carried on tottering towards another small gathering of religious men in white thaubs and turbans with different colours and officials, among them the Chief Minister of the Kingdom. When she approached them, the Chief Minister picked her up, and he said, 'Our little princess, happy birthday to you.' Her parents, who followed her wherever she went and guests attracted by her beauty and her energy, joined the Chief Minister, holding her up. Afterwards, people at the party began to talk about how gorgeous and active she was.

Beneath the congenial late afternoon weather, her party went on as planned, and Dhudi was at the centre of the people's attention until the party ended. In the evening, when the family returned home, her parents gave her a nice bath, rubbed special oil on her body, fed her well and put her in her bed, then told Dhudi, giggling at them, that she was going to be the Queen of the nation one day.

When she became a toddler, they taught her reading, writing, good manners, and other necessary life skills. Her two parents gave her everything she needed physically, emotionally and spiritually. Unfortunately, her world started crumbling when Dhudi, now eight, her mother died. It was a terrible, shocking death that left behind a void that no one could fill for her and for her father. Although Dhudi loved her mother so much and would miss her every day, she accepted her death after weeks. Sadly, her father, who loved his wife so dearly, was depressed and remained in unusual mourning. A sorrow that refused to go away hung over him as he was convinced life without his beloved Hibo was tasteless. He always remembered her and occasionally carried a bouquet of flowers to her grave in a cemetery behind an army camp on the south side of his Palace's compound.

2

CHAPTER

Two years after his wife's death, members of his council and chiefs, bothered by their King's loneliness, decided to help him. They came to him sitting in his private chamber, and the Chief Minister, Councillor Asseyr, speaking on behalf of the others, said, 'Our King, we're truly worried by your loneliness. It's more than two years since the death of your wife, and you're still unmarried. Your majesty, the council, has a proposal for you.'

'What do you have in mind?' The King asked uneasily.

'Your council wants to find a mother for your young princess. We want you to marry an intelligent and beautiful wife who can give you the support any great man like you would need.'

The King replied, 'Thank you for coming to help me, but you forget something important, my councillors.'

They looked at each other in surprise, and the chief minister asked, 'What have we forgotten, O king?'

'You don't realise that I'm too old to marry again and that there's no woman who can fill the void left behind by Hibo. My councillors, I don't want another woman to comfort me,' the King lamented.

'O King, although Queen Hibo was so special to you, please don't give up all hope of future happiness. Age doesn't matter. We want you to marry the most beautiful and intelligent woman in our land. Please respond to our plea and let light enter your home again.'

The King still loved his passed-away wife and wasn't interested in marrying again. Nevertheless, he respected his council members' proposal and accepted their offer. Weeks later, they married him to Idil Gabadah, a beautiful and intelligent woman who was cruel and greedy in the heart. She was a widow with two children, a girl with a small head that elongated forward and thin legs and a boy with a flabby belly. Idil tried to be a good wife to the King, and she endeared herself to his daughter. Disappointingly, her kindness came to nothing because the old King wasn't in the mood to entertain a woman, and Dhudi never liked her stepmother and her children. She treated them like aliens who had intruded into her family's life.

Idil was ambitious, and she ultimately aimed to take over the kingdom. So she continued to be nice to him and his daughter. Whatever she did, there was no love lost between them. Dhudi, avoiding her stepmother and her children, made herself busy with learning or going out with friends. The King wasn't interested in his new wife and stayed in his chamber most of the time. Idil, who loved the material world and wanted to have quality time with her husband and enjoy the wealth of the kingdom, detested the situation of the sad old King.

She went back to the council that had arranged her marriage with him. She explained to them his condition, and then they advised her not to give up the hope of making the King happy. They encouraged her to be patient with the King in this challenging situation. Idil Gabadah took their advice and carried on her marital responsibilities. However, her efforts changed nothing. As time went by, after one year, Idil made a horrible decision. She decided to get rid of the old King and take the kingdom. So, she spiked his food with poison, and he became seriously ill. Unaware of what his wife did to him, the King decided to relinquish his responsibilities to her before he died.

He called her and gave her the keys to the kingdom's stores, and he explained to her that there were two separate storerooms in the building. One next to their private chamber and a larger one in the building's west wing. He told her that there were two treasure chests and bottles full of dangerous poisons for battle arrows in the small storeroom, and there were new guns and other sophisticated weapons for defending the kingdom from the enemies in the large one in the west wing. He also gave her the list of other essential things in stores in the city and other properties of the kingdom. He requested her to look after his daughter and run the kingdom properly after his death.

Happy she had the keys to the kingdom's treasure, Idil promised that she would do whatever she could. When he'd finished with her, he asked her to call for him, Yusuf Saeem, the keeper of the kingdom's stores. She brought Yusuf in minutes, and the King looked at Idil, who remained in the room after getting the keeper for him and said, 'Can I have a private word with Yusuf?'

'Sure.' said Idil and walked out of the room, and the King continued, 'Yusuf, I think I'm going to die. Work with the Queen. She's in charge of the kingdom now.'

Yusuf replied, 'Your majesty, I will.'

The King went on, 'Dhudi's savings box and her special scroll do not include the assets taken over by the Queen. Keep them for Dhudi and give them to her when she's fifteen.'

'I will.' Replied Yusuf, who was a trusted man.

'One more thing. Never let my daughter know your secret name until she turns fifteen,' the king repeated, and Yusuf answered, 'I will, my king.'

'Now you off to go,' the King concluded, and Yusuf went away.

Hours later, Dhudi returned from school and came to her father grimacing in pain on his bed. As she usually did in the evenings when she returned home, she sat on the side of his bed and asked him, 'Father, are you alright?'

Finding it hard to breathe, the King turned his head on her side and said in a weak voice, 'I'm glad you came, Dhudi. Listen to me carefully.' He paused, groaned, and continued, 'It seems my time of being in this world is coming to an end. I shall be leaving you in a treacherous world where you'll be without your parents. Anyway, don't be afraid to face the challenges ahead of you. Be strong and resilient. You can be who you want to be.'

'Father, don't worry about me. I know I can be who I want to be if I work hard. What happened to you? You were fine when I last saw you.'

'My daughter, I don't know what happened. Anyway, it seems that I'm departing from this world. Try to live a good life and follow the instructions on the secret yellow scroll, which Wiseman keeps for you when you grow up.

You'll only have access to it when you're fifteen, four years from now. At that time, you'll be mature enough to understand the instructions on the scroll. Until then, your stepmother will take care of you.' He paused.

'*I hate my stepmother*,' Dhudi was about to say. Instead, she asked, 'Father, who is Wiseman and what is writing in the scroll you've mentioned?'

He winced with pain, and as though he'd planned to answer her question later, he continued advising her. 'After I die, if you need help, there are good people who can help you. Sultan Kandhafo of Awsa, remember the sultan, who came to us after your mother died with his wife and the son you liked to play with, my Chief Minister, and my cousin, the Governor of Thorny Land and the City of the Five Gates, can help you when you need help.' He paused again, breathed hard and carried on, 'Not only will Sultan Kandhafo and Governor Ebbie or the Chief Minister help you, but there are other reliable clan chiefs and loyal members of my council in this city. Remember, all the information you would need is in the secret scroll.'

Before he could tell her the names of the other reliable people and what was exactly written in the scroll and about the scroll keeper, he gasped for breath. He gripped her hand for support and began shaking. He convulsed and gasped for breath for seconds, then stopped breathing. Dhudi understood that something had gone wrong. She wailed, 'Father, please don't die.' She shook his emaciated body and tried to resuscitate him, but her efforts were in vain.

The news of the King's death spread throughout the country quickly. People in faraway villages and towns streamed to the White Palace to pay their last respects and express their condolences to his family. Over a thousand mourning people followed his coffin on the day of his funeral. Queen Idil, her two children and the King's heiress, Dhudi, were among those solemnly walking behind the coffin.

Following his request, the King was buried next to his wife's grave. That day people were coming to Dhudi, standing by her father's graveyard and were saying to her, 'We're sorry for your father's death. No one can stop death. Be strong and face up to your new life.' One of those who advised her was her father's cousin, Governor Ebbie, the ruler of Thorny Land and the City of the Five Gates. He was an uncle she had heard about him but she couldn't remember if she had seen him before.

People extended their condolences to Dhudi, now eleven, and they talked to her as the most important person the King left behind. Only a few people, including members of the King's council, extended condolences to Idil, and to her disappointment, no one paid attention to her children. At the graveside and on their way back to the White Palace, Idil could see Dhudi in the centre of the people's attention and that no one cared about her children. She started to think about what she saw unusually. She grudgingly looked at Dhudi and those who poured kind words on her several times. Then, afraid people to notice her actions and feelings, she told herself, *'Relax and think about this later.'*

3

CHAPTER

Her father's death was another terrible blow for Dhudi, who had now lost both of her parents. She felt emptiness, and her world began shrinking. However, the young princess took her father's advice of 'be strong, you can be who you want to be', and the advice was given to her by the people who spoke to her at her father's funeral. She decided to face reality ahead of her. 'Be strong. You can be who you want to be,' she repeated her father's words to herself. Tragically, things got out of her control immediately after returning from the funeral. An unbearable feeling of grief, worry and other unpleasant thoughts streamed into her head, and then these feelings turned into a gloomy sadness that prevented her from making the right decisions.

She couldn't sleep at night. The food she ate became tasteless. The Palace she had lived in since birth turned into nasty dark walls facing each other, and she didn't know anywhere else to go. Confusingly Dhudi only wanted to think and stay in her room. Unfortunately, the more she thought, the more she became confused, and she hated the world without her loved ones. On top of these, she couldn't get on with her stepmother and her two children.

As her sorrow and the worry of her solitary life took their grip, and there was no one to talk to, she wished to see the scroll her father had mentioned before he died in case there was a clue of help. In fact, there was vital information in the scroll as it enshrined the family's assets and hoards, the names of their friends and foes, and how her ancestors ruled the country for many generations. Also, there was exceptional advice for her in it. Disappointingly, there was no way she could have access to either the information on the scroll or the man trusted by her parents to keep it for her. The system allowed her to see the scroll and its keeper only when she was fifteen or over.

Thank goodness. Eventually, the young princess's painful grieving attracted the attention of some of the servants working in the White Palace. The first person who stepped in to support her was a female servant called Ladan. Ladan, worried about her well-being, one day went to her room. She came to her sitting on her bed with her head down. She sat with her and told her to stop grieving. She explained that things would get better instead of sitting in her room if she went out more often and made herself busy with activities outside the Palace and talking to people. Ladan not only advised her and left her alone to handle the situation herself, but she took her out of the Palace.

The kingdom's Palace was a two-storey rectangular white building with large arched windows and wooden doors. Its actual name was The White Palace, and it stood alone in a sprawling compound with several watchtowers. The harbour of Zaila and the city centre were spread-eagled on its north side. The camp of the kingdom's regular army and the cemetery were neighbouring it in the southeast. On this palace's west side, there was a horse racing track, an archery field and a stream that supplied water to the city during the rainy season.

It had a rear garden and two small rooms with metal doors, where the kingdom temporarily imprisoned people who had misbehaved. The bedrooms of the family and the monarch's private chamber were on the top floor of the Palace. The servants' quarters, a massive chamber for official meetings and arms stores were on the ground floor. The security men and their families were housed in shack houses on the northwest side of the compound.

Dhudi's bedroom was on the top floor, and it was a well-decorated and spacious room with all the things she needed. On the first day, Ladan took her to the back garden and narrated encouraging stories to her.

The following day they went to the beach to swim. On the third day, they went to the archery field and later watched a horse racing competition. After that, they kept going out together, and Dhudi began taking an interest in things outside the Palace. Before long, Dhudi decided not to remain in sorrow and sit in her room anymore. She started going out alone and joining friends she had in the city. She swam with her friends and participated in archery, running and jumping over hurdles races. She engaged very well in the community activities.

Within two months, she'd become a fully active and popular girl in the competitions and earned respect for her performances. Her vigorous daily activities, her good manners and the fact that she was stunningly pretty had drawn people's attention to her once again. In public gatherings, folks talked of her excellent skills, beauty, and intelligence. They dubbed her 'Beautiful Princess of Zaila', and they respected her as an influential person even while she was a simple teenager. Apart from her positive community engagement, Dhudi visited her parents' graves occasionally. She would sit beside their graves and pray to God for them whenever she went there, and after her prayers, she would tell them that she was doing well and not to worry about her.

She hugely benefited from her engagement with the community activities, but this was a wake-up call for her enemy. Queen Idil, who always disliked Dhudi but kept her feelings secret, abhorred hearing that people had dubbed her 'the beautiful princess of Zaila' and that they adored her exceptionally when no one was paying attention to her own children. She wanted her children to be respected as royal figures and be the kingdom's future leaders. She'd found it unbearable that people respected only Dhudi while her children were treated as though they didn't exist. She began to think of ways in which she could deal with her. It didn't take her long to devise a horrible, creepy plan to degrade Dhudi and boast of the quality of her children. She decided first to cut her from the outside world. Second, make her a servant who works for her and her children.

So, one day she called Dhudi and told her that her actions were not what a girl of her status should do. She explained to her that she was a member of the royal family, and for that reason, she shouldn't be mixed up with common people. Dhudi never believed that going out with her peers was wrong and didn't want to stay in the house the whole day. She rejected her instructions, arguing she loved the people she met outside and everything she did out. Sadly, Queen Idil, using her powers as the head of the royal family, instructed her to stay in the house and not to mingle with the ordinary people anymore. Even though Dhudi tried hard to gain her freedom to go out, ultimately, she unwillingly accepted the order of her stepmother and stayed in the Palace.

Another day, Idil came to Dhudi sitting on a bench in the White Palace's back garden, and as part of her brutal secret plan, she instructed her that she should assist people working in the Palace instead of sitting idle. Then Dhudi, who had no idea of her stepmother's hidden agenda and felt bored staying in the house without doing anything, agreed to work with the servants. She helped the cooks and servants. Every day, she assisted those working in the kitchen or others doing gardening and building repair services. She'd found it exciting to learn cooking and gardening skills, and the servants she helped liked her.

Queen Idil's covert plan wasn't over yet. Another morning she fired Ladan and another servant working in the kitchen, and then she instructed Dhudi to do their jobs until other servants could be recruited. Once again, Dhudi, unaware of her stepmother's creepy plan and expecting someone would take over the job soon, did what her stepmother told her to do. A week later, Dhudi, tired of doing alone the workload for two servants and wondering why on earth there were no people coming to take the job, went to her stepmother. She told her that she couldn't continue doing the job. Unfortunately, Idil, who had no intention of recruiting servants to do the work, became angry and screamed at her, 'Do the job. It's yours now.'

'No. It isn't my job.' Dhudi protested.

'It's yours now, and you must do the kitchen work and scrub floors,' Idil screamed again.

'No. I don't want to do it,' Dhudi screamed back.

Idil slapped her on the face and said, 'Do it, or you'll see the consequence,' and Heeto supporting her mother, hit Dhudi repeatedly with a broomstick.

Idil and her daughter beat her with sticks, punched her in the face and kicked her repeatedly until she fell. Queen Idil and her children forced her to scrub floors, wash their clothes and do the kitchen work, and at the same time, they took everything valuable away from her. Heeto took her well-decorated and spacious room on the second floor. They threw her clothes and books on fire, banished her to live in one of the two small cold rooms with metal doors for the prisoners, and forbid her from visiting her parents' graves.

Dhudi was now humiliated and had no choice have to work hard every day. In the daytime, she did the kitchen work and scrubbed the floors. At night, she used to sleep in an old bed with a tattered dark sheet in the small cold room, and when she could get some spare time, she would sit on a rusted chair also in the room and read a book that survived from the fire that consumed her other items.

4

CHAPTER

E nslaving Dhudi and confining her in the house didn't stop people from talking about her qualities. Visitors coming to the White Palace or others who had seen her elsewhere would mention how she was pretty and gracious. The people's comments bothered Queen Idil, who wanted her biological daughter, Heeto, to be the number one princess and inherit the kingdom after she died. She saw Dhudi as a real threat to her dreams. So, she hated people talking about her qualities, even after she made her a servant who scrubs floors. Feeling this unacceptable, she thought of what else she could do about her.

Before long, she hatched another horrible plan, but she decided first to consult with a fortune-teller, a lady who had a translucent Red Round Ruby, which, when you look into it, would show you what may happen in the future. Idil summoned the Fortune-Teller to the Palace and asked her to predict if there was a person who could challenge her leadership by any means and if Heeto could be the Queen of Zaila and the Thorny Land after she'd retired from power.

The Fortune-teller pulled out her Red Round Ruby from a pouch she carried. She put it between them and began reading some magical words she usually reads before looking into it. Dhudi, now fourteen and beautiful, entered the room with a kettle of herbal tea and two empty mugs on a wooden tray, the Fortune-teller in the middle of her reading. The fortune-teller stopped her reading at once and looked up at her. Dhudi was surprised by the quick look of the strange woman. She put down the tray next to the unique Ruby and walked away. As Dhudi was almost exiting the door, the fortune-teller twisted her neck to the side of Queen Idil and said surprisingly, 'This is the house of beauties. Is this the daughter you want to be the future Queen?'

'I didn't bring you here to ask questions. Look at your Ruby and tell me if there's anyone who can challenge me by any means and if my daughter will be the Queen after me,' Idil hissed angrily.

'Okay, my queen,' the woman said, turning her head back to the Ruby. She continued her reading of the magical incantation. 'The truth-teller, my good Ruby, Her Majesty the Queen of Zaila, wants to know if there is anyone who can challenge her by any means and if her daughter will be the future Queen of Zaila and the Thorny Land. Show her the truth and everything that may happen to her in future.'

In response to her request, the Red Round Ruby had shown Dhudi in a glamorous red dress, with a golden crown on her head and holding a bright sword in her right hand, dancing in the centre of the Ruby. It also had shown

Queen Idil, wrapped in ragged black cloth and her face heavily wrinkled, watching her in dismay from a corner.

'Your majesty... the Ruby has got something funny for you! It has shown you very old and wrinkled. But don't worry. Your daughter is going to be a queen after you get very old,' mumbled the Fortune-teller, still looking at the images in the Ruby.

'Show it to me,' she'd snatched the ruby from the Fortune-teller and looked into it, and then Idil surprisingly cried, 'This is ridiculous. How can it happen?'

'My queen, your daughter, is going to be a queen when you get old,' the Fortuneteller repeated.

'The in the picture is my servant,' said Queen Idil, shocked by what she had seen in the Ruby.

'The... then w… what I see isn't good for you, my queen,' the Fortune-Teller stammered. 'The good Ruby, look at the future again and show the queen the truth of her future,' she commanded the Ruby.

'Show it to me,' barked Idil reaching for the Ruby before the Fortuneteller could even look into it.

They simultaneously looked into the Ruby, and the Fortune-Teller was terrified by what she'd seen. Carefully selecting her words, she said, 'My Queen, I'm sorry. What I see doesn't look good.'

'What's it? Explain it to me,' demanded Idil, squinting at the picture in the Ruby.

'My queen, it shows the same things, and each thing signifies something else.'

'Tell me what these pictures represent for,' The Queen, still peeking at the Ruby, said.

'The red dress on the girl represents blood. This means there would be a dreadful war in your kingdom. The slender figure and the happiness on the young girl's face are symbols of rare beauty and joy. The golden crown and sword in her hand symbolise power. Your sad face, wrinkles and black dress represent despair, emptiness and powerlessness. My Queen, I think your servant will take the kingdom from you by force.'

'This is impossible. Look in your Ruby again. What should I do to stop this from happening?' demanded Queen Idil, who was shocked by what she'd heard.

The Fortune-Teller then peeked in the Ruby again and said, 'My queen, to break this dreadful curse and the sadness heading to you must make a sacrifice.'

'What kind of sacrifice needs to be done?'

'You need to spill huge blood, feed many people, and celebrate God's goodness with your heart pure and sincere. The curse will break if you slaughter at least twenty large animals, feed many people, and create happiness in your kingdom. Your Highness, make your subjects happy, then the curse will break up.'

'I see! If that will solve the problem, I'll do it,' Queen Idil, feeling relieved, replied calmly.

After the fortune-teller had left, Idil, outraged by her ugly image in the Ruby, went to her dressing table and examined her face with a mirror. She found no wrinkles or creases on her cheeks and under her eyelids. She was still pretty. However, she was petrified by what she had seen in the ruby and worried about her children's future. Still studying her image in the mirror, she silently mumbled, 'Dhudi is a haunting problem.'

5

CHAPTER

The moment of breaking up the curse came. Two weeks later, Queen Idil, following the instructions given to her by the Fortune-teller, ordered her butlers and servants to slaughter over fifteen fat oxen and fifteen camels with large humps and to cook food enough to feed hundreds of people. She also ordered them to invite the people in Zaila to the palace. So the servants sent invitations to the people in Zaila, slaughtered the animals, and cooked enough food for many people. Then in response to the special invitation, citizens from different parts of the city and its surrounding areas streamed to the White Palace. Community elders, Queen's councils, army officials, youths, mothers and fathers with their children, male and female dancers in traditional dresses, people from all social groups matched to the White Palace, and Queen Idil smiling constantly, received them warmly.

Believing the curse would break up once everybody was happy, and she had done what the Fortune-Teller of Zaila had told her, she greeted people with her face flashing with unusual happiness and her heart glowing with remarkable kindness. 'It's a happy day, everyone, enjoy,' she said to the visitors. Even as part of her bid to make people in the kingdom happy, she gave Dhudi a nice fluffy blanket that day and told her not to work during the special occasion. The Queen, smiling constantly, kept telling people to feast as much as they wanted. The folks relished the warm welcome of the Queen and took her advice, then gorged on food, drank taste sherbet, and danced on the white sandy beach after they'd filled their stomachs.

The feasting and dancing continued until the sunset. Afterwards, Queen Idil, as happy as the feasted people, went to her private chamber. She sat on a couch and reflected on the way she'd handled the event. She evaluated the service of her servants, her performance during the feasting and if people were pleased. She was satisfied with the result and started to think about other things and the future.

While she was thinking, she realised that Dhudi would become fifteen soon and could lead an independent life. Afraid this might instigate a problem, she further thought about it. Then all of a sudden, a strange idea popped up in her mind. It wasn't a good idea, but she immediately liked it because she thought it would forever end her worries. That night she slept with the idea in her mind. In the morning, she summoned a servant whose name was Bedel Subagleh to her Private chamber. Bedel was a big, strong man with a serious face and bulging hazel eyes. He was the sailor of the Kingdom's fishing boats. Only the two of them in her private chamber, Idil said, 'Bedel, you are a chosen one. I selected you from many people who work for this kingdom because you have the qualities I need. I have a little job with a big reward for you. If you do it for me as I tell you, I will make you rich, and you will be one of those close to me. Are you ready to do this little job for me?'

Servant Bedel was thrilled with the Queen's request and that he would be rich. He smiled at her and happily cried, 'Your majesty, I'm more than happy to serve you. Just tell me what you want me to do.'

'Listen to me carefully. I want you to follow the instructions I'm going to give you exactly as they are,' The Queen said.

'Don't worry, my Queen. Just tell me what you want me to do,' he interrupted her impatiently.

'Well, I want you to take Dhudi on the boat tonight at midnight with this machete and get rid of her while everyone is in a deep sleep!' She put a big sharp machete wrapped in canvas in front of him and continued, 'Chop her head off and feed her to the hungry sharks in the far sea! She's a cursed person with many problems.'

Bedel, never expecting to hear such a thing, was shocked. His bulging eyes popped out of their sockets, his chews dropped, his body numbed, and he lost the words.

Noticing that he was in shock, Idil said, 'Bedel, answer me,' and then he uneasily growled, 'Your majesty...I...I can't.'

'You've already promised to do this. Remember?' She said.

'My queen, I can't,' he moaned.

'You must do it. Bedel because you'll be a rich man after you do this little job for me.'

'My Queen, I can't. I don't want to be rich for doing this.'

Queen Idil knew how to blackmail people. She thought for a moment and said softly, 'Bedel, you've children and a wife you love. I bet you don't want trouble for them, do you?'

'No, Your Majesty, I don't want trouble, but I'm not a killer. Please find someone else.'

'You already heard my word. As I told you earlier, you're the chosen one, and I'm giving you a big reward. Do the job if you want your family to be safe.'

Bedel was frightened when she threatened his family. He felt he had no choice but to do what she asked him to do.

He lifted his head up and grunted, 'Okay. I'll do what you want.'

'Take her with this machete. Cut her head off in the deep sea and feed her body to the sharks. Afterwards, bring me the machete with her blood. After that, you'll have your bounty and never be a poor servant again.'

Bedel was disgusted at what he was going to do. He told himself to be brave, do what the wicked Queen wanted at once, and never do such a thing again. Bedel took the machete to his boat at the city's pier. He put it in the boat's cab and began preparing other items he needed for the horrible killing. At midnight carrying a rope, a sack and a piece of cloth, Bedel went to Dhudi's small darkroom at the rear of the building. He came to her in a fast sleep. He gagged her with a cloth and tied her legs and hands together with the rope. Bedel put her in the sack and took her away to his boat. He bundled Dhudi writhing in the bag onboard and sailed the boat towards the deep sea. The sea was relatively calm that night, and the wind blew gently from the south to the north, and a bright moon, shining down from a clear sky, was sparkling on the water.

Thinking the girl gagged in the sack and frequently glazing at the machete beside him, he sailed the boat with the wind northward. When he reached far into the deep sea, he took the machete and went to Dhudi, still writhing in the sack. Holding the machete in his right hand, he dragged her to the boat's edge. He stopped in a corner, put down the machete, opened the sack and pulled Dhudi out. He sat her upright. He picked the machete up with his right hand, lifting it to sever her head in one blow. As he swung with the machete in midair, Dhudi, whose eyes dilated with horror, struggled to say something under the gag. She'd screamed an unheard scream and shook her head sideways in shock.

Bedel wondered what she was trying to say. He lowered the machete and stooped down to remove the gag from her mouth with his spare hand. As he took the cloth off her, he asked, 'What?'

'Bedel, what's going on? Why are you killing me?' She hysterically cried.

'Don't call my name. I'm a different person tonight, and I must kill you.'

'Before you do what you've decided to do, tell me your reasons. Why do you want to kill me?'

'I'm a servant, and the Queen has ordered me to kill you!'

'Why does she want to kill me?'

'You're a curse to her kingdom, she said.'

'That's unfair. You're breaching the trust my parents put in you. Don't kill me.'

'If I don't kill you, she'll kill my whole family, and I won't get the fortune she promised to give me after I kill you.'

'Do you know that taking the life of an innocent person is a big sin?'

'Girl, I've no choice. Stop talking,' said Bedel, who hated what he would do but was determined not to show mercy.

'That isn't true. Still, you've got a choice.'

'What kind of a choice do I have?' He asked.

Her eyes scanned things on the boat with the help of the moonlight and saw a piece of wood, and then thinking desperately, Dhudi said, 'Think of this. If you drop me in the ocean and leave me here, sharks will eat me in seconds. Don't be a cursed one, a murderer. Let the sharks and this dangerous sea kill me instead.'

Bedel didn't want to be a murderer. He felt that her idea was reasonable. So he said to himself, 'If there is another way that she could die why should I be a murderer?' After a brief silence, he said, 'That's fine, just wait.' He sailed the boat a bit further into the sea. Once he believed that there was no way she could survive in such a faraway deep sea full of monsters, he returned to her. He untied her and ordered her to jump into the water.'

Dhudi, dressed only in her flimsy night garment, grabbed the wood and dived into the water. It was a metre-long piece of flat wood and she put it under her chest when she got in the water.

He watched her holding the sides of the wood and the waves pushing her away towards the deep sea. He didn't lift his eyes from her until she disappeared in the distance into the deep sea. When he ascertained that she'd drifted away with the waves to the epicentre of the sea, and in his opinion, there was no way that she could survive in such dangerous water, he sailed the boat back to the town.

Frequently glancing back, just in case his eyes might catch a glimpse of something happening to her, he sailed away.

Her chest rested on the plank, and both of her hands gripped tightly onto its sides, and she floated away with the gentle waves towards the deep sea. Dhudi didn't know what would happen next or where she was heading. However, she decided to be calm and not lose her grip on the plank. Waves kept pushing her further and further into the deep sea. After she'd been in the water for two hours, she felt freezing cold and sick. She endured the pain with great determination. Sadly Dhudi started to faint, and the gentle waves changed into violent tides. 'Be strong, Dhudi, keep in control. Everything will be fine,' she mumbled, but she couldn't hold back the feeling that she was about to faint. Before completely blackening out, she managed to mumble again, 'God, protect me in your water. I'm in your hands, and that was it.'

6

CHAPTER

B edel Subagleh was sickened with what he'd done to the orphan princess. He could not avoid thinking about her figure, receding in the sea and the reward he would get for her death. Trying hard not to think about her and the prize, but he couldn't. Queen Idil's words 'You'll never be a poor servant anymore, Bedel,' and Dhudi's desperate question of 'Bedel, why are you killing me? You breached the trust my parents put in you' ringing in his mind he sailed his boat back to the city. His head reeling with these disturbing thoughts and wondering what would happen next, he carried on his journey.

Bedel in a state of confusion reached the city at dawn. He moored the boat on the side of the pier, and then carrying the machete he was supposed to chop Dhudi's head off, he walked to his house, which wasn't far away from the city's harbour. Not wanting to wake up his wife and children, he quietly opened the front door and entered the house. He silently closed the door behind him, and then, hardly making any noise, he tiptoed towards another door that opened onto the house's backyard. He passed the door and went to a chicken coop and a shed for his family's goats in the backyard. He approached the cage, opened it quietly, and grabbed one of the chickens inside.

The chickens, frightened by the hand that took one of them, clucked and ran around in the coop. Leaving behind the clucking birds, Bedel carried away the one he'd grabbed. He brought it near the goats' shed, and he slaughtered it. Bedel had spilt its blood on the machete, carefully spread it all over the blade, and then put the bloody machete on the roof of the goats' shed. He turned back to the dead bird lying on the ground and thought about what to do with it. Before he decided what to do next, his wife, who had heard the chickens clucking and the commotion in the backyard, and thought a badger was attacking their chickens, came out with a kerosene lamp in her left hand and a club in her right hand.

'Bedel, what are you doing here?' she asked, surprised to see her husband. He jumped over to the chicken, began plucking it and said, 'I'm preparing breakfast for our children, dear.'

She came close to him. She shone the lamp in his face, and suspiciously she asked again, 'Where have you been all night? I was worried about you.'

'Sorry darling, I should've told you before I left. I went fishing,' he replied, pulling up the chicken's feathers.

She looked around the fence and asked once more, 'If you went fishing, where is the fish you've caught?'

'I was unlucky last night. I didn't catch any. That's why I'm making the chicken for our breakfast,' he lied.

It didn't surprise her that her husband went fishing at night because he used to do that, but she wondered about the way he acted and why he didn't tell her in advance that he would be away fishing that night. He never went fishing without telling her first. Unsatisfied with his answer, she walked back to the house, leaving him yanking feathers from the chicken.

After he fed the family in the morning, he secretly went to where he'd put the machete. He grabbed it from the shed's roof and examined its blade to check if the blood had dried on it correctly. Satisfied with the result, he wrapped it in canvas and sneaked out of the house with it, heading to the White Palace. Hate and fear full in his heart, he came to Queen Idil, sitting in her private chamber upstairs. Then looking down to avoid their eyes meeting, he growled uneasily, 'Your Highness, the job is done.' He unwrapped the canvas and put the machete with the dried bloodstains in front of her.

'Well done,' she said. 'Now you've done what you've promised to do. I must do what I've promised to do.' She stood up from her seat and went to her bedroom. In minutes she returned with a pouch containing gold and money. She handed it to him and said, 'This is your reward, Bedel, but there's one more thing I must tell you.'

Bedel, frightened when she mentioned one more thing, hastily said, 'What's it, my queen?'

'Listen carefully to what I'm going to say.'

'Okay, my queen,' he replied hastily.

'Shut your mouth and spend the fortune I gave you wisely. Any mistake you make can cost your life and the lives of your whole family.' Never let anyone know or speculate about what you've done to the dead girl and the reward I gave you.

Her stark warning scared him. Anyway, Bedel never wanted to advertise the crime he'd committed. So he gladly promised that he would never let anyone know their horrible secret.

'You can leave now,' she said, and Bedel, grateful that his ordeal was over, got on his feet. As he exited the room, Queen Idil, feeling that something wasn't right in him, called, 'Bedel!' He stopped and turned. 'What's it, my queen?' he asked, his heart thumping with fear.

'I can read on your face the trouble you have inside. Handle yourself well.'

'Okay, my queen. I will,' he said and walked away.

Servant Bedel was not good at lying. He did not like those who tell lies, nor had he ever murdered anyone. Bedel was a man who cared for his family and his job as a servant. He started working in the White Palace at age fifteen, and even before that age, he often came to the palace with his father, a former butler working for King Erek. His job was as a fisherman for the king's family and others who lived in the kingdom's palace. He used to go fishing in the mornings and the evenings with his boat, and he would hand over the fish he caught to the cooks in the palace. He was one of the most trusted servants of the kingdom.

Today he hated himself because of what he had done to Dhudi. He also hated Queen Idil, who had used him to commit a serious crime. He wished that he'd never been involved with her. Cursing her under his breath, he walked away with the treasure to his house. On the way, he thought about what he would do with the prize and how he could conceal it from his wife. Unable to figure out a good plan, he arrived home and found that his wife and the children were not there. He felt relief at their absence. He entered the house, and he straightaway went to the backyard. He took a small shovel and dug a hole between the goats' shed and the fence's wall.

He buried the treasure in the hole and cleaned the fresh sand to make things look normal. Afterwards, he went to his room and stretched himself on the bed. In minutes he fell asleep, but it didn't last long. He woke up frightened and sweating. He dreamed of Dhudi saying, 'Bedel, why are you killing me? Do you know that taking the life of an innocent person is a big sin?' Not only had he heard her voice, but he also saw her image gliding before him, coming close to him and accusing him of what he had done to her.

He sat in bed, looked around the room, and when he realised he was alone, he went back to sleep. However, the nightmare returned. He heard Dhudi's voice saying, 'Bedel, why are you killing me? Do you know that taking the life of an innocent person is a big sin?' And her image sweeping down around him. He jolted from his sleep again, sweating. This time he was not alone in the room. His wife and their two children had just returned from the market and were in the room with him. She came to the side of the bed and said, 'Bedel, are you alright?'

He sat up in bed, breathing heavily and trying to focus. 'Yes, I'm fine. I just had a bad dream. Check the kids,' he said and returned to his sleep, wondering how he could cope with the torments of the nightmares that had begun to haunt him.

7

CHAPTER

I t's hard to expect that Dhudi would have survived the snapping sharks and the monstrous crashing tides that battered her in the middle of the sea. If you believe in miracles, it was a sheer miracle that she didn't die in the water that night. At midday the following day, she found herself lying on a yellow sand beach, basking in the warm sun shining down from a clear sky with the plank she'd grabbed on the boat at her side. Even though she'd lost consciousness in the sea, Dhudi didn't lose her grip on the plank. The raging tides kept pushing her away and away until they tossed her out of the water with her plank and left her lying unconscious on that strange beach.

Surprised at how she could survive in such a dangerous sea, she stood up and tested her limbs to check if they were functioning properly. Luckily she was okay, though she felt weak, and her legs were a bit numb. She looked around the beach and saw to the east that it was a green island. Amazed to see this beautiful land, she grabbed the plank and staggered inland. Curiously gazing around her from side to side, she walked a bit unsteadily into lush green woodland. After walking for a while, she approached three huts that stood inside a large fenced enclosure made of dry branches and logs. She stopped at the entrance and shouted, 'Hello, is anybody there?' But there was no reply.

She looked down and saw fresh footprints of people who went in and out of the entrance. 'Hello, is anybody in?' she repeated, though again there was no answer.

When she'd ascertained that no one was in the house, she leaned the plank on the side of the fence and walked in. She passed a recently made fire by the enclosure and went straight to the door of the closest hut. She cautiously pushed the door open and went in. She stopped near the door and looked around to see what was in the room. She saw two wooden beds, a big one and a small one, each covered by a white sheet. Also, she saw a table with two stools and a small fireplace close by the door. Under each bed, there was a small wooden box with a padlock.

On the table was a frying pan with a red cover and several coconuts, two of which opened on the top side. She went to the table and lifted the lid from the frying pan. She found in it some still warm lobster and juicy fillets of salmon. She sat on one of the stools, gobbled up the salmon fillets, and then guzzled the juice from one of the opened coconuts. After that, she turned to the lobster and drank more juice from the second coconut. When she'd gorged on the lovely food and the coconut juice, she explored inside the room once more. She looked at the two beds of different sizes and the two boxes, and she concluded that two people, probably an adult and a child, lived there. She began to feel tired and dizzy as she studied the things in the house. She rose from the stool, crawled onto the big bed and tucked herself up in a sheet. Immediately she fell asleep.

The house wasn't a safe place for a girl of her age. It was a house of thieves that lived on this forlorn Island. Nearly at sunset, Dhudi, still in a deep sleep, two of the five thieves who lived on the Island came back. They saw her footprints entering the fence and the plank she'd left at the side of the fence. One of them was a short man, and his name was Jamanjug. Jamanjug, staring at her footsteps, said, 'Gabi, look. It's a child. How did she get here?'

Gabi, wielding a club in his right hand, looked at the footprints and growled, 'Look at it properly. It's a woman, not a child, and she must have carried this piece of wood.'

'If it's a woman, she must be a jinni woman? And possibly she's in our house,' Jamanjug, gazing at her footprints, speculated.

Puzzled at this, Gabi asked, 'What makes you think she's in our house?'

'Because there're no returning footprints, the woman must still be inside,' Jamanjug replied.

'She could be in one of the two other huts. I'll check in our room. You go to and check Shaman, Daweel and Kalah's huts,' Gabi said to Jamanjug. Before they went in, the other thieves carrying their hunting spoils of that day arrived too. 'What's going on?' Shaman asked, and Gabi replied excitedly, 'Today, we have a visitor.'

'What do you mean we have a visitor?' Shaman asked.

'It's a woman, and she's in one of our rooms. Let's check the big room first,' Gabi said.

They all looked at her track and then marched to the door of the room she went in. Gabi in front, they stopped at the doorstep, and Gabi said quietly, 'Wait here for me. I'll check inside.' Hardly making any sound, he crept into the room. He lit a kerosene lamp hung on the centre pole of the house, and with the lamp's light, he examined the room. He saw a woman's head on the pillow of his bed. He froze with surprise. He slowly and silently walked backwards and mumbled to the others, 'It's a real woman, and she's in my bed.'

'Let us see her,' Kalah said, and they all entered the room and saw her head sticking out from under the bedsheet. Gabi was amazed at what he saw and grunted, 'Wow, she has a pretty face and long black hair.'

Before one of them said another word, she turned over, pulled up the sheet to cover her head, and continued soundly asleep.

Jamanjug looked at the table and uttered, 'Hey guys, she ate our food and drank our coconut juice.'

'She was hungry and thirsty and tired, I guess,' Gabi speculated. 'Why don't we leave her alone to rest?' Shaman added. 'I agree with him. Let us wait until she wakes up,' Kalah mumbled, and they all left the room. They gathered around the fireplace by the fence, and Daweel, who couldn't believe she was a real woman, said, 'Guys, I think she's a jinni impostor who assumed the shape of a human. If she isn't a jinni, how could she come to this Island?'

'Jinni doesn't eat food. She's a real human and could be a thief banished here by the Kingdom of Zaila,' Jamanjug guessed.

'There was no boat that recently came here,' Shaman argued.

'Then she's a mermaid who fell in love with Gabi,' Jamanjug joked.

'We'll find out who she's when she wakes up. Let us make our dinner,' Shaman suggested. So after that, they began making dinner.

These five thieves were criminals banished to this Island by the kingdom of Zaila, which had no mainland jails to keep the offenders. The kingdom used to send criminals to the faraway islands in the sea to separate them from the public for safety reasons. The Kingdom of Dhudi's father, King Erek, sent these five thieves here after committing various offences. They'd all lived on the Island, and each had unique characteristics and a nickname reflecting his physical or behavioural attributes. For example, Shaman was calm. He had a long, white beard and prominent eyebrows that rolled upward. He was a self-appointed healer and inaccurate fortune-teller, and his real name was Talah Faalshow, but they called him Shaman.

Daweel was tall and had legs as thin as sticks and a long neck. He was less intelligent than the others. They called him Daweel, which means 'the tall one,' though his real name was Ahmed Dhuubow. Kalah was a medium-sized man with big eyes, a stubby nose, and a massive bald patch, which mostly consumed his head. His real name was Takar Bisleh, though this name was history because everyone called him Kalah. He was a natural clown, but he was without the colourful dress for clowns. The name of the fourth man was Jamal Goley. He was a large man with tiny red eyes. They called him Gabi, which means 'the boulder', and he was a close friend of the group's smallest and shortest man, Jamanjug, whose actual name was Yarow Falah-Falah.

Jamanjug was a mischievous dwarf with fat fingers and flat feet. He always carried a quiver full of arrows and a big bow. He shared a hut with Gabi, and even though they ruthlessly insulted each other, they usually went hunting together and enjoyed being together. They'd grown up in the same village in Thorny Land. Both were tricksters who used to perform different hustling tricks before the security men arrested them. Jamanjug's father, who was also a trickster, had taught them their hustling skills when they were young. Kalah and Daweel were also hunting buddies, and they shared a hut. The oldest Shaman always hunted alone and lived in a separate house.

That night, after they ate dinner, they sat in a circle at the fireplace by the fence. They talked with their voices as low as a whisper about the strange woman in their house. They speculated further about how she could end up on this Island and how they would deal with her when she woke up. Before they went to their beds, they agreed that Gabi and Jamanjug would be vigilant, and If one of them noticed any strange things happening in the room or saw her wake up, they would instantly alert others. After that, they went to their beds, and Gabi took a small mat and stretched himself out by the door of his room.

At midnight in a time, the men were in a deep sleep Dhudi woke up. In the darkroom, she heard the men breathing and snoring around her. She listened to their sounds for a while, and then, not knowing what else to do, she returned to her sleep.

8

CHAPTER

———❧———

Dhudi woke up early the following morning while everyone else was still sleeping. She sat up in bed and looked around the darkroom. She couldn't see much as it was still dark, but she could hear the sounds of the two men snoring from different sides of the room. She listened to their noises and noted that one was in the small bed, and the other was by the door. She then slowly climbed out of bed and tiptoed to the door. Not wanting to wake them up, she quietly opened the door and stepped out of the room. Immediately after she exited the door, Gabi noticed her movement. He jumped from his sleep and yelled at once, 'Jamanjug, she's leaving!' Then Jamanjug expecting to hear such a call, jumped out of his bed too.

Dhudi, startled by Gabi's yell, stopped in the enclosure of the huts and turned back to face the man shouting behind her. Gabi and Jamanjug came out of the room in a hurry, and the other three men who heard what was happening also came out. Now the five men dressed awkwardly, and some of them rubbing their puffy eyes gathered around her and then Jamanjug asked her, 'Who are you, young woman?'

'I would like to ask you the same question,' she replied.

'I'm Jamanjug, and these are my friends. We're the owners of this place. Tell us who you are.'

'My name is Dhudi. I'm from Zaila. I drifted on this Island yesterday.'

They looked at each other in surprise, and Gabi growled, 'Hey, young lady, you're not a dead fish or an object just washed up on the shore. How did you get here?'

'I swam with that piece of wood,' she said, pointing at the plank she'd left by the fence's entrance.

'No one can swim with that little piece of wood all the way from Zaila to here. How did you get here? Tell us the truth,' Jamanjug grunted suspiciously.

'I told you how I got here. By the way, can you tell a bit more about who exactly you are?'

'We're thieves sent here by the kingdom of Zaila, and we live on this island,' said Shaman. 'Tell us more about you.'

'*Thieves from Zaila!*' She thought and then asked, 'Is that true? How long have you been here?'

'We're indeed thieves, and we've been here for four years, ' Shaman repeated.

Dhudi'd heard stories of nasty thieves that the kingdom of Zaila sent to Islands in the faraway sea. She was scared when she heard they were thieves. She said softly, 'I was a servant working for the Queen of Zaila and one night at midnight, a man, whom the Queen had sent to kill me, came to my room. He gagged me and put me in a sack...' Dhudi told them her story. However, she didn't tell them that she was a princess and the daughter of the late King of Zaila and The Thorny Land.

'I don't think you're telling us the truth. The ruler of Zaila is a king, not a queen,' Jamanjug said doubtfully. The King passed away four years ago, and his second wife is the Queen of the country now,' she replied.

'What was the reason the Queen wanted to kill you? Have you committed a serious crime?' Jamanjug asked her once more.

'I didn't commit any crime. The queen thought I was a curse to her kingdom,' she answered.

Shaman found it hard to believe her story. However, he felt pity for her and said, 'Whoever you are, and whatever reason you're here, welcome to Faay Island.'

On the other hand, Gabi had a different feeling about her. He was pleased that she was a real girl and became interested in her. His eyes dancing on her, he said, 'You're one of us from now on, miss. Feel free, and you can keep my bed until you get your own one.'

'No, Gabi, she's a girl. She can't share a room with two men. She will have my hut until she builds one of her own,' Shaman insisted.

'If that is the case, I'll sort out her lunch,' Gabi added.

'She can eat with Gabi and me,' Jamanjug offered, and Kalah yelled, 'Young lady, I'll show you how to hunt.'

They were kind and generous to her, yet there was a secret behind their offers. Each of them was interested in her, and Dhudi was unaware of their feelings. She happily said, 'Thank you, that's very kind of you.'

After they got to know each other, the men made a good breakfast, fed her generously, told her to stay home, and then went hunting. After they left, she began exploring the Island. Carefully studying her environment, Dhudi walked through the woods. She saw different kinds of lush green trees new to her, tempting wild fruits, but she didn't touch them as she thought they could be poisonous and charming flowers. She kept roaming in the forest, her eyes wandering until she emerged onto the beach. She walked along the shore, wondering how she could live on this Island with a bunch of thieves. Dhudi continued her tour until she felt tired and returned to the huts.

She ate some food and stayed in for the rest of the day. In the evening, she had a nice dinner with the thieves, and after they had finished eating, the thieves began telling funny jokes and entertaining stories at the fireplace by the fence. Their silly jokes and stories amused her. After enjoying their jokes, Dhudi went to the hut given to her by Shaman. She lay on his ragged bed and thought about the island and the thieves she found there. After thinking for a while, she felt uncomfortable living with five strange men in the same compound. So, before falling asleep, she decided to get her separate space as soon as possible and figure out what else to do later.

9

CHAPTER

***

Back at home, in Zaila City, Queen Idil did not doubt that Dhudi had died and that her problems were now over, but she had to cover up her death. As part of a misleading plan she devised after Dhudi's disappearance, she summoned the servants working in the White Palace and asked them if any of them had seen Dhudi lately. They told her that they hadn't seen her in the last couple of days. Then she instructed them to look for her. One of those she sent to find Dhudi was Bedel, who was disgusted at his role in her disappearance, and whose stomach churned up when she told him to look for the girl he left in the deep sea to die. He was among a group that went to the city and asked people there if they had seen the missing princess. Another group went to the archery field and the areas around it.

When the servants were exhausted looking for her, they returned to the White Palace. Then Queen Idil, pretending she was so worried for the safety of her stepdaughter, summoned the heads of the security forces and her interior minister and ordered them to look for her stepdaughter everywhere in the country. In response to her command, the army forces and many volunteers took to the streets to find Dhudi. One of those who gave their time to support the manhunt was Heeto, the queen's daughter. Heeto never liked Dhudi, but she did this for her mother, who advised her to show how she was anxious about the disappearance of her stepsister. Heeto, frequently twisting her little head from left to right to have a good glimpse of her surroundings, led a group of volunteers who went again to the Archery and Horse-Race Field and the area behind it.

Others, including Dhudi's friends, who genuinely worried about her wellbeing, went to the city outskirts and dump sites. One of these friends was a girl called Hani. Hani said to a friend with her, 'I think Dhudi escaped because her stepmother forced her to stay in the Palace after her father died.

The friend replied, 'Hani, you don't understand these people. They're aloof and snub ordinary people. They kept her inside only because she was a princess. There is surely another reason for her disappearance.'

'I disagree with what you said,' Hani replied. 'Dhudi wasn't aloof. She respected everybody, and her parents liked to be with ordinary people. I think the problem is her stepmother. Things have changed after the death of the King.'

Dhudi's search intensified day after day. Many volunteers came out to lend a hand to the efforts to find the missing princess. Unfortunately, whatever they did or wherever they checked, no one got the slightest clue of what had happened to Dhudi or where she was. The interior minister wondering what had happened to the young princess extended the search to other towns and villages around the country. Sadly, they ultimately gave up any hope of finding her.

When the minister and the security forces returned with nothing, Idil vowed not to give up easily. She organised men on horses and ordered them to look for her stepdaughter in the faraway villages and forests. After much travel and pursuit, the horse riders found nothing and returned to Zaila. Eventually, Idil, convinced that she had done enough and that her plan had worked well, sat back on her luxurious cushions in her private chamber. Then sipping a special aromatic tea she usually drank, she asked herself, 'What else should I do now?' And then, answering to herself, she said audibly, 'Nothing but have fun.'

10

CHAPTER

Dhudi would have giggled if she had been aware of her stepmother's false search back home. Instead, she was planning how to settle down in her new place. On her third day on the Island, Dhudi thought about how she could learn skills to hunt and get a place of her own. Her mind figuring out what to do, she left the house after the men went hunting. She walked towards the seashore, and then when she'd reached the beach, she turned left and kept walking alongside the sea without knowing her destination. Shaman has worried about her safety since she first came to the Island. He covertly followed her this morning and watched her from a distance. He did so because he thought she was vulnerable and afraid the thieves might harm her. After watching her loitering on the beach aimlessly for hours, he decided to share his concern with her. He approached her and said, 'Good morning, young lady. Did you sleep well last night?'

She smiled at him and replied sarcastically, 'I shared my accommodation with five strange men, and the bed I slept on wasn't mine. How could I sleep well?'

He smiled and enquired further, 'Do you have any plans to change the situation?'

'Maybe, if I get some help.'

'I'll help you if you tell me your plans,' he said.

'I would like to have my own hut and learn hunting skills.'

He again smiled at her and said, 'That's a good thought. Come with me.' Together they went to a large rock overlooking the sea from the sunrise direction, a spot he usually used to sit when he was fishing. They sat side by side on the edge of the rock, and then he gave her his fishing pole and a rod with a long string, and he showed her how to draw the rod with bait into the water. While they patiently waited for the fish to fall into their trap, he said, 'Dhudi, you're a young girl, and you live with thieves who have committed different crimes. I advise you to be careful.'

'Thank you, Shaman, but they're kind to me. Do you think they're dangerous?'

'I don't know. Even though we've been together for years, I haven't asked them about their crimes. Anyhow be careful.'

'Okay, Shaman,' she replied.

He carried on teaching her some necessary fishing and hunting skills that she would need to survive on the island. He told her of the resources available for her to build her hut. They talked more about life on the Island, what she could do, how he could help her, and what support she might get from the others.

At midday, Shaman and Dhudi getting on well with each other and carrying two medium-sized fish they'd caught, left the rock and went home. On the way, they further discussed her hut's shape and how quickly it could be built. Their plan was almost complete when they reached the house and started making their lunch.

In the evening, when everyone had returned from hunting and had dinner, Shaman said to the other men, 'Dhudi must have her cabin, and she needs our help to build it.'

The men looked at each other, and Gabi growled, 'No problem. We can help her; it won't take long to build the hut if everyone offers some effort.'

'Where should we build it,' Talah asked. Jamanjug pointed at a space by the enclosure door and hurriedly said, 'Just over there. That's a good place.'

'No. I don't want to share the same fence and toilet with five men. I need my own secluded area.'

'We can build it anywhere you want, but it's safer for you if we all share the same fence.'

'I need a separate room and toilet in my private enclosure,' Dhudi insisted, and the men happily agreed to her idea.

The next day they started building a small cabin with a toilet and private enclosure outside the men's huts. Each of the men worked hard to complete it quickly, and her hut was completed within three days, and then Dhudi moved in.

When settled in her new place, she carried on going fishing with Shaman, who became her close friend and cared for her more than anyone else. He taught her more hunting skills and told her educational stories, which widened her understanding of the world. He encouraged her to be strong and self-reliant. Dhudi absorbed his word and did whatever she could to survive and be safe.

Two months later, one day at late noon, Dhudi and Shaman were sitting on the rock where they used to sit when fishing and casting fishing rods in the water, Dhudi saw a boat sailing towards them. 'Look, there's a boat in the sea,' she shouted.

'Concentrate on your fishing line. Boats sail in this sea all the time. Perhaps it's one of the boats of the Southern Kingdom,' Shaman grunted as he wiggled his fishing pole sideways to increase his chance of catching a fish.

"When you said the Southern Kingdom, do you mean, it belongs to the Ajuran Kingdom," enquired Dhudi knew most kingdoms in the region but never heard of a kingdom named the Southern Kingdom.

'Yes, it's Ajuran boat, probably it's from Hamar to Aden. Anyway, forget about the boats in the sea. Let us focus on our fishing,' He replied looking at the sea under him.

The boat continued sailing towards the Island. 'Look, it's coming closer,' Dhudi shouted minutes later. He lifted his head and squinted in the direction of the boat. He recognized its flag and softly said, 'It's the supply boat. I didn't realise it's already the time when it used to come.'

'The supply boat!' Dhudi asked surprisingly. 'What does it supply for?'

'Sorry, I should have told you about it earlier. It's the boat that brought us here, and it comes here once every three months to supply some essential things for the prisoners scattered on the islands in the sea. The Captain counts the prisoners every time his boat comes and he brings some essential things to the prisoners in exchange for precious stones, shells and other nice things they find by the sea. You can order things you want from him, and then he'll bring them to you on his next trip in exchange for whatever you've got.'

It's from the kingdom of Zaila, and it's Idil's boat. What should I do? Dhudi thought about the boat worryingly. After moments of silence, she said, 'Please don't tell anyone on that boat about me. I don't want the Queen of Zaila to know I'm alive and live here.'

'Don't worry. I won't let anyone on it know about you. Go to your hut before Captain Boon and his men see you, and don't come out until they leave the Island,' Shaman explained. Dhudi hastened to her place without delay but it was too late. Captain Boon, standing on the bow of his boat and scanning the Island with old-fashioned binoculars, saw her leaving from the rock. Wondering about the uncounted female on the Island, he kept eyeing her until she disappeared into the woods. When the boat came close enough to the shore, he ordered his men to anchor it, bring down two canoes from the deck, and load the supplies for prisoners of this Island. After the men loaded the various items onto the canoes, he cried again, 'Get your weapons and let us go!' Each of the two canoes carrying three armed men and the things for the thieves on this Island, he started towards the Island.

Boon and his men approached the beach. They got off the canoes and went to Shaman and the other thieves who had arrived at the beach in a hurry when they saw the boat and stood there with their precious things for the usual stock exchange. Captain Boon, interested in the strange woman he'd spotted more than the lovely things the thieves had collected, gazed at Shaman and asked, 'Who was the woman perched on the rock with you?'

Shaman was shocked by his question. He decided not to tell him about Dhudi and said, 'What woman?'

'Don't play a game with me, old man. Who was the woman with you on that rock?' Demanded the Captain pointing at the rock they sat on.

'She's nobody,' said Gabi trying to help Shaman.

'I'll find out who she is. Are there other uncounted people living with you on the Island?' Captain Boon asked.

'No,' Gabi, grinning at him, replied.

Boon believed that something unusual was going on on the Island. He called his men to come with him, and then they matched towards the huts of the thieves. As they reached the huts, Boon ordered his men to spread out and search the area. Then, with one of his men assisting, he searched the men's houses one by one and went to Dhudi's hut. He found her sitting on her bed and asked, 'Who are you, young lady?

Dhudi, scared and unsure of what to say, remained silent.

'Answer me, girl. How did you get here?' He screamed.

'I'm an islander who lives here,' she replied.

'This place is a home for thieves. Are you a thief?'

'I am what they are,' she replied.

'You're not listed with us as a thief. What is your name?'

'Dhudi'

'Dhudi…' He paused, 'Dhudi who?'

'You can just call me Dhudi.'

'How did you get here?' He repeated.

'That's none of your business, mister,' she shrieked.

He carefully studied her facial profile and her physical complexion. He guessed her age, noted her height and hairstyle and colour, and asked her, 'How long have you been on this island.'

'Two months,' she replied.

'I think I know you. However, I'm asking you once more, how did you get here?'

'Please, leave me alone. I don't want to answer your questions,' answered Dhudi suspecting that he recognised her.

'Are you the missing princess?'

Instead of answering his question, her face fell, and she sobbed.

'Your stepmother, the Queen, is looking for you. Come with us. We'll take you back.'

'No, I'm not going anywhere,' she protested.

'You must come with us, princess. You're the princess of the nation. I cannot leave you here with a bunch of thieves.'

'I'm not a princess of a nation. I was the servant of Idil Gabadah. Leave me alone.'

'I'll take you back,' Captain Boon insisted.

'No, you can't. Go away.'

After she refused to go with him, he turned back and said to Shaman and the other thieves who huddled next to him, 'Guys, she's a princess. I can't force her to come with us. Keep her safe while I report this situation to the Queen. I hope the Queen will come to collect her very soon. If anything bad happens to her, you'll be severely punished.' The thieves were surprised to hear that she was a princess and didn't know what to say, but they promised she would be safe with them until someone came to take her back to the mainland. On the way back to the canoes, Boon asked the thieves, 'How did she get here?' and Jamanjug replied, 'She drifted onto the beach with a piece of wood.'

'That's very strange! Did she tell you about what had happened to her?'

Jamanjug attempted to answer his question, but before any words came out of him, Shaman poked him in the ribs. Jamanjug understood what that meant and then replied, 'No, she didn't.'

Captain Boon continued asking questions that no one was willing to answer until they came to the beach and started exchanging goods for supplies. After each side got what they wanted, Captain Boon headed for his canoe and shouted, 'Take care of her properly. The kingdom will come to collect her.'

11

CHAPTER

In Dhudi's opinion, the arrival of the boat from Zaila was a disaster for two reasons. First, her stepmother would know that she was alive and where she was and then she would come to get her. Second, the thieves she'd befriended would now think that she was a dubious person who had lied to them when she hid her true identity from them. Afraid of facing the thieves, she remained in her room after Captain Boon and his men had left. Thinking about those thieves who were banished to this lonely island by her father's kingdom and her stepmother who would come to kill her, Dhudi remained in the room.

At sunset, once the dinner was ready, and there was no sign of her, Shaman went to her room. He knocked on her door, but she didn't answer. He banged it harder, and then Dhudi, whose head hanging down with shame and fear, slowly opened the door.

'I'm sorry for what happened today. I should have told you about the supply boat prior to its arrival,' lamented Shaman, who could guess what she'd been through.

'It wasn't your fault,' she said.

'Let us go. The food is ready,' Shaman said, but her answer was, 'I'm not hungry.'

'Stop worrying. You can't change what happened. Come and eat something,' explained Shaman thinking she was only worried about the boat.

'Shaman, can you forgive me?' She muttered.

'What! I don't understand. What have you done to me?' He asked surprisingly.

'Because I hid my true identity from you and your friends. I shouldn't lie to you. It's shameful to lie to people who were helping you.'

'You didn't have to tell us everything, princess. We're a bunch of strange thieves, and you were running for your life. Come and eat some food.'

'Do they think the same as you do, Shaman?' Asked Dhudi feeling relief to hear that he wasn't holding a grudge for her.

'I think so. However, if there's anyone unhappy with what you did, say sorry to them.'

Belief the situation was different from what she thought she said again, 'If that's the case I'm coming with you.'

They came to the four men sitting in a circle at the fireplace by the fence and eating dinner. They sat with them, and Shaman served food for himself and Dhudi and said, 'Gentlemen, Dhudi is in trouble.' No one bothered to say a word. The chatty men usually played silly jokes on each other and were nice to her were utterly different that evening.

Dhudi, guessing that they were angry with her, said, 'My friends, I guess you're angry with me because I didn't tell you who I truly am?' She paused, waiting for their reaction, but no one said anything. She continued, 'I'm sorry I didn't tell you exactly who I am. I should have told you everything about me when I first met you. I missed the point. Please forgive me.' Even though her words were touching and reasonable, it seemed they had changed nothing. The men looked at each other as though they were silently asking among themselves what to say to her. Unfortunately, they just continued with what they were doing without saying a single word.

They were not angry with her because she didn't tell them her true identity. Most thieves initially saw her as a potential female partner and each one of them secretly wanted to form a family with her, but they stopped being interested in her when they realised she was a princess. So the beauty living among them tonight turned out to be an alien belonging to a different world.

Shaman decided to break the silence. 'Princess, can you tell us exactly why your stepmother wanted to kill you?' He asked.

'I think she hates me. As I told you earlier, the man she hired to kill me told me that I'm a curse to her kingdom, so she decided to end my life.'

'We're very sorry about what happened to you,' Shaman said sadly.

'Please forgive me. I didn't mean to lie to you,' Dhudi repeated, her eyes brimming with tears.

'Don't cry. You didn't do anything wrong,' Shaman, gazing at her, said. Then he looked at the men and continued, 'Guys, stop ignoring her. She didn't do anything wrong. She's a child in danger, and she apologised for not telling us her true identity.'

'I think we should talk without her first,' Gabi growled.

Then Shaman, who wanted to hear what was in their minds, said, 'Princess, would you please go back to your room,' and Dhudi, getting to her feet, quickly replied, 'Certainly.'

As she walked out of the enclosure, Shaman grunted, 'Mates, I don't understand why you were so mean to her. You didn't respond to her apology. She hasn't done anything wrong. She's a child in trouble.'

Kalah spoke first. He said, 'She's a princess, and we're thieves imprisoned here by her father's kingdom. Why do we care about her?' And the mischievous gnome, Jamanjug, hurried to say, 'I have an idea. She's a princess. We can use her as a pawn to get our freedom.'

'You're crazy. No one cares about her. She's a helpless orphan,' Shaman screamed angrily.

'Shaman,' Jamanjug interrupted him. 'She's a princess. If we hide her somewhere on the island and demand our freedom in exchange for her life, the queen will make us an offer.'

'That's a good idea,' Daweel mumbled, and Kalah added, 'She never told us who really she is. Why do we care about her?'

'Shut up! That's not a good idea. It's inhumane. Although we're thieves, we're good men. We must do what's right,' Shaman argued.

'Shaman's right. She's a young girl running away from someone who wants to kill her. We should treat her better,' growled Gabi, who had consulted his conscience and changed his mind.

'How about if I don't want to help her?' Kalah queried.

'You're free to choose what you want, Kalah,' said Gabi.

They kept talking until most men agreed to accept her apology, and then they went to bed. The following evening, after they ate dinner, Shaman yelled, 'Princess, we accepted your apology. Is there anything else you want to discuss with us?'

'Yes. Thank you all for accepting my apology, but I wonder if you can help me build a boat. I must disappear before my stepmother finds me here,' she explained.

'A boat! What made you think we could help you to build such a thing? We've been on this island for four years, and we never thought of making a boat to escape with,' Gabi explained surprisingly.

'Not a real boat. I just need something that can float with the waves and some food. I must vanish before Queen Idil comes to get me,' replied Dhudi, who had already weighed all the options open to her and decided to disappear before her stepmother came to find her.

'Why didn't we make one for ourselves and escape if we can build a boat?' Gabi repeated.

'People can do anything if they have the desire and a necessity compel them to do so,' Dhudi explained.

'Where will you go if you get a boat?' Shaman asked.

'I'll go wherever the waves and the wind take me. I may land in a safe land or Ajuran boats towards Hobyo and Hamar find me stranded in the sea. '

'That's insane,' Jamanjug said.

'She isn't insane. She has no choice. She's running for her life,' Shaman defended her.

'If I'm dying anyway, it's better to die in the sea,' she lamented. 'Please help me to improvise something that can take me on the water.'

In response to her request, Shaman said, 'Guys, let us talk about how we can make a small boat for her.'

'I don't know how to make a boat, and I don't think making a boat is that simple,' Kalah suggested.

'We can find poles, logs, sticks, bark, palm leaves and other things on the island and then we can build a small boat from them. Please help me,' Dhudi pleaded.

'I don't think making a boat is that easy,' Jamanjug mumbled.

'A piece of wood has carried me all the way to this island. Putting those things together can make a boat that can carry more than even a person. Please help me before she comes to kill me,' Dhudi implored.

'Let us begin it tomorrow. The Princess must leave the island before the queen and her people come to get her,' Shaman said in her support.

'Relax, guys. It'll take a month or more for those people to return to the island. There's no rush,' Gabi suggested.

'I doubt it'll take long for her to come here. Please let us hurry,' Dhudi, fearful, chirped.

'Princess, the captain of that boat, has to visit six more Islands in the sea prior to returning to the mainland. His journey will take a month. Don't worry. Your boat will be ready before he gets back to Zaila. Go to bed,' Gabi explained reassuringly.

'Wait a minute, Gabi. You're all wrong. If we help her to escape, the kingdom will punish us,' said Kalah remaining quiet since they were talking about her escape boat.

'He's right. Captain Boon will severely punish us if we help her escape,' Daweel having the same feeling added, and Jamanjug realising the danger her escape may result cried, 'I agree with them. Her escape will ruin our future release.'

'You're right, my friends,' said Shaman. 'But we can't allow that wicked queen to kill this innocent orphan girl.'

Gabi agreed with him, 'Shaman's right. We have got a moral duty to help her, even if we're going to be punished by the queen.'

They split up into two groups, two in favour of her escape and three against it. Shaman and Gabi attempted to persuade the others to help her, but sadly they refused. Gabi, who had made his mind up, stood up and growled, 'Don't worry guys, Shaman and I will help her. Good night everyone. I'm off to bed.'

The next day, Gabi, Shaman, and Dhudi began building her escape boat in a secluded region of the island's north side.

12

CHAPTER

———❧———

Captain Boon cancelled all his visits to the thieves scattered on the other islands in the Red Sea and sailed his boat back to Zaila City. He kept his journey for the rest of that day and the following night. He reached the city while people were still sleeping. Boon moored the boat at the harbour, and then thinking about nothing but the princess he'd found in Faay Island, he stretched himself on a small mat on the ship, waiting until the city woke up. In the morning, when people had begun their daily activities, he went to the house of the kingdom's Chief of Prisoners and Detention Centres. He came to him, eating breakfast in the living room. After they quickly exchanged the usual greetings, Boon excitedly said, 'Chief, I found the missing princess. She's well and lives on Faay Island with a group of thieves.'

The Chief was Surprised by his claim. He said, 'Captain, are you sure you've found the missing princess?'

'Yes, I found her yesterday. I tried to bring her home, but she refused to come with me.'

'How did she get there?'

'I don't know how she got there. However, I think she'd been on the island since she went missing. She has even got her own hut on the island, and the prisoners she stays with told me that they found her sleeping in their house,' he further explained.

'That's interesting. If what you're telling me is true, then you've got a big story for the kingdom. Is the princess safe there with those thieves?' the Chief asked anxiously.

'I'm not worried about her safety at the moment. I told them to look after her until someone comes to collect her.'

'Good. Now we must go to the Queen and tell her that you've found her stepdaughter. Wait for me for a minute,' said the Chief as he rose from his seat to prepare himself. The Chief thought the Queen would be thrilled once she heard that her stepdaughter had been found alive, and he would get the credit for the big news. He hurried to his bedroom, put on his best attire and quickly returned to Captain Boon, eagerly waiting for him in the sitting room. 'Let us go. The queen must get this news immediately,' the Chief shouted from the doorway. After that, the Chief striding in front and Captain Boon keeping him up, they started for the White Palace.

They continued walking as fast as they could until they approached the main gate of the Palace and the Chief shouted at the guards, 'We've urgent news for the Queen. We must see her quickly.' One of the guards picked up the urgency in his voice and led them to the Queen's special butler, Mr Hoob. They came to Hoob at the main chamber, and the Chief shouted excitedly, 'Butler Hoob, we have big news for the queen. We must see her quickly. Butler Hoob wondering about the big news, showed them where to sit and went to the Queen's private quarters. He came to her reclining on luxurious large cushions and sipping the aromatic red tea she usually drank in her private chamber.

'Your majesty, we have visitors who want to see you urgently,' Hoob cried from the doorway.

'Why have they come to see me at this hour of the day? Tell them to come back later,' she replied, daintily sipping her special tea.

'Your majesty, the Chief of Prisoners and Detention Centres and his assistant said they have big news for you.'

She thought for a moment and said, 'I don't like people coming at the wrong times. Alright. I'll come down. Tell them to wait.'

Minutes later, she walked into the main chamber and shrieked, 'Chief, I've been told that you have big news for me. What is it?'

'My queen, the missing princess is safe and well. We found her on a faraway island in the Red Sea,' he explained, his face flushing with excitement.

Queen Idil was shocked by the unexpected news. 'Impossible! How could that be?' She screamed.

'Everything is possible, Your Majesty,' said the Chief and the queen, trying hard to manage her feelings, sat down. Then the Chief began retelling the story he'd heard from Captain Boon. She listened to him calmly, hanging on each word that came from his mouth. When he'd finished telling Dhudi's story, she glanced at Captain Boon and said, 'Captain, I think you've found an impostor. Can you describe the appearance of the girl you've seen on that island?'

Captain Boon, who had seen Dhudi before and was confident that he'd found her, described Dhudi in detail to the Queen.

Now believing that the girl he'd found was the real Dhudi, she said calmly, 'You told the Chief that she has a hut of her own on that island. Tell me more about the place where she lives. Does she live with the thieves in the same compound?'

'No,' he replied and explained more about Faay Island, where Dhudi's hut was located, and about the men she lived with. When he finished, she asked him curiously, 'How far away is Faay Island from here?'

'It's a one-day non-stop sea voyage away when the sea is stable,' he said.

'Captain, it sounds like the girl you've seen is my stepdaughter, but I doubt Dhudi is alive. You may have seen someone who resembles her. I want you and your men not to tell anyone about the girl you've found until we discover the truth,' explained Queen Idil, who decided to keep things secret.

'Okay, my queen,' Captain Boon grunted.

She looked at the Chief in slow motion and said, 'My Chief, thank you for coming. Please don't mention this story to anyone until we can ascertain who that girl is,' and the Chief obediently promised that he wouldn't mention it to anyone.

'You can go now,' she said to them, rising from her seat to leave the room too. Feeling dizzy due to the disturbing news, she went to her bedroom. She lay on the bed, and with her eyes fixed on the ceiling, she started to think about Dhudi and Servant Bedel. She wondered how he'd helped her to get to that island. Unable to control her anger at Bedel, she mumbled quietly, 'This bugger betrayed me. He must pay the price,' and she carried on thinking about him and Dhudi to figure out what to do next.

13

CHAPTER

Queen Idil didn't stop thinking about Dhudi and Servant Bedel until an immature idea struck her. It wasn't a brilliant idea. Anyway, she liked it, and she began acting upon it. The following morning she opened a coffer next to her bed, pulled out a bunch of keys from it and went to the kitchen with the keys in her right hand. She picked up a small empty bottle from a shelf and walked with it to the little storeroom next to her private chamber. She unlocked the door and went to a wooden box in a dark corner of the room. She opened it and took out one of three bottles in the box marked 'Rijzi, the death medicine.' She sat on the floor and put the two bottles in front of her with the keys.

After that, she unscrewed the lid of the big bottle with great care and put it next to its bottle. In a similar move, she unscrewed the small bottle's cap and put it next to it.

Then she picked up the big bottle containing the 'death medicine' with great care and poured the liquid in it into the small bottle, filling it close to the brim.

She carefully put down both bottles and screwed their lids back on them. She tightened the caps securely, returned the big bottle back to its box and locked up the room. Afterwards, carrying the small bottle and the keys, she returned to her bedroom. She placed the bottle and the keys on a bed stand next to her bed and stooped down to open her late husband's coffer at the side of her bed. She pulled out a curved dagger with a golden grip in a shining sheath and a white handkerchief with blue and black coloured patterns on its sides. She put the cloth beside the small bottle on the bed stand, drew the dagger out of its sheath and examined its sharp edges. She put it back in the sheath and placed it next to the bottle containing the Rijzi poison. Then gazing at the poison and the dagger, she said under her breath, 'If one of these misses her, the other must end Dhudi's life.'

She stuffed the dagger, the handkerchief and the little bottle into a leather handbag with a long strap and soft fringes that hung down from its sides. Ready to leave the room, Heeto knocked on the door and shouted, 'Mum, can I come in.'

She quickly stashed the bag under the bed and shouted back, 'Come in, darling.'

'Mum, I'm going shopping for the Royal Parade. Can I take Beautie to the city?' The Royal Parade was a yearly event a few days away, and Beautie was a special horse wagon used by the royal family.'

'Of course, you can take it, darling. Get the best outfit in town. You're the only princess of this kingdom, and you will be the Queen after me,' said Idil, whose heart was glowing with motherly affection as she turned to open the coffer which contained the royal regalia. She pulled out a dazzling crown from it and said, 'Come here, sweetheart.' Heeto came closer, and the mother placed the crown on her small head though, oddly, it was too big to fit her. Idil laid the crown down on the bed and picked a smaller one from the coffer. Unfortunately, it wasn't fit either for Heato's head as well. Idil, disappointed, sighed and said, 'Don't worry, princess. I'll order one that is your size soon.'

'Can I be a queen, mum?' Heeto, unsure if she could be a queen, asked.

'Yes, you'll inherit my kingdom when I die. Get ready for it.'

'Thank you, mum,' cried Heeto, burying her little head between her mother's right shoulder blade and her neck. Idil, whose eyes were moistening with affection, held her tight and adoringly. After they'd clung to each other for half a minute, the mother detached herself from the daughter and said, 'My princess, I'm going on a tour. Tell the servants that I'm not receiving any visitors today and tomorrow.'

'Okay, mum,' said Heeto, turning away to leave.

After Heeto left the room, Queen Idil summoned her special bodyguard, Kirkir Gambieh, a strong, tall man, to her private chamber. She explained to him how her stepdaughter had been found on a faraway island and that she needed his help to bring her home. Then Idil, in a hooded black dress and carrying the bag containing the death medicine, the handkerchief and the sharp dagger, and Kirkir slipped secretly through a back door of the White Palace and set off for the harbour. They took a boat, and they sailed away to Faay Island. After they'd been at sea all day, nearly sunset, they saw Faay Island looming in the distance. Idil anchored the boat, and she said to Kirkir,

'The men on the island are dangerous thieves. We'll move close to the island when it gets dark. Afterwards, I'll go to the island alone and get my stepdaughter quietly. For now, let us make dinner for ourselves.'

'No, my Queen, the thieves are dangerous, as you said. If they capture you, it means they've captured the whole kingdom because you're the head of state. Instead, I'll go and get your stepdaughter for you,' he explained.

Queen Idil planned to kill Dhudi in her room, and she didn't want anyone to know her plan. She thought for a moment and said, 'I appreciate your concern, but I must go by myself. I'm the only one my stepdaughter can trust. I'll sneak into the dark night, get her place quietly and secretly bring her out. Cover me from a distance.'

'My Queen, I'll do the job for you. I'm a specially trained man. I'll silently look for her room, muffle her with a special technique I know to make her quiet and bring her to you without any trouble.'

The Queen, impressed by his skills, thought about what to say again. After a long silence, she decided to test Kirkir's loyalty. 'Kirkir, can your queen trust you with her crucial secrets?'

'My queen, don't put in question my trustworthiness.'

She came close to him, put her right hand on his shoulder, stroked his neck and said, 'Even if your queen asks you to kill someone on her behalf, will you do it?'

'My Queen, don't keep me repeating myself. I'll do everything you want,' said Kirkir, who was a ruthless individual.

'In that case, we'll work together closely. Keep our little secrets between us,' she said, still tenderly stroking around Kirkir's neck.

'I'll never let you down, my queen,' he boasted, and the Queen, happy with his unwavering loyalty, said, 'Let us make our dinner. We'll plan things after we eat.'

14

CHAPTER

Princess Dhudi and the thieves had spent most of the day hunting and building the boat for her escape, gathered at the fireplace in the evening. They ate their dinner, and when they'd sorted the dishes, the mischievous dwarf Jamanjug, looking at Kalah's face, said, 'Kalah's head always reminds me of a big frog's countenance when it's ready to croak. Look at his eyes perching way above where they should be on his skull, his stubby flat nose and his bald head like an unsown field. Isn't that a frog's head?'

They all laughed. It was usual for these men to make fun of each other after dinner.

'Shut up, silly dwarf,' Kalah screamed angrily. 'When you're with Gabi, you look like a little child with a giant father.' And in support of his comment, Daweel added,

'That's how they seem to me when they're together.' Some of them laughed again.

Jamanjug stared at Daweel furiously and said, 'Do you know what, Daweel? Whenever I see your long scraggy legs and your tall skinny body reminds me of a lank tree standing alone in the crosswind.'

They all laughed, and Dhudi, who used to avoid laughing at their hurtful jokes, laughed too unintentionally.

After the thieves exchanged some more cruel jokes and insults, Dhudi, who always wanted to know what crimes they'd committed, asked, 'By the way, my friends, how did you end up on this island? What crimes have you committed?'

They looked at each other, and Shaman said, 'She has the right to know who we are. Why don't we get to know each other a bit more?'

Then Daweel decided to express himself first. He said, 'I always regret what I did. Before I was taken to court in Zaila, I entered a farm full of watermelons and all types of crops. I was so thirsty and hungry. I cracked a giant watermelon, and it tasted sour. I broke another one, and it was so bitter to eat. Again, I sliced another big one, over-ripened and tasted too bad to eat. At last, I opened a sweet one, and I ate it. After I filled my stomach, the farm owner caught me, and he took me to Judge Koshin's court. He told the judge that I ate his watermelons and that I'd destroyed many of his watermelons. I confessed to my felony, and then the horrible judge said to me, 'You've stolen or destroyed the watermelons of our hardworking farmer. You're a bad thief. You must live in a place with no watermelons to steal or smash. I'm sending you to an island in the far sea. That's how I got here.'

'Tha's amazing. What about you, Shaman?' She asked, twisting her neck to his side.

'You don't need to know what I did because it isn't that important,' he simply answered.

'It's important to me. I need to know about my friends.'

'Okay, this is what happened to me,' Shaman began telling his story. 'On a Friday morning, six and a half years ago, my wife and I went to visit my father, who was critically ill. We stayed in his house most of that day, cooking food for him and washing his clothes. After my wife and I had prepared to go home in the evening, he called me from his bed. I came to him, breathing hard and coughing. My wife came to him too. He said, 'My son, I think I'm going to die. Keep my Red Round Ruby. It will help you to help other people.' The Ruby was an unusual thing. It worked with magical words, which helped it to reveal everything you want to know when you read them and look into this Ruby. Not only did my father give me the Ruby, but he also taught us the incantations you would need to read before you look into it.'

Shaman paused and continued, 'My wife was a quick learner. She immediately picked up the incantations and started working with the ruby after my dad died. Even though I sometimes worked with the ruby, my wife was the main operator, and I didn't mind that as long as she was my wife. She became a famous fortune-teller in Zaila City, and sometime later, she asked me for a divorce without good reason after we'd been married for nineteen years. I divorced her and asked her to give me my Ruby, and she refused to give it back to me. It was unthinkable. She dumped me, and at the same time, she wanted to keep the only thing I inherited from my father.'

'What have you done then?' Dhudi asked.

'I just grabbed the Ruby from her hand and walked away with it. After that, she went to the court of justice and told Judge Koshin that I'd robbed her special Ruby from her. Then the security men took me to court, and the judge said, 'Return her Special Ruby. You've robbed the property of a good citizen. I must send you where there's no Ruby to rob and no woman to harass.' I tried to tell him that the Ruby was mine, but Judge Koshin said, 'She has many witnesses. Do you have one?'

I said 'No,' so he sent me to this island. I think it wasn't his fault. People in Zaila thought the Ruby she used for her fortune-telling was hers, so they testified in court against me.' He paused, sighed and continued, 'I'm a loser. She dumped me, and she took my Ruby, and now I'm nothing because of her.'

Dhudi remembered the day she saw the Fortuneteller with the Red Round Ruby and was about to say, 'I've seen your Ruby.' Instead, she said, 'Shaman, don't give up hope. My father told me to be strong and resilient and that I could be who I wanted to be. I'm advising you the same. Be strong. One day you may get your Ruby back.'

She turned to Kalah and asked, 'How about you, Kalah?' Kalah twisted his upper lip upward, showing his heavily stained and rotten teeth, and he said, 'I used to do comedy acts. It was the only talent I had. Children in my town and even the grown-ups liked what I did. My appearance and my acts amused them, and they used to pay me whatever they had to make me act for them repeatedly. One day, the security men caught me doing funny acts and collecting money and other things from minors. They accused me of tricking money from innocent young people. They took me to court, and Judge Koshin said, 'You deceived our good citizens. You took their things after you brainwashed them with your evil performances.

You're a bad thief. I must stop you from stealing money from our innocent people. I'm sending you to a desolate island where there are no people for you to swindle their money.'

I said to him, 'I didn't steal anything. The fools gave me voluntarily whatever they gave me,' and he replied, 'Article fifteen of Zaila and the Thorny Land law says thieves must be sent to a forlorn island in the far sea. Don't argue with me. You'll be going to Faay Island.'

Princess Dhudi, fascinated by their stories and wanting to hear more, looked at Gabi and asked, 'How about you, Gabi?

Gabi smiled and said proudly, 'I was a conjuring trickster and a wrestler.' He paused, turned his head towards Jamanjug, and carried on. 'With the help of this little man, I earned money and food through my skills. Then these silly people, who paid me willingly, later accused me of being a magician and that I tricked them into paying me.' 'You were a big, brainless idiot. It was all my planning,' Jamanjug interjected.

'Forget about him, princess. Let me finish my story,' said Gabi, grinning at Jamanjug. 'One day, some fools had paid us money in exchange for our tricks. When we'd finished the performance and prepared to go home, an imbecile came out of the group and told us to return the money he gave us. I refused his demand, and then he approached me aggressively. I beat him up. He was a security officer, so he got help from others, and they took us to court, and Judge Koshin said, 'You're a big man. You've beaten up our community security officer after you took his money. Additionally, you and your friend tricked other people with your evil skills to take their money. You cannot live where there are people to cheat with your magical skills. I'm sending you to an isolated island in the far sea.'

'We tried to tell him we didn't steal anything, and he said, 'taking what isn't yours is stealing, and article fifteen of Zaila and Thorny Land law states that the thieves must go there.'

'Article fifteen doesn't categorise levels of theft. That's why Jamanjug and I ended up here, and our world shattered afterwards.'

'Your world didn't shatter. Still, you can be who you want to be.'

Dhudi, fascinated by their stories, smiled at Jamanjug and said, 'Jamanjug, you were a clever trickster, weren't you?'

'He gave us the same sentence,' Jamanjug answered.

'What does he look like, this strange judge who sends people to forlorn islands in the Red Sea?' Princess Dhudi asked curiously. Jamanjug visualized the judge's image and laughed before saying, 'He looks like a mole rat, and he has front teeth the same as the beaver's teeth.'

They all laughed, and Gabi said, 'He's an old man with a massively bald head and a long, wonky nose. His front teeth are a bit pointed forward like those of beavers, as Jamanjug said, and when he's in his robes, he looks like a mole rat emerging out of its hole.'

They all laughed at the judge's description and Princess Dhudi, amazed by their stories. She stood up to leave and said, 'Thank you all. I'm off to bed. Good night.'

'Good night, princess,' the thieves replied.

15

CHAPTER

Idil, convinced that Dhudi and the thieves on Faay Island were deep asleep, sailed the boat at around 10:00 pm, closer to the island. She stopped it near the seashore and ordered Kirkir to drop the anchors. When he'd done what she'd told him to do, Idil grabbed the handbag with the Rijzi poison, the dagger and the handkerchief and said to him, 'Bring down one of the canoes,' which he did. After that, Idil and her bodyguard had a plan they devised together over dinner, rowed towards the seashore. They moored the canoe in a sheltered place and walked onto the island. Before long, they emerged into the huts of the thieves. She stopped and pointed the head of her torch at Dhudi's little house, silhouetted in the black night and said, 'She's in that separate hut. As you said, I'll cover for you from here. Go and take care of her, and don't leave any traces behind you.'

'Don't worry, my queen. I'll do it as you said,' he responded.

'Excellent,' she said. She gave him the bag that contained the dangerous items and added, 'Kill her with the poison. Use the dagger only if needed. Make sure she dies.'

'My queen, I don't need the dagger. The poison is strong enough to kill her instantly, and if needed, I'll strangle her.'

'Alright. Anyway, keep it with you in case you need it. Go, I'll cover you from here,' Idil advised him.

Kirkir had precise instructions on how to take Dhudi's life in his head took the bag and hastened towards the target hut, leaving Idil hiding behind some shrubs with his bow and arrows in a case. He'd reached Dhudi's fence, opened the front gate slowly, and then carried on to the door of her room. He opened it and then, hardly making any sound, he went inside. He sat down near the entrance and listened for Dhudi to make a sound, to locate where she was in the room. He detected her breathing on the right side of the room. He silently crawled to the middle of the room. He stopped again and listened intently to her sounds to assess the distance between her and him.

Again he crept soundlessly further toward her bed. He stopped by the side of her bed, removed Idil's handbag from his shoulder and opened it to get out the weapons they'd planned to use for Dhudi's killing. He first brought out the small bottle with the Rijzi poison and the handkerchief. He soaked the cloth with the poison in the bottle, and then, holding the poisonous handkerchief in his right hand, he crawled to Dhudi's bed until he accidentally touched her arm, and Dhudi jumped and screamed.

Her scream woke up the men in the other huts, and they got out of their beds, but she didn't make any sound again.

Kirkir jumped over her swiftly, muffled her mouth with the poison-soaked handkerchief and pinned her down on the bed. He suffocated her with the poisonous handkerchief to make her die. Dhudi tried to avoid swallowing the liquid seeping from the wet cloth and wriggled as hard as she could to free herself from the attacker. Sadly, whatever she did, it was too late. The liquid penetrated her system through her mouth and nostrils, and her body began losing strength.

The thieves wondering what had made her scream at once, flocked to her room. Before they reached her hut, a flying arrow from nowhere struck Gabi on the right arm, and another was barely missing Kalah's head flew past them. They quickly sought cover, except for Shaman, who ran to Dhudi's room. He instantly reached her door and shouted, 'Dhudi, are you alright?'

Kirkir, sitting on Dhudi's powerless body and considering whether to break her neck, saw the man approaching the door. He dropped the handkerchief and ran from the room heading out. He shoved Shaman aside, slipped between him and the doorframe, and ran away into the black night, leaving behind the bag and the poison on the floor. He sprinted as fast as he could towards the sea, and the queen saw him running, got to her feet and followed him. Jamanjug, crouching in the darkness with his bow and arrows, spotted them dashing one after the other and shot both of them in quick succession, injuring them. However, even though his shots were painful and made Queen Idil cry out, they didn't stop them from escaping. Idil and her bodyguard kept running to the canoe, and on reaching the beach, they hastily threw the canoe into the water and rowed it away.

Shaman reached Dhudi lying on her bed, frothing at the mouth and coughing and saw the handbag on the floor. 'Dhudi, are you alright?' he anxiously asked.

'He gave me a bad poison. I'm dying,' Dhudi moaned.

'No, you ain't dying, dear,' he said, picking her up from the bed. He carried her with the bag to the men's enclosure. He put her down near the fireplace, lit a lamp in a hurry, and pulled out a box from underneath the bed in his room. He grabbed a small bottle from it and poured a liquid in it into Dhudi's mouth. 'Swallow it,' he said. 'It's a medicine for all poisons.' He repeated, 'Swallow it.' It was true that his medicine was an antidote for all poisons. Sadly, Idil's poison was the most potent potion ever found in the region. Only a few drops of it could kill or paralyse a person in minutes. The small amount that had slithered into her throat had already disabled parts of her body. Her limbs had stopped functioning, and her tongue and lips had started swelling. After giving her the medicine, Shaman built a fire and continued assessing her situation.

Shaman continued hovering over her and checking her if his medicine had worked until the other men returned from chasing the midnight attackers. They returned with Gabi had an arrow sticking out of his arm. 'What happened to the princess? Did she get hurt?' Gabi growled, and Shaman explained that an unknown assailant had poisoned her. He showed them the handbag he'd found in the room with her and explained about the antidote he gave her. The men were stunned at the midnight raid. They talked over and over about the attack. They speculated on who the attackers could be, and at the same time, they worked out the arrow on Gabi's arm. They managed to remove the arrow from him and dabbed his wound with medicine. Thereafter, Kalah, Jamanjug and Daweel took lamps and went to investigate the area, starting with Dhudi's hut.

Dhudi survived the dangerous poison. If Shaman didn't give her his antidote, she could die instantly. When Kalah, Jamanjug and Daweel left, Dhudi glanced at the bag and dagger by the fire. Too weak to talk she mumbled, 'Shaman, the attacker was my stepmother. She came to kill me. That's her bag, and the dagger is my father's dagger. If I survive this poison, I must disappear before she returns to kill. Will you come with me? I'm too weak to travel alone.'

Shaman was impressed by her courage. He smiled at her and said, 'You cannot travel now. You need some time to heal before you travel. We'll think about what we can do when you get better.'

'I must find a place to recover if I don't die now. Please help me. I must leave before Idil returns,' Dhudi, closing her eyes to rest, bemoaned.

'I'll do whatever I can,' he said.

Jamanjug, Kalah and Daweel, holding their lamps in front of their faces, entered Dhudi's room. They found the wet handkerchief and the small bottle lying apart from its lid in the room. They carefully collected the things and continued searching the area. After thoroughly investigating the site, they returned to the fireplace, carrying what they had found. They assembled the things they had found by the fireplace, and then Shaman holding the curved dagger in the bag, said, 'Be careful. Those things are coated with a dangerous poison. If you touched them, wash your hands right now. The attacker came to kill the princess with the poison in that bottle and this dagger.'

Jamanjug, gazing at the curved dagger with the golden grip and the bottle, said, 'Who were the attackers?'

'I don't know, but they came to kill the princess,' Shaman explained.

'One of them was a woman,' Jamanjug said.

'How do you know?' Gabi asked.

'She whimpered when my arrow struck her,' Jamanjug explained.

'This is the queen's bag, and this is the dagger of her late husband. The attacker could be Queen Idil with an accomplice,' Shaman explained.

'Oh my God, I shot the queen of Zaila?' Jamanjug said alarmingly.

'How could the queen know that her stepdaughter was here?' Gabi asked curiously.

'I don't know. However, Dhudi knows her better than us, and she has confirmed that this is her bag and the dagger belongs to the royal family,' Shaman added.

'The queen is ruthless. If she came to kill her stepdaughter, we're all in danger now,' Jamanjug speculated alarmingly.

'That's true. We're all in real danger. We must do something quickly,' Shaman explained.

'Why do you think we're in danger? Daweel demanded.

'This wicked queen will tell her supporters that we attacked her while she was trying to bring her stepdaughter home. She'll come back and do horrible things to all of us. We must do something immediately,' Shaman said worryingly.

'What can we do?' Gabi asked.

'I don't know. Anyway, I'll go with the princess. She wants to escape, and anyway, she needs my help,' Shaman grunted.

'We can't breach the law,' Kalah protested. 'We're not allowed to leave the island.'

'The queen already breached the law when she tried to kill her stepdaughter,' Gabi declared. 'I'm coming with you, Shaman. Where are we going?'

'Anywhere. We'll finish her improvised boat quickly and take the sea. We may find another island,' Shaman replied.

'I'm coming with you too,' Jamanjug, afraid of the queen, hissed. So eventually, they all decided to escape.

16

CHAPTER

Idil wincing from unbearable pain in her right flank, where Jamanjug's arrow had struck her, scrambled up a rope ladder hanging down from the side of her boat to reach the deck. In a similar move, her bodyguard had two arrows sticking out from his body, one in his right buttock and another in his left buttock joined her on the boat. Immediately after they reached the deck, they winched up the canoe and the rope ladder and started working out the arrows protruding from their bodies.

Firstly Kirkir managed to remove the arrow from the queen's left flank and dabbed the wound. Secondly, the queen taking her turn, removed the arrow in his left buttock. Sadly she found it more challenging to pull out the one in his right buttock. She wriggled it and tried to yank it out. Strangely it didn't budge, and Kirkir growled with excruciating pain. 'Be strong, Kirkir. It will come out,' she assured him. Then trying to dislodge the arrow from where it jammed, she pulled it up forcefully. Only its wooden shaft without the metal head came out, and Kirkir growled with pain again. Idil realised that the metal part remained in his buttock. So, she said, 'The arrowhead's still inside. It's a strange arrow different from others. Anyway, don't worry. We'll sort it out when we get home.'

It was true that this arrow was different from the others. That night Jamanjug had two types of arrows in his quiver, and he had fired both at the attackers. Some had smooth edges, but others had unique three-pointed heads, one point faced forward, and the other two points faced backwards like hooks. The arrow in Kirkir's buttock was the latter type, and it intertwined with his flesh and refused to come out. She wrapped her scarf around his wound to stop the bleeding, and then, leaving him lying face down on the floor, she went to the cabin and sailed the boat back to Zaila.

The following morning, the thieves, afraid that Queen Idil to return, started enlarging Dhudi's getaway boat to make it enough to carry all of them and their belongings. That day no one of them went fishing. They all went to build the boat. At midday, once they were on lunch break, Shaman decided to find out what the future held for them by using his fortune-telling skills. He went to a secluded site behind a cluster of trees, then using his fingertips and frequently looking up at the sun shining down from the sky above him, he began making marks on the soft sand. He marked three of his right-hand fingertip prints on the sand, leaving three parallel dots on the ground.

Again he traced two more finger imprints after the first three dots, and then he put one more fingertip print after those two. He repeated the same process, creating similar parallel dots on the right side of the first marks, and then he looked at the sun again. Nothing occurred to him. He repeated the process again and again and eventually sank into a deep trance, and then suddenly, he had a dramatic vision that scared him. He envisaged his friends and himself cowering with fear and a giant dark wave towering over them. Shaman, troubled by the ominous signs he had seen, went back to his friends. He came to them, thinking about whether to tell his friends about what he had seen or not. After thinking for a while, he decided not to tell them, and they went back to building the boat.

CHAPTER

Queen Idil, whose journey was slowed by seasonal winds and her injury, reached the coast of Zaila City in the late afternoon of the day following the night of the attack. Idil, unwilling people to notice her movement stopped the boat far from the harbour and told Kirkir that they would move in when it turned dark. They remained in the water until sunset and soon it turned dark, she sailed the boat to the harbour. She moored it at a deserted pier, and afterwards, they sneaked away into the darkness of the night, heading to the White Palace. They entered the building supporting each other from the back door and eventually ended up in her private chamber. She gave Kirkir pain remedies and told him she would find a healer to deal with the arrowhead in his buttock in the morning. She also told him to show the Healer only the wound with the arrowhead and not to mention or let him see the other one.

Thereafter, she went to bed. In the morning, after breakfast, she called her butler, Mr Hoob. She ordered him to bring in a medicine man who lived on the city's east side. Hoob hurried to get the healer. It didn't take him long to find him and bring him with tools to Kirkir lying on his stomach in the queen's private chamber. The medicine man asked, 'What's your problem, my patient?'

Kirkir, pointing at his right buttock, shyly replied, 'Healer, I've got an arrowhead embedded in my buttock.'

The medicine man looked at the wound and asked again, 'How did you get this injury, my patient?'

'A colleague accidentally shot me at army training practice,' Kirkir lied.

The medicine man, about to start his work, mumbled, 'This area of the body is delicate. Be patient with me while I'm doing the work.'

'Okay, my healer,' Kirkir grunted.

The medicine man removed the scarf that Idil had put on the wound and enlarged the opening of the cut with one of his sharp scalpels. Then using vascular clamps, scissors and tongs, he searched for the arrowhead lurking deep in Kirkir's flesh. Kirkir couldn't resist the pain caused by the wriggle of sharp blades in his buttock and accidentally revealed the wound on his other buttock. The medicine man saw it, and with surprise asked, 'What happened to your other side?'

'It was another accidental shot,' Kirkir bemoaned.

The medicine man wondered how that could happen. Anyway, he carried on with the operation. After much long and painstaking work, the Healer brought out the arrowhead with a piece of flesh hanging around it. He cleaned the wound with antiseptics and stitched it up. When he'd completed his job, he packed his things up and said, 'Mister, your injuries are in a sensitive area of the body. Sleep on your chest, and don't sit on your bottom for one month.

'Okay, healer,' replied Kirkir, grateful that his ordeal was over.

Queen Idil approached the Healer, ready to leave and chirped, 'Healer, he's my bodyguard. I want him to recover rapidly. Please give him your best medicine.'

'Don't worry, my queen. I already gave him strong medicine, and I'll give him some more powerful medicine again before long. Hopefully, he will be fine soon.'

Idil had a plan for Kirkir when he got better, but in the meantime, she had to solve another problem. Since they left Faay Island, she has been worrying about the things Kirkir had left in Dhudi's room, and she wasn't sure if he had killed Dhudi. She went to her bedroom, sat on an armchair next to the bed, and started to think about her mission to Faay Island and how to fix what went wrong. It didn't take her long to figure out what to do. She decided to return to the island, ascertain Dhudi's death, and eliminate all the witnesses on the island.

So, as part of her plan, she summoned the head of the Palace's security guard, Farah Shalaqbeen, to her chamber. She gave him a cup of tea and said, 'Farah, I should have told you about this earlier. However, I'm telling it to you now. Please listen to me carefully. Two days ago, I got information about my missing stepdaughter. I'd been told that she was on a faraway island with a group of thieves. I went there with Kirkir to bring her home. Sadly we were attacked by dangerous thieves on the island. We escaped with our lives, but I think they killed the young princess. I'm returning to the island and need your help.'

Farah Shalaqbeen was surprised at the news and asked, 'My queen, how did the young princess get there?'

'I don't know. Please let us act quickly. We don't have time,' Idil made a pretence at sobbing.

'My queen, don't cry. My men and I will go now, and we'll bring your stepdaughter home if she's still alive.'

'I'm coming with you, and we'll go in the morning. Organise your men,' she hastily ordered him.

'I'll, my queen. Which Island is she?' he asked, rising from his seat to leave.

'She's on Faay Island. Prepare a strong army. We must leave early in the morning,' she emphasized.

The following morning, he came to her as she was waiting for him and then together, they went to her royal wagon, Beautie, which was ready for them outside the building. As she lifted her right leg to climb in, she saw Servant Bedel walking past them. She stopped and stared at him grudgingly. Bedel saw her and wondered why the queen looked at him that way, but he kept walking, feeling worried. When he had disappeared, she climbed into the wagon, and they started out for the harbour. They took a vessel and sailed away to Faay Island.

On the way, Queen Idil was thinking of ways to control Farah. After they had been in the water for about an hour, she began a careful conversation with him in the cabin of the boat to figure out what kind of man he was. After talking to him for a long time, she decided he was her man, a man she could twist to her liking. After ascertaining his character, she said, 'Farah, if those thieves have already killed my stepdaughter, they must all die on the spot because they've killed her.'

'My queen, it's better to take them to trial,' he answered.

'As the queen of the nation, I order you. They must pay the price if they killed my stepdaughter. They're horrible criminals,' she screamed.

'We'll do what you want, my queen,' he replied obediently.

They carried on their journey. In the late afternoon, once the ship was tearing through the water smoothly with Faay Island just a few miles away, ferocious gales from the southerly direction came and struck them repeatedly. It wasn't a good time to be in that sea. It was a time when the Indian Ocean's seasonal winds, known as Summer Monsoons, began. The storms and angry tides battered them continuously, and the army scrambled to protect their ship from capsizing. The cruel waves continued hitting the vessel hard, and Farah and his men fought hard to save the ship. At last, they had survived the mayhem, but the turmoil of the turbulent sea had delayed their journey.

18

CHAPTER

If Faay Island was a home and a place to tell funny jokes over evening meals, now the thieves and Princess Dhudi, critically ill, must flee from it. The group, unaware of the enemy boat heading towards them, gathered at the fireplace in the evening and discussed nothing but their daunting escape plan. They anxiously talked about how soon their getaway boat could be ready. When their journey would begin, where they should go, what they would carry with them and whatever else they thought might affect their unavoidable escape. After a lengthy discussion, they sorted out the most pressing issues but couldn't figure out where to go and exactly when their journey was to begin.

Jamanjug and Shaman insisted they should leave instantly as Queen Idil could return at any time. Kalah, Gabi and Daweel argued that the queen wouldn't come back so soon because she was injured. They advised Shaman and Jamanjug not to worry and to wait until their improvised boat was ready. Once Shaman and Jamanjug almost succumbed to what the majority wanted, Dhudi paralysed by Idil's poison and unable to talk but in stable condition, pulled Shaman's hand to get his attention.

Shaman understood that she intended to tell him something, lowered his head down close to her mouth, and asked, 'What's it, Princess?'

She directed her mouth to his ears and slurred, 'Shaman, Idil may return faster than you think to ensure I'm dead, and no one will be safe if she returns. Please, we must leave as quickly as possible. Remember when Gabi said that Captain Boon's journey would take a month, and then she came just three days later."

Shaman listened carefully to her distorted speech and afterwards shouted, 'My friends, the princess is reminding us of what Gabi said regarding Captain Boon's journey. Remember, he said that the queen would get the news of the missing princess after one month, and three days later, she came to kill her. The princess believes Queen Idil is returning quicker than you think. We must leave immediately.'

Her words not only increased their fear but also squarely nailed down those who were reluctant for their journey to begin immediately. Believing what she said was very likely to happen, they unanimously agreed to speed up building the boat and take the sea within two days.

Before they went to bed, Shaman remembered the huge dark wave he envisaged in his fortune-telling vision on the previous day and said, 'My friends, there's something I didn't tell you.'

'What is it?' Jamanjug hastened to ask.

'When we decided to abscond from this island, I tried to predict what the future held for us, and in the process of my prediction, I saw a huge black wave towering over us in the sea. It was so fearsome, and I saw all of us cowering with fear.'

Jamanjug didn't want to hear anyone casting doubt on their escape. So to trivialise Shaman's prediction, he asked, 'Have you seen some of us dying?'

'No,' Shaman replied.

'Then your prediction has nothing to do with our escape,' he repeated, and Gabi supporting his comment, added, 'Shaman, Jamanjug's right. Your fortune-telling scheme is always lousy. Remember, it didn't work several times properly in the past. Relax. There's nothing to be afraid of. We'll take to the sea immediately when our boat is ready.'

'I didn't mean to alarm you or to change our getaway plan. I just wanted to tell you what I've seen,' Shaman, getting up from his seat, explained. He went to his hut, and in a minute, he returned with a shovel and a lamp. He stopped near the group, ready to go to bed and said, 'Kalah and Jamanjug, come with me. I got something to do.'

'What is it?' Kalah asked.

'Stop asking questions. Just come with me if you are willing to help.'

'Okay, old man. However, you should know that I'm entitled to know what I'm going to do,' Kalah rising from his seat, said.

With Shaman in front, they walked towards Dhudi's hut. They stopped at a spot behind her house, and Shaman said, 'We're going to dig her grave here.'

'What?' Kalah asked shockingly.

'I said, we're digging her grave here.'

'I don't get it. What do you mean?' Kalah repeated.

'Just do what I say. You'll understand what I mean later.'

'Are you out of your mind, Shaman? Tell us what's going on. The girl is alive. How can we did her grave?' Jamanjug, also surprised at his instructions, demanded.

'Okay, listen to me carefully. We'll dig Dhudi's fake grave here to mislead the queen. I want that horrible queen to think her horrible medicine has killed the princess when she returns.'

The two men, satisfied with his answer, smiled at him, and together, they started digging the false grave on the selected spot. Heaping fresh dirt on the sides of the hole, they kept digging it until they had made it one metre deep. After that, they filled the grave with sand and rocks they collected from nearby places, and again they heaped the fresh dirt on it and shaped it like a real grave by smoothing its sides with their hands and fixing slabs of stone at both ends. In addition to these, they put fresh branches on it, and lastly, Shaman holding the lamp wrote with black charcoal on one of the slabs, 'God bless Princess Dhudi, the daughter of late King Erek. Keep her soul in your best paradise.' Then Kalah laughed at him and said, 'Shaman, you're a terrific faker .' After that, they went to their rooms.

19

CHAPTER

E arly next morning, Kalah, Daweel, Shaman and Jamanjug, leaving behind the two injured, Gabi and Princess Dhudi, went to what they called 'the boat, but was a small platform made from logs and beams they tied together with green strips of bark. They engaged in working on the boat without sparing any effort. At around 10.30 am, Gabi, feeling better and considering joining those building the boat, came out of his hut. He stopped outside the fence of the houses and looked out to the sea. He saw a vessel heading towards the island in the distance. He went to the top of a nearby small hill to ascertain whether it was heading to the island. The vessel kept moving towards him.

It continued coming closer and closer, and then Gabi established that it was aiming at the island. He ran back to the huts and picked Dhudi up. He bundled her slim body on his shoulder and sprinted away to where the building of the boat was going. On the way, he shouted, 'They're coming… they're coming!' Then the rest of the men scrambled to their huts to pick up whatever they could grab. They quickly pulled their half-built boat, which still needed some essential work for the water and aggressively paddled it away using improvised wooden oars. As they inched along in the water, Gabi looked at the boat coming and shouted, 'Faster, they're approaching the island.' Thereafter, they frantically rowed the boat.

Shalaqbeen was standing on the boat's deck and was gazing at the island as they approached the shore. He stopped the ship and ordered his men to drop the anchors and bring the canoes down. Soon after that, Queen Idil was in one of the canoes with him, and they rowed to the beach. When they reached the beach, they rushed to the island looking for the thieves.

The men spread on the island to find the men and Queen Idil want to ascertain Dhudi's death went to her hut. She found the fresh grave in the backyard of the Dhudi's hut. Believing that her poison had killed her, she longed to gaze at the tomb with great satisfaction. Her thoughts with the grave, she heard Shalaqbeen talking to some of his men behind her. She turned around and when saw him approaching her, she tenderly cried, 'Shalaqbeen, I found her grave. They killed her. We must get them and kill them all.'

He hastened to see what she saw, and his blood boiled with anger when he saw the grave. He stomped away to a group of his men who were with his deputy in the huts of the thieves and shouted angrily, 'They killed the young princess. Find them.' His men were shocked at the news and dashed into the woods, looking for the perpetrators.

Joining other men, who had already spread out on the island, they actively started searching for the thieves. They looked behind rocks, in the bushes and in every other place they thought someone could hide. But the more they tried to discover someone hiding somewhere, the more their hope thinned.

An hour later, his deputy returned with a broken axe, a worn-out shirt and freshly cut pieces of wood. He held the things in front of his commander and said, 'Commander, we searched everywhere and found these things. We also found fresh footprints and the mark of something large that had been dragged into the water. We think the thieves may have escaped in some sort of raft.'

'Show me where you found the markings,' Shalaqbeen demanded and then together, they trudged to the secluded section where the thieves had made their getaway boat. He saw the footmarks, the remnants of the things they used to build the boat and the mark left behind by something that had been dragged into the sea. He carefully considered these signs and said, 'They've escaped in an improvised boat. I wonder how they could make it. Let us find them.' He led his men back to the seashore. He approached Queen Idil and explained, 'Your Highness, it seems that the thieves who killed your stepdaughter have escaped in some sort of an improvised boat. They can't travel far with such a thing in the turbulent sea. Let us take the vessel and find them.'

'Shalaqbeen, where do you think they went to?'

'I don't know. Possibly the thieves took to the sea to find another Island.'

They hurried to their boat and started in the direction they thought the thieves had gone. Before they could go far, the Indian Monsoon winds with violent tides came and hit their ship very hard, and the captain and his men worked crazily to keep the vessel safe. After they struggled with the tides for quite some time, Queen Idil gazing at the sea, asked Shalaqbeen, 'Do you think their improvised thing can survive in these ferocious waves which almost capsized our big vessel?'

'It's unlikely, my queen,' he replied.

'Then let them die in the water. Call off the search,' said Idil, who had no intention of chasing a bunch of thieves who would die anyway in the raging sea.

'No, my queen. Even if the heinous men die in the sea, still we need to find their bodies,' he replied.

'Shalaqbeen, there's no need to waste our time looking for dead bodies. Let us go home. I need a private space to grieve for my stepdaughter,' Idil explained.

'But my queen...' he tried to argue, and she interrupted him, 'stop it. Leave them to die in the sea,' and that was the end. They sailed back to Zaila.

On the other hand, Dhudi and the thieves went to an unknown destination with the waves. Sometimes using their oars and other times relying on the restless tides pushing them away and away, they kept moving. At late noon, once they'd cut a long distance, their little boat became out of control. Tides taking turns, continued hitting it one after another and tossing it away, and the men tried hard to keep it under control. Unfortunately, the waves of the furious sea flung it away so madly. Everyone was silent with fear and clung to the boat's sides. With their chests flat on the floor, a gigantic wave rose high from the sea, towered over them like a wall and crashed down on them, washing away most of the things they carried. Shaman and Gabi thought the waves might either wash Dhudi away like they had washed away their items or destroy the floorboard. They tied her to one of the larger logs of the improvised boat and stayed close to her. They tied her to the log because they thought she would remain afloat with it if the waves destroyed the floorboard and it fell apart.

Another huge wave came, and it swept away everything on the boat except Jamanjug's bow and quiver, which he strapped across his chest and Queen Idil's bag, which strapped across Shaman's chest. Everyone was speechless as their floorboard flew with the battering waves. No one knew what to expect next their boat crashed on a large rock among a chain of rocks, and it broke into pieces but no one was seriously hurt. Dhudi broke away with the log she was tied to, and the men either fell into the water or scrambled to safety. Shaman saw Dhudi floating with the wood somewhere not far from him. He swam to her and dragged her towards the rocks.

As he neared the closest rock, Kalah joined him, and Daweel had already landed on top of a reef and yelled, 'A land! There's land.' Then Gabi and Jamanjug got out of the water and joined him. Together they investigated how to winch up Dhudi, and eventually, they managed to bring her in. The group, happy they survived the mayhem of the crashing tides, huddled on the rock. After that, Gabi looked towards the sunset and roared, 'We aren't on a small island anymore. We're on a mainland open to the world. Let us settle somewhere.'

'Can we settle here even if it's part of Zaila Kingdom?' Jamanjug asked suspiciously.

'Anyway, we're tired and cold. Let us find a warm place to rest. We'll think about other things later,' said Shaman, looking at Dhudi, who was very weak and curled up next to him.

They picked her up and trooped behind Kalah, whose left knee had bumped into the rock that destroyed their boat and limped in front of them. They settled in a sandy spot approximately a hundred yards away from the beach.

'It's a lifeless desert. We can't stay here. We must look for somewhere else to live,' complained Jamanjug feeling that the place was stuffy and lifeless.

'Jamanjug, we're in the land of hope and a better future. Get some rest. Everything will be fine,' Gabi responded.

20

CHAPTER

It was unbelievable that Dhudi and the thieves didn't die in the cruel sea and that they'd found a mainland but the question is can they cope with the heat of the strange empty desert? After having rested the group feeling hungry came together the following morning, and Jamanjug, who spoke first complained, 'The place is salty and hot. I couldn't sleep last night.'

Daweel yawned and grumbled, 'I couldn't sleep too. It's a breath-gagging desert. We must find a better place to live in.' Afterwards, other men talking one after another, recounted their negative experiences about the place. After they had talked enough about how they felt, Gabi suggested they should walk alongside the sea to find a suitable place to settle. Kalah disagreed with him. He argued that everywhere alongside the sea was salty; therefore, it was better not to waste time looking for another location near the sea. Dhudi heard their conversation. She pulled Shaman's hand to get his attention. He lowered his head close to her mouth, and she slurred, 'Let us look for the Kingdom of Awsa. Sultan Kandhafo will help us. He's a friend of my father.' Shaman then repeated what she'd said to the others.

'Princess, why do you think the Sultan will help us?' Jamanjug asked, and she replied through Shaman, 'My father told me that Sultan Kandhafo will help me if I ask him for help.'

'We don't know how to get to that Kingdom,' Gabi said.

Dhudi pulled Shaman's hand to get his attention again, and, as usual, she slurred, 'I can guess where we are. Let us go westward. We'll find it.' He passed the message on to the others, but it didn't go down well with everyone. Daweel looked in the direction she mentioned and grunted, 'It's a suicide travelling through that vast desert while we don't know where we're going. Think of something else.'

'We don't have another option, Daweel. Here isn't the right place to stay. Wherever we go, let us hit the road before the energy drains out of our bodies,' Shaman said.

'If there's no other option, then let us face the desert,' Jamanjug added, and that settled their differences.

Kalah carried Dhudi on his left shoulder as they started walking to the west. After they'd walked for a mile, they found a path. They took it, and it led them to the southwest. When they'd been on it for nearly three hours, Dhudi doubted the direction they were heading and slurred through Kalah, 'I heard the stories of this region. It looks like we're in the Danakil Desert. We must go to the west. The Kingdom of Awsa is in the west direction.' Kalah listened carefully to her distorted speech and said, 'Let us go to the west. Awsa is in the west.'

Then leaving the track, they started to the west. Each man taking a turn to carry Dhudi, they continued their journey. Once they were exhausted, hungry and thirsty at midday, they settled under a dry old tree in the desert. After they regained some strength and the scorching sun of the desert cooled down, they carried on their dreary journey. They trudged until the night fell on them in the middle of the sprawling desert.

At dawn the next morning, they restarted their daunting trek. With their tongues dried and exhausted at midday, they found some sporadic trees in the vast desert. They helped Daweel put down Dhudi under the shade of one of the trees, and then they fell side by side to rest. An hour later, once they'd restored some energy, Kalah worrying about the endless desert, said to Shaman, 'Do something, Shaman. Use your fortune-telling skills. Check what the future holds for us.'

'I'm not in the right mood, brother. I can't concentrate,' Shaman, who was in horrible shape, grumbled.

'Come on, Shaman,' said Daweel, coaxing him to do it. 'We're in a dire situation. Make the prediction. Remember, you did it in Faay Island and what you predicted actually happened when we were in the sea.'

Shaman looked at Jamanjug, who was curled up next to him and said, 'Jamanjug, if I do it, will you believe in what I'll say?'

'Just go and do it,' Jamanjug grunted hopelessly, and Shaman stood up to find a suitable place for his prediction. He went under the shade of a tree and began his fortune-telling feat. Chanting the incantation that he used in his prophecy, Shaman printed three fingertips on the sand, two after them and one more fingertip at the top end. He repeated the same finger markings in parallel with these and looked at the sky, searching for signs to show him what the future held for them. Nothing occurred to him. He repeated similar fingerprints to the side of those he had already created, and again he looked up into the sky. He visualized himself and his group in a pen and unhappy. Startled by his vision, he stood up and went back to his friends.

He told them what he'd envisioned, and Gabi got to his feet and said sarcastically, 'Shaman, whatever is going to happen to us, we need to keep going while we can still move. Let us go.'

Before the rest of the group got on their feet too, Dhudi, now dehydrated and disoriented, pulled Shaman's hand, and she sadly mumbled, 'Shaman, I want to die here. Leave me alone, please.'

'Are you out of your mind? Why are you saying such a thing?' he replied.

'I'm a girl and a princess. It's disgracing and sickening for me, men who aren't my close relatives, to carry my filthy and stinking body on their shoulders. I lost everything. Let me die here.' Since the night she was poisoned by her stepmother, she couldn't go to the toilet by herself or feed herself. She felt worthless and disgraced because the thieves were taking her to the bathroom, feeding her with their hands and carrying her everywhere. Shaman understood her feelings and was saddened by her decision. With a frown on his face, he gazed up at the sky. Then the other men, attracted by his gesture and wondering what she'd told him, asked, 'What did she say?' And Shaman repeated what she'd said to him.

While others were still thinking about what to say, Shaman twisted his head back to her and said, 'My princess, you didn't lose everything. You have us. I want to adopt you as my daughter, and I'll die with you in this desert if we can't make it,' and Gabi growled, 'If you accept me, I'll be your good brother. Don't give up hope.' 'Me too, we all like you,' Jamanjug shouted. Before she could say something Gabi picked her up, dangled her on his healthy shoulder like a small blanket and walked away and the others followed him. They trudged in the hot desert for the rest of the day. At sunset, as they were looking for a place to sit Daweel blurted out, 'Look at the fire!' They all looked in the direction where he pointed but they couldn't see any fire.

Unbelieving what he said Jamanjug looked at him and said, 'Daweel, there's no fire. You either hallucinated, or you've seen a firefly.'

'Shut up, Jamanjug. There's no firefly in this scorching desert. You're too short to see it,' screamed Daweel, turning his head to Gabi. 'How about you, Gabi? Can you see it?'

Gabi turned his head to the direction where Daweel pointing at and replied, 'I can't see anything except the increasing darkness of the night.'

'You're all blind. It's an intermittent light. Let us keep walking towards it. You'll see it soon.' Daweel insisted.

After they walked for a while, Kalah cried unexpectedly, 'It's there. I can see it.' This time they all saw a small flame that was sometimes rising and other times disappearing in the distance. Feeling hopeful, they hurried towards it. As they came closer to it, they saw more fires and lights on their way, and afterwards, they emerged into an area with clumps of trees and huts. They hastened to the nearest house, standing in a large enclosure with a big tree. They stopped at the entrance, and Kalah screeched, 'Hello, water, please.'

People in the house rushed out to see the strangers at their gate. They brought them inside and gave them water. While drinking the water, the family's father sent one of his two sons to call the village's chief. The place was an oasis in the desert, and it was a custom agreed by the people who lived there to inform their leader if strangers came to the oasis.

The boy brought a chief dressed in traditional attire with red and black tartan patterns. The father of the family gave a stool to his leader and said, 'Chief, we have these miserable people."

The chief sat opposite the strangers and asked them, 'Where are you come from?'

The group didn't bother to answer his question. Instead, they begged for food.

The chief stood up, picked up an oil lamp and shone it at them to see their faces. He was astonished when he saw how miserable they were. He instructed the father of the family to feed them and provide them with a place to rest for the night and that he would be back in the morning to interrogate them.

The people that lived in the oasis were not wealthy. So it was hard for one family to feed six people. The Father of the family sought assistance from his neighbours and fed them well that night.

21

CHAPTER

The Next morning the chief returned with two elderly men. They sat under the big tree with the thieves and Dhudi curled nearby, and then the chief asked, 'Who are you, guys? Tell us about you.'

'We're travellers going to the Awsa Kingdom,' Shaman replied.

'Where are you come from?' The chief asked again.

Shaman, avoiding mentioning the island they'd escaped from replied, 'We come from the sea. Our boat had broken up after it hit a rock.'

'What happened to this girl,' the chief, gazing at Dhudi asked yet again, and Shaman hesitantly answered, 'She had a terrible accident.'

'We're speaking the same language. Are you Zailians?' he asked once more. Shaman was frightened when he talked about Zaila and replied, 'That's right but we're heading to Awsa.'

'At which port did you begin your voyage?' The Chief asked searching for a hint of a lie in his face.

Shaman found it hard to answer his question. He remained silent thinking what to say. The chief longing for his answer snarled, 'I'm waiting for your answer.' Then Daweel, trying to help Shaman, naively rushed to say, 'It started from Faay Island.'

'Are you thieves put on that island by the kingdom?' The Chief questioned.

Daweel almost to answer the question Gabi said, "It's where our ship wrecked."

"Whoever you're and wherever you come from we'll deal with you properly,' said the Chief. 'Stay where you're while we're deciding what to do next.' He stood up and walked away with the two men already with him, leaving behind the thieves silently blaming Daweel for his off-guarded response. They went to a tree that stood near a well in the centre of the oasis. They sat down under the shade of the tree, and the chief said, 'My colleagues, what do you think about these men and the powerless girl with them?'

'I think they're merchants whose boat capsized,' one of the elders said.

The other speculated, 'They don't look like merchants.Perhaps they're thieves escaping from their detention island in the sea. Remember one of them mentions that they started their journey from a place he called Faay Island.'

'I disagree with you,' said the chief of the oasis, 'if they're thieves running away from a detention island, why is this young woman with them? The kingdom doesn't put women on the detention islands. They're the bandits of Hamash Ghedi Hamag. We must stop them.' Hamash was an outlaw hiding with a group of violent militia in a mountainous zone called 'The Triangle', a no-man area between the kingdoms of Zaila, Awsa, and Abyssinia.

'How do we stop them,' asked one of the two.

'We'll hand them over to the kingdom's security force in Jibuti,' answered the chief, who had already made up his mind. He stood up and added, 'Let us go to tell them our decision.'

They came to the thieves huddled where they left them and the chief delivering their verdict, yelled, 'Strangers, we suspect that you're are Hamash Ghedi Hamag's militia.' We'll take you to Jibuti tomorrow morning. Stay where you're while we're arranging your transport.' Jibuti was a seaside town between the oasis and Zaila City.

The thieves were terrified at his decision. They looked at each other, and then Gabi desperately roared, 'We don't know Hamash Ghedi, and we ain't going to Jibuti. We must proceed on our journey to Awsa.'

'You can go to Awsa only if the queen's army in Jibuti lets you go there,' replied the chief turning towards the father of the family hosting the thieves. 'Disarm them and guard them in your enclosure until we're arranging transport for them,' he added.

The father replied, 'Okay, chief' and straightaway he went to Jamanjug and snatched his quiver and his bow from him.

'One more thing. Don't let them talk,' the chief turning away to leave with his colleagues grunted harshly.

22

CHAPTER

It was an unexpected terrifying twist that people they thought would help them turn out to be their enemy's agents. After the Chief and those with him left, the five thieves looked at each other, a look that meant, 'What can we do?' Before one of them could say a word, they covertly glanced at the Father of the family, who was watching them from a corner. They said nothing. After some time, they saw him fidgeting, and they thought he was leaving, but ahead of he did so, his older son came, and the Father whispered in his ears, and then the son looked at the Thieves warily.

The Father went to an allotment at the back of his family's house leaving behind the boy eyeing the thieves cunningly. Minutes later he returned with a bowl full of corn cobs. He sat next to his son, and together they began shelling out seeds from the cobs. The families that lived in this oasis had allotments to grow crops and chicken coops in the backyards of their houses. When they finished shelling the corn cobs, the Father went back to the allotment to collect more cobs, and his son went to a latrine in a far corner of the house's enclosure. Jamanjug seized this opportunity. He said, 'We must do something. We can't allow them to take us to that cruel queen.'

'What can we do?' Kalah asked, and the Father, who probably saw his son left for toileting, came back in a hurry. He sat where he was sitting earlier, and afterwards, his son returned before long. The Father angry with his son mumbled, "Don't leave them alone again." From that moment, when a member of the family leaves another pretending was busy with something in their hands eyed them from a close range.

In late noon, Shaman convinced that there was no way they could discuss what to do, went to the toilet. While he was toileting, he curiously studied the wall of the toilet and understood that it was made of twigs, straws and easily breakable beams. Thinking about the wall of the toilet, he returned to the group. He sat next to Gabi and said audibly, 'My friends, as the Chief said, it's going to be a long journey for us tomorrow. Let us have a long nap,' and in support of his statement, Shaman winked at Gabi, and Gabi passed a similar signal to Jamanjug, who was next to him. They lay on their backs, and Shaman avoiding looking at him whispered to Gabi on his side, 'We must take the plunge tonight.'

Gabi whispered back, 'How?'

'Through the Latrine. It is made of straws and breakable beams, and nothing is behind it.'

'The whole group cannot escape through it while someone is watching us. Do you have another plan?' Gabi whispered again.

'No, but we have to leave tonight.'

Gabi thought a moment and said, 'Let us see how it works.'

The Father woke them up in the evening and gave them dinner, and over the food, they quietly shared the information about the restroom's breakable wall. When they finished eating, The Thieves lay on their backs again, waiting for a chance. Nearly midnight night, once the village was in a deep sleep, Shaman went to the latrine to assess the situation. He saw two guards, one sleeping on a mat at the fence's entrance and the other dozed off against the wall of the family's house. Shaman slowly tiptoed into the latrine, and after he had done what he was supposed to do, he silently broke the back wall and returned to his group. He whispered in Gabi's ears, 'I broke the back wall of the toilet, and the guards are fast sleeping. Let us move.'

'Okay. You go first and walk in the northwest direction and wait for us outside the oasis. Kalah carrying the princess will be the next.'

After Shaman disappeared into the darkness, he pulled Jamanjug's earlobe and whispered in his ears, 'Hey, little man, it's time to move.'

'Okay, Mr Gorilla?' Mumbled Jamanjug longing to hear this.

'The guards are fast sleeping. If they wake up we must kill them before they can a sound. The one sleeping against the wall of the house is yours. Take him if he wakes up. I'll take care of the one at the entrance of the enclosure.'

'Okay,' replied Jamanjug crawling towards his man.

Gabi pulled Kalah's hand and instructed him to take the girl, sneak with her through the toilet, and join Shaman outside the village. Moments later, he sent Daweel away, and then on his way to the latrine, he said in a hushed voice, 'Jamanjug, let us go.'

When they got out, Gabi saw him carrying a bow and a quiver and asked, 'How did you get these?'

'I nicked them from the boy. He had them beside him,' Jamanjug replied proudly.

Gabi laughed at him and said, 'Let us hurry up, little nicker.' In minutes, they joined others waiting for them outside the oasis. Together, they ran in the northern direction. Jamanjug and Gabi, frequently glancing back to check if they were being followed the group kept running as fast as possible. Once they descended a hill created by the desert sand dunes, Jamajug asked, 'What will happen to us when we get to Awsa?'

'I don't know,' said Gabi. 'Maybe the princess can tell us.'

'Don't you think that kingdom will send us back to Zaila?'

'Why it will do that?' Shaman queried.

'Kings and queens are friends,' Jamanjug repeated cunningly.

'No, the Sultan of Awsa is a good friend of my father. He won't hand us over to that ruthless queen. I'll tell him everything she did to me,' Dhudi drawled from Gabi's shoulder, and Gabi relayed her message to others.

Jamanjug unconvinced the Sultan would listen to such a miserable young girl with a bunch of thieves, again asked, 'Dhudi, can you really talk to the kings and sultans?'

'She's a princess and the daughter of a king. What stops her from speaking to them?' Shaman snarled. They kept running, sometimes bantering over trivial things while jogging and other times glancing back to check if they were being followed.

An hour later, the man sleeping at the house's entrance woke up, and when he noticed the thieves were missing, he ran to the other guard. He woke him up and asked, 'What happened? Where're the thieves?' and the young guard replied, 'I don't know. Sorry, I dozed off.'

'You let them escape, imbecile,' said the older guard, who grabbed a lamp and started to find their footprints and where they made their way out. He couldn't see where The Thieves exited. Wondering how on earth the five men and the ailing girl could escape without being noticed, he searched their footprints outside the house's enclosure. He saw where they broke the latrine's wall and the direction they went. 'Come on, boy. Let us catch them before they go far,' he shouted, and together they followed the track of the getaway men. After they pursued their footprints for quite a while, and there was no sign of them, the older guard decided to go back and report the matter. They came to the Chief's house, and they told him what happened, and The Chief, so upset, busted, 'How could they get out of your sight? If you couldn't guard them as it should be, why did you take the job?'

'Sorry, Chief. They benefitted a few minutes this young lad dozed off.'

The Chief then rushed to the houses of eight families who lived in the oasis one after another to gather warriors. Within minutes he brought together six armed men, one of whom had a rifle. He ordered them to chase the escaped thieves and get them back to him immediately. The six village warriors began their chase. They were fast desert men. Once they covered a long distance and the day broke out a mighty whirlwind of sand battered them in the desert. Half an hour later when the high wind passed, they ran as fast as possible to catch the thieves before entering Awsa territory. Sadly they lost their footprints. However, they kept to the direction of Awsa Kingdom.

In late noon, the chasers saw in the distance the Thieves already crossed a dry valley that divided the two countries. They dashed towards them and as they approached the edge of the valley the thieves saw them too and ran away. One of three fast chasers who had a gun fired several shots at them in the valley and shouted, 'Stop where you're before we kill you.' The thieves ran away with Dhudi, leaving Jamanjug ducking behind a shrub with a bow and arrows to slow down the chasers. As the first three chasers almost crossed the valley Jamanjug shot the gunman in the chest, and his flying arrows forced others to dodge.

While they were ducking from his arrows, Jamajug got out of his hideout and ran after his group. One of the chasers fired an arrow at him, and at the same time, they chased him until their leader on the side of the valley shouted, 'Warriors, come back. The other side of the valley is Awsa's territory.' After that, the chasers returned with their wounded comrade.

23

CHAPTER

J amanjug wondering what made those chasing him stop caught up with his group and together, they trouped westward. At sunset, they settled in a soft sand spot and the following morning, they continued their journey. After walking for two hours, they emerged into rolling maize fields and sporadic human settlements. They kept walking through the fields. After walking for a while they turned to a shackhouse by the entrance of a maize field. They came to a family having breakfast. They greeted them and asked them for water. The family gave them water, and after drinking water, Shaman asked the family's father to direct them to the capital of Awsa Kingdom. He showed them the way and told them it would take one hour on foot to get to the city. The group, delighted with his information, thanked him and proceeded with their travel.

An hour later, they'd emerged on the outskirts of Awsa City. They carried on walking, and afterwards, they mingled with people flocking towards the city centre. As they advanced into the town, a handsome young man dressed in an embroidered brown jacket that hardly fit him and a hat designed like a royal crown approached them and asked, 'Where are you come from, brothers? You look like strangers.'

'We come from the Red Sea. Who are you?' Jamanjug asked him.

'I'm Prince Hanad. I live in this city.'

'Ask him. Is he Prince Abacha's brother?' Dhudi hung down on Gabi's shoulder drawled, and Gabi repeated, 'Are you Prince Abacha's brother?'

Prince Hanad looked at the miserable girl dangled from the man's shoulder and asked Prince Abacha. Wondering how she knew him and what happened to her, he asked, 'How do you know Prince Abacha?'

'The princess knows him. Answer her question,' Gabi replied.

Hanad, looking at her with his eyes dancing on her high cheekbones, her flowing black hair, her big intelligent eyes with perfect eyelashes and her powerless stunning figure hanging down from Gabi's shoulder, asked again, 'Is this suffering girl a princess?'

'Yes, she's the Princess of Zaila, ' Jamanjug replied proudly.

'What happened to the princess?' He asked once more, gazing at her interestingly.

Gabi annoyed at his many questions, replied, 'Answer the Princess's question first. Are you Prince Abacha's brother?'

'No. I'm not a member of the royal family, but I know Prince Abacha,' Prince Hanad explained.

'The Princess is going to Sultan Kandhafo. Can you direct us where the royal family lives?' Jamanjug interjected.

'Come with me. I'll show you the way,' said Prince Hanad curious about them and happy to help them to know more about them. He led them to the kingdom's palace, and within a short time, he brought them the entrance of a compound with thick cobblestoned walls and defence towers on its various corners. Then he said to one of three security guards dressed in a red jacket with brass buttons, a black crown hat and a white thobe, 'This girl is the Princess of Zaila, and the men with her are her assistants. She has come to see Sultan Kandhafo.'

The watchman looked at the group despisingly and enquired, 'Who are you, guys? Tell me who you are in your own words.'

'We're thieves from the Red Sea. We brought the Princess to Awsa, and she came to see the Sultan of this land,' Shaman explained.

'You are a crazy bunch of people. Go away,' the watchman screamed.

Dhudi flustered with the guardsman's abusive comment, demanded Gabi put her down and help her stand up. She stood up with the help of Gabi and Shaman, who flanked her on both sides. Then her legs wobbling, she mumbled, 'We ain't crazy people. I'm Princess Dhudi of Zaila and The Thorny Land, and these are my friends. I come to meet Sultan Kandhafo, a friend of my father. Let us go in,' and then Shaman repeated what she'd said as usual.

The security man was baffled by her situation and her claim. 'Wait for me. I'll take your message to the throne hall,' he said and walked away.

He came to the butler of the Sultan and said, 'Butler Zaman, there's a sick girl with five strange-looking men at the gate. She said she's the Princess of Zaila and The Thorny Land and wants to see The Sultan.'

'Did she say her name?' Butler Zaman asked.

'Yes, her name's Dhudi.'

'If she isn't an impostor, she must be the only daughter of King Erek. Wait here for me,' said Zaman. He went to the Sultan and told him about Dhudi and the men with her. Then the Sultan instructed him to bring them in. After that, the butler hurried to the gate. He came to the group huddled around the ailing princess and told them to follow him. They followed him without thanking the young man who had shown them the way. Zaman, bewildered by the appearances of the five funny-looking men and the condition of the ailing princess in front and the thieves frequently glancing at things on their sides with awe, trouped to the official chamber.

The Awsa Kingdom's home was a two-storey large building that stood in the centre of a sprawling compound on a hill in the west of the city, and its name was The Citadel. It had three sections and a large open forecourt. The main chamber of the king where he works in the day time and his house were in the east wing of the building. The second large section was a guest house in the west, and it had female and male subsections. The third was in the middle of these two sections, and it contained a court hall, the office of head security men, a health post and a dungeon for prisoners. Moreover, it had heavily fortified bulwarks and defence towers erected in different corners of its compound.

Butler Zaman brought them before the Sultan, and Gabi put Dhudi down. After that, Gabi and Shaman flanking her and her feet hardly holding the ground, she slurred, 'Your Highness, my name's Dhudi Erek. I come to you for help,' and Shaman carefully listened to her slur and interpreted what she said.

The Sultan didn't rush to respond to her. He looked at Shaman, who was badly dressed and flanked to the right side Dhudi rocking back and forth. He glanced at Kalah, the clown who smiled at him, displaying his rotten black teeth. The Sultan then stole a look at Daweel, the skinniest of all, and then his eyes shifted to Gabi, who towered over Jamanjug next to him. The Sultan marvelled at the selection of people they were, turned his head towards Dhudi and said, 'All of you sit down.'

They sat down on a carpeted floor, and the Sultan repeated, 'Princess, I can recognise you, but you're in terrible shape. Tell me what happened to you and how you met these strange-looking men?'

'An accomplice of my stepmother poisoned me, and these men saved my life. They're the only family I have now.'

'Before you came to my chamber, some of my ministers warned me that you could be an impostor. However, I do not doubt that you're the daughter of King Erek and Queen Hibo. Why did that accomplice poison you?'

'Your Highness, it's a long story.'

'Okay, we'll come back to it. How did you meet these men?'

'I met them on an island in the Red Sea,' she said through Shaman.

The Sultan disliked the Shaman's awkward interpretation and decided to question the men directly one by one instead. He said, 'Gentleman, stop translating what the princess says. Just answer my questions. Tell me who you are and how you met the princess, and I must warn you, if you lie to me, I'll punish you.'

Shaman then grunted, 'Your Highness, I'm one of these five thieves, and we come from Faay Island.'

The Sultan, shocked by his claim, opened his eyes wide and said, 'Did you say we're thieves?'

'Yes, your honour,' Shaman repeated, and Dhudi slurred, 'Your highness, they're not bad thieves...' and Shaman relayed her message to the Sultan.

'Shut up, Princess, there are no good thieves. I want every one of you to tell me what crime you've committed and how you met the princess,' the king screamed.

'Your Highness give me a chance to explain to you about them and why they're here with me before they tell you the crimes they've committed,' Dhudi decided to protect them, slurred, and Shaman repeated what she said.

'Why can't they explain themselves?'

'I'm afraid they may confuse and give you wrong answers,' Dhudi explained, and the Sultan respected her word and said calmly, 'Go on.'

'Sultan, it's true these men are petty thieves, but they're harmless good men. I found them on an island where my father's kingdom banished them once they had been accused of committing minor crimes. They protected me from my stepmother, who tried to kill me twice. They carried me in the sea and in the deserts, and they're here to help me. Before he died, my father told me if I needed help, you and a few other people would help me. I came here to ask for your help. The kingdom of Zaila fell into

127

the hands of a wicked queen. I want to liberate my people from the rule of this terrible queen. Please help us.'

The Sultan, impressed by her courage and wanting to know more about what happened to her asked, 'You said your stepmother tried to kill you twice. Tell me what happened and how you got on that island where you found these thieves.'

'It all began at midnight and in my room in the Palace of the Kingdom Zaila,' she started telling her whole story through Shaman. Without leaving any essential part of it when she finished, the Sultan felt pity for her, ordered Butler Zaman to take care of her and her friends properly, and then the butler led them to the guest house.

24

CHAPTER

Sultan Kandhafo was a kind man with good moral values and integrity, but he had a wife who could twist him to her ways. The Sultan, disturbed by Dhudi's terrible state and thinking about how best he could help her went to his house after the meeting. His wife, holding a brightly coloured small quilt in her left hand, opened the door for him and then the Sultan passing her to enter the house, said excitedly, 'Nadia, I have big news for you today.'

'What is it, my dear?' asked his wife, Nadia, who followed him to help him take off his royal robes.

'But I must warn you, somehow it isn't good news,' he told her.

'Whatever it is, tell me at once, my dear,' she chirped, taking off his robes and crown from him. Nadia was a tall, brown woman with a long neck and was sensitive to unexpected news stories. She had been known for getting over-excited when she heard something new was happening somewhere in the world. She couldn't wait to listen to his big news.

'Princess Dhudi's alive. Sadly she's in terrible shape,' he said sadly.

'Impossible! Where has she been for such a long time?'

'More than that, she's here in our Citadel.'

'Here in our Citadel!' Nadia, who was surprised and already getting overexcited, screamed. 'That's incredible. How did she get here?'

'She came with a bunch of thieves who have been helping her since she went missing.'

'Thieves! How did she come to be with thieves?' Almost jumping out of her clothes in surprise and excitement, Nadia asked.

'I asked myself the same question at the beginning.'

'You didn't answer my question, and I am repeating it. The girl is a princess. Why was she with thieves?'

'The thieves helped her to escape from Zaila.'

'You said she's in terrible shape. What happened to her?' Nadia asked worryingly.

'She said she had been poisoned by her stepmother, Queen Idil.'

'This is unbelievable. Are you telling me that the Queen of Zaila has poisoned her stepdaughter, the only child of her late husband?'

'At the beginning, I found it hard to understand it. However, I have accepted what the Princess told me.'

'The fiancée of our son, the girl we've chosen for him, turns out to be a very mysterious person. Why did she get involved with thieves? Is she a thief now too?' Nadia, feeling confused, asked.

Five years ago, when Dhudi's mum died, Sultan Kandhafo, his wife, Nadia and their youngest son, Prince Abacha, came to Zaila to extend their condolences to King Erek and his family. At that time, Abacha was eleven years old, and Dhudi was nine. While Abacha was with his parents in Zaila, he got on well with Dhudi. He played with her and shared stories of his country with her, and in turn, Dhudi told him folk stories about her country and dined with him as her guest while he was at the palace. They developed a strong bond quickly, and Abacha's parents observed the chemistry between their son and Dhudi. Amazed at her relationship with him, her beauty and intelligence, they decided to make them a couple in the future. So, they proposed to King Erek that their son marry his daughter when they grew up, and the king accepted their proposal.

After the family had returned from Zaila, Abacha missed Dhudi, and he asked his parents if he could see her again. They told him that he would see her again, and more than that, she would be his wife when they were grown up. Abacha was delighted to hear that Dhudi would be his future wife, and he couldn't stop thinking of her from that moment on. He always remembered how nice she was to him, her excellent gaming skills, and her smartness at everything. When she went missing, and the news reached Awsa weeks later, he was desperately worried about her.

'Can you sit tight and listen to me? I'll tell you what I heard from her and the men with her,' the Sultan said to Nadia.

'Go on,' said Nadia, wriggling her bottom in the seat and trying to sit tight.

'Dhudi is now paralysed. She's crippled by Rijzi potion, and her speech has distorted so badly.' He paused, sighed and went on telling her the rest of her story, starting with the night Servant Bedel kidnapped her from her little cold room and ending it with her journey to Awsa. When he'd told her everything that he had heard from Dhudi and those with her, Nadia sat forward and said, 'She isn't the fiancée of our son anymore. She' is invalid, and she's been with thieves. We must find him another girl for him.'

'Let us find treatment for her first. She may get better.'

'No, she's paralysed, and she has been with thieves. We don't want her anymore.'

'Let us try it, please. The poor Princess may respond to the treatment well.'

'No, my husband, forget about her.'

'Ok, Nadia, but what can we tell Abacha? He'll be devastated when he hears what happened to her. Even though he only met her once, he loves her,' the Sultan said, trying to avoid succumbing to his wife's pressure.

'He'll stop loving her when he sees her crippled,' said Nadia, spreading the colourful quilt in her hand on the armrest of a wooden sofa.'

On the other hand, for Dhudi the Guest House of Awsa Kingdom was like a sanctuary run by merciful angels. Immediately after Butler Zaman and Gabi had carried her to the women's section, a patron in charge of the building ordered two maids to take her to a self-contained room on the building's ground floor and clean. The maids put her in a bed in the room. They stripped off her filthy rags, wrapped her in a clean and soft sheet, and afterwards took her to the bathroom. They sat her on a wooden chair and washed her thoroughly. They dried her up, wrapped her in the clean sheet again, and returned her to bed.

They applied a soothing oil to her body, dressed her up in a lovely garb and combed her tangled hair. Afterwards, they fed her a hearty stew, rice and sweet sherbet. When she had enough food in her stomach, Dhudi, who had been deprived of a good night's sleep for many days, dozed off quickly. The maids then crept out of the room and closed the door quietly for her. She slept deeply for the rest of the day and the following night. The next morning she woke up to find the two pleasant maids hovering over her. They took her to the bathroom, washed her and helped her brush her teeth. After that, they fed her porridge blended with honey and milk. When she had finished eating, one of the maids, a plump young lady with dimply cheeks and an oval face, shrieked, 'Princess, what's your name?'

Dhudi, trying to make her distorted speech understandable drawled, 'My name's Dhudi. What are your names?'

'I'm Marian,' the woman with dimply cheeks said happily, and the other maid added, 'I'm Amran.'

'Thank you both for caring for me,' Dhudi said gratefully.

Marian wondered why Dhudi's body lacked strength, and she had difficulty speaking. 'Princess, what happened to you? You can neither talk nor walk,' she asked anxiously.

Dhudi, making her speech as audible as possible, explained that her stepmother, the queen of Zaila, had given her a potion that paralysed her body and distorted her speech.

Marian asked again, 'Princess, why did your stepmother poison you?'

Princess Dhudi replied, 'I don't know exactly why she wanted to poison me but a man she arranged to kill me in the sea told me that I'm bad luck for her kingdom.'

At that moment, the two maids understood that she was indeed a helpless orphan princess and a victim of a cruel queen. They decided to help her to the very best of their ability. They massaged her body with a nice cream from head to toe. They applied special oil to her hair and combed it caringly. They spread a soft sheet on her bed, and from that day forward, they gave her the best care they could.

25

CHAPTER

Three days later, Prince Abacha returning from Afambiya, a village by Lake Afambo where his aunt lived came home his parents sitting in their private chamber and had two cups of tea and a kettle on a table in front of them. He happily greeted them, and his father greeted him back with hints of sadness in his voice. Abacha, wondering what made him so sad sat down. He poured himself a cup of tea from the kettle and animatedly talked about a hunting game he went with some distinguished landlords, including his aunt's wealthy husband. To make his story even more enjoyable, he told them about a giant antelope he had shot down by the lake, how he roasted it, and how the landlords exchanged entertaining jokes over the feast of the roasted antelope. It was a topic his parents usually enjoyed thoroughly. Strangely nothing he said had cheered them up. To discover what made their moods low, he asked, 'Mother and father, have something wrong happened? You aren't happy.'

His mother, Nadia, slowly turned her long neck towards her husband and shrieked, 'Sultan, tell him what happened to the girl.'

'Mother, you tell me what happened. Who's the girl you're talking about?' he demanded wanting to hear what had happened from his mother because unlike his father she would tell him everything she knew unreservedly.

'Darling, your father knows better ways to say things than I do. Let him tell you what happened to the girl,' his mother replied.

'No, mother, you tell me,' he insisted.

'Son, it's about King Erek's daughter,' she shrieked.

'Did they find her?' Abacha hastened to ask.

'No. We found her but she isn't your fiancée anymore,' she added with her speech full of sadness.

'What happened to her?' He asked worryingly.

'My son, we tried to find the best girl to marry for you. Unfortunately, the girl we've chosen for you has been crippled by Rijzi poison, and she's been living with thieves since she went missing. Forget about her.' His mother explained, and his father added, 'My son, don't be disappointed. We'll look for you another good girl.'

'Father, I know you've chosen a good girl for me. However, you didn't answer my question. I want to know what happened to Dhudi. Who poisoned her? And where is she now?' He demanded worryingly.

His father sat forward in his seat and said, 'Listen to me, son. A Rijzi poison given to her by her stepmother paralysed her, and she's in the Guest House.'

'You mean she's here in our Guest House?' Abacha interjected impatiently.

'That's right and I'm ready to tell you her whole dark story if you want to hear it,' his father replied.

"Go ahead, father. Tell me everything you know about her,' Abacha said anxiously.

His father started telling him about Dhudi's misadventures, beginning with the night Servant Bedel took her away in a sack to kill her in the deep sea. Without leaving out any vital part of her sad story he concluded, 'Sorry for the bad news, son.'

Abacha then said calmly, 'It's a miracle that she's still alive after getting through these many dangerous incidents.' Saying this he stood up from his seat and walked away, heading to the door.

'Where are you going?' His mother asked.

'I'm going to see the princess,' He replied, almost exiting the door.

'Don't be disappointed, Abacha. There're plenty of nice girls to marry in Awsa,' his mother cautioned him.

He strode out of the house heading to the Guest House. Minutes later he knocked on the door of Dhudi's room, and Marian entertaining Dhudi with local folk stories at that time, opened the door for him and respectfully said to him, 'Hello my prince. Welcome.'

Stepping into the room he asked her, 'How is the princess?'

'The princess is paralysed by Rijzi poison. Otherwise, she's fine,' Marian answered before she hurried back to Dhudi sitting upright in bed with her back against the room's wall. She covered her body quickly, put a chair for him next to Dhudi's bed, and said, 'My prince, please take a seat.'

Abacha gazing interestingly at Dhudi rested well and nourished in the past three days she was in the Guest House sat on the chair and asked, 'My princess, how are you feeling?'

As Dhudi saw him mixed feelings flooded into her mind. In one way she was happy to see him and in another way, she was saddened by the terrible health condition he found her. However, the memories of the good times they spent together in Zaila streaming into her head she drawled, 'I'm good, my Prince.'

Also random sweet memories of the days he was with her in Zaila gushing into his mind and his eyes dancing on her powerless beautiful figure in the bed, Abacha said, 'I'm sorry about what you went through, Princess. I heard your story from my parents.'

Dhudi wriggling her bottom with all the strength her feeble limbs could have to sit properly and making her voice as clear as possible replied, 'Thank you for your kind visit, my prince.'

From that moment, Dhudi saying less, and Prince Ababcha talking the most, they had a long conversation about what they had done together in Zaila. Things happened to her after the death of her parents. How he worried when she went missing and more, and at the same time while they were chatting Abacha disturbed by the illness that maimed her abilities was thinking nothing but how he could help her. As they were close to the end of their long conversation he looked up at the ceiling and said, 'Princess, Rijzi is a potent potion. You need a strong anti-Rijzi medicine to restore your strength. I'll look for you a good healer.'

'Thank you, my prince. Please do whatever you can. I want my legs to carry me again and my tongue to sing as it used to be before the Rijzi poison distorted my speech,' said Dhudi whose face flushing with hope.

'I'll do whatever I can. Wait for me, I'll be back tomorrow with a healer,' said Abacha getting up from his seat to leave.

The following day, Abacha went to a lady healer who lived in Awsa. She was a good healer and her name was Saba. He found her in her house and explained to her about Dhudi's situation. Then Saba confident that she could cure the ailing princess came with him in a hurry. When they arrived the healer told him to wait outside and then with the help of Marian, Healer Saba first examined Dhudi's incapable body thoroughly. Second, she pulled out two bottles, one full of a brown liquid, and another containing black seed oil from a pouch she carried. She opened the lid of the bottle with the brown liquid and gave Dhudi two full spoons from it. She screwed the lid back on the bottle and put it down on a small bedstand by Dhudi's bed. She then unscrewed the other bottle's cap, poured some oil into her palm and applied it to Dhudi's body. She repeatedly massaged her stiffened limbs with the oil using both hands.

When she finished medicating her, she put the lid back on the bottle and instructed Marian to give the princess two spoons from the bottle containing the brown medicine in the mornings and massage the black seed oil onto her whole body in the evenings. Afterwards, Saba went to Prince Abacha, who waited for her on a wooden bench outside the building. She told him that she had given the princess two different medicines. A brown syrup that would clean the Rijzi poison from her blood and restore the strength of her limbs and ligaments and a black seed oil would make her skin shine and be healthy again. She also told him how she'd directed the maid to administer the doses. Lastly, Saba confidently assured him that her medicines would heal the Princess.

Abacha was delighted to hear that Dhudi would recover with the help of those medicines. He thanked Healer Saba and paid her handsomely. When she left, he went to Dhudi's room to check if Marian understood properly how to administer the medicine. He asked her some questions about the use of the medicines and Marian answered his questions correctly. After he confirmed that she knew what to do, he said to Dhudi, 'Princess, take your medicine. I hope it'll work well for you,' and exited the room heading back to his house. He came to his parents having lunch in their private chamber. He joined them and over the food, his mother asked him, 'How is the crippled girl?'

'She isn't crippled, mum. I got a good healer for her. She would be fine soon,' he replied with confidence.

'If she can't stand up or talk, isn't she crippled, son?' His mother repeated.

'Stop this, mother. She'll be fine soon, I promise,' he shouted angrily.

'Two of you, stop this conversation. Let us talk about other things,' his father snarled then they continued eating their food quietly.

26

CHAPTER

H aving plenty of food to eat and a bed to sleep on is surely good, but staying in the same limited space for a long time without having things of interest to keep you busy must be boring. Jamanjug found it dreary sitting in the Guest House all the time and couldn't resist his urge to explore the vicinities of the Citadel. 'Gabi, let us stroll out to see the surrounding area,' he said to his friend, Gabi, after they had been in the Guest House more than a week.

Gabi had never been in the palace of a kingdom before and was afraid that they might breach some rules unknowingly. He looked at his friend and said, 'Jamanjug, we've been given food and a place to sleep. We mustn't look for trouble.'

'We're not looking for trouble. We'll just stroll out to see what's behind this damn wall. We've been in this building for around ten days,' said Jamanjug, poking his forefinger against the wall beside his bed. Gabi, though, held his ground. He turned away from him and growled, 'No, my friend, forget it.'

Despite his friend's protests, Jamanjug refused to give up. He kept coaxing him to come with him until Gabi eventually succumbed to his pressure, and they began their first little adventure in the Citadel's vicinity. As they left the building, Gabi said, 'Let us see the princess first,' but Jamanjug rebuffed him, 'We'll see her after we return. Let us go.'

Gabi, getting annoyed with his response, turned towards the women's section. He approached Marian, who smiled at him when she saw him coming. 'Good morning Marian,' he greeted her.

'Good morning,' she greeted him back, smiling admiringly at him.

'How's the princess?' He asked.

Marian answered, 'She isn't in good shape. The medicine has stiffened her muscles. So, Prince Abacha called Healer Saba again this morning.'

'I'm sorry to hear that. Can I see her?' he said.

'Healer Saba is with her now. You can see her later,' she explained.

'I'll come back later,' Gabi halted at her and walked away.

He joined Jamanjug, who was waiting for him nearby, and together they took a footpath towards a garden by the west side of the building. Both enjoying a gentle breeze caressing their faces and strolling relaxingly, Jamanjug said, 'Isn't it a lovely day?'

Gabi didn't answer his question and Jamanjug repeated, 'Are you still afraid of going out, big boy? Why didn't you answer me?'

Gabi then replied, 'Jamanjug, frankly speaking, I've got a bad feeling about all this.'

'Stop thinking negatively. Enjoy your day,' Jamanjug said. After that, one chattering with excitement and the other sulking like an angry child, they continued rambling in the garden. As they went a bit further, they saw a group of men huddled around a juggler in a spot between the garden and the army bulwark in the west corner of the Citadel. They approached them and watched the performance of the juggler who was dressed in a collarless loose shirt that was too big for him, dirty trousers that looked like pyjamas and a worn-out brimmed straw hat. He was performing with two juggling stones and was stomping in the centre of the group in an awe-inspiring way. With the stones leaping up one after another from his hand before landing in his other hand, he had played the juggle-stones for a while, and then he took off the straw hat from his head. He put it in front of him and shouted, 'Friends, Just drop in it whatever you can.' Some of the men stepped forward and dropped what else they wanted to offer into it.

He stashed the coins and whatever else was offered into a leather pouch he carried, returned the hat to his head, and pulled out a little wooden flute from a sack lying next to his right foot. He placed its small flat side between his lips, put his fingers on its tiny holes, and then breathed in it with his fingers now moving up and down alternately. The flute released a lovely melody that captured the attention of his audience. The entertainer playing his instrument passionately and the crowd listening to him, a tall man with a large moustache and bushy eyebrows in a royal army uniform approached him from behind and yelled, 'Otel, I told you not to do this in the compound during the work time. Leave now.'

'It's a Friday. Everyone is off duty, mister,' Otel argued.

'You're distracting the security men. Even on Fridays, you aren't allowed to perform in the Citadel. Leave now,' the officer screamed.

'Sorry, mister,' said Otel, who quickly picked up his things and hastened to leave.

Gabi and Jamanjug were interested in talking to the entertainer. They followed him and caught him up just as he was about to reach the Citadel's main entrance, and Jamanjug shouted behind him, 'Hey, Otel, wait.'

Otel stopped, and Jamanjug approaching repeated, 'My friend, we're entertainers like you. Can we talk to you in a minute?'

Otel frowned at them and grumbled, 'Before you talk to me, who are you?'

'I'm Jamanjug, and this is my friend, Gabi. As I said, we're entertainers and the supporters of the Princess of Zaila,' Jamanjug replied proudly.

'I see,' Otel said with interest. 'What do you want from me?'

'Is it legal to entertain people with tricks in Awsa and take money from them?'

'Yes. If you have good entertaining skills, people will pay you.'

'That's amazing. Can we work with you? Maybe we know what you don't know,' Jamanjug added.

'Tell me what you know first,' Otel demanded.

Jamanjug hurried to say, 'We play four-piece juggle-stones, a flute, a fire-breathing game and acrobat dance.'

Otel, astounded by their skills, then said, 'Wow! That's amazing. You know strange things. How is it possible for a person to breathe fire?'

'We'll show you how to do it. Can we work together?' Jamanjug desperate to get money, asked.

Otel thought for moments and decided to make money from their skills. 'You can come along and perform with me if you want,' he said casually.

'But we don't have kits to perform. Can you help us?' Jamanjug said, and Gabi yelled out, 'Are you out of your mind, Jamanjug? We ain't going anywhere.'

'Come on, Gabi. We've got plenty of time. Let us just pay a quick visit to the city centre, do some tricks with our new friend, and then go to the palace, Jamanjug cajoled reasonably.

'No, we can't,' Gabi protested. 'Remember, we agreed to return to the Guest House after we get some fresh air.'

'How far is the city centre?' Jamanjug asked, twisting his head towards Otel.

'It's less than fifteen minutes away,' Otel answered.

'You see, Gabi. It isn't far away. Let us go and perform with him. At least we would get some money for soap and other essential things,' Jamanjug reasoned and Gabi attracted by the money eventually accepted his proposal.

On the way, Otel asked them how they acquired their rare skills and if they earned money with them. Jamanjug then explained to him that his father, who was a woodcarver and birthright trickster, had taught them their skills in a remote village in Thorny Land when they were both young. Also, Jamanjug, who wasn't shy to talk about the dark side of their past, told him how he and Gabi had played tricks secretly in Zaila and earned money with their skills until a judge in a court in Zaila City found them guilty of swindling money from people with their illegal tricks and sent them away to an island in the Red Sea.

Otel listened to him with interest and then said, 'Guys, the judge who sent you to that island was wrong. You've just entertained people, and they pay you after you make them happy. Nothing is wrong with that. Here, even you can entertain the Sultan, and he'll pay you if he likes your performance.' Gabi smiled when he heard that the Sultan of this land liked the entertainment. He thought that maybe he and Jamanjug might one day amuse the Sultan with their best tricks as a thank-you for treating them well in his Citadel.

When they reached the city centre, Otel said, 'My friends, I think we can make good money if you play the four-stone juggling act and do the fire-breathing stuff. I've only got two stones. Can you get anything to play with?'

'No, please. Get the things for us. We need four Juggle-stones, a half litre of Kerosene oil and three flame torches, and you'll lend us your flute whenever we need it. We'll compensate you later.'

'We can find the extra stones from the craftsman, and the kerosene oil is everywhere, but I've no idea where to get the strange fire torches.'

'Any woodcarver can make them easily,' Jamanjug said, and Otel cried, 'I know a good woodcarver. Let us go.'

They came to a craftsman who had a shop near the city centre. Then Otel, acting as the leader, explained to him that they needed four juggle stones and three short clubs, about the size of a kitchen pestle with a piece of cloth on the head of each of them.

The craftsman, who had never made such clubs before, demanded an accurate description. So Jamanjug helped him to understand how to make the clubs. When the craftsman mentally pictured the torches' shape, he asked for a down payment and Otel gave him some advance payment and told him they would return to collect them after lunch.

They went to the city square, where people go to chill out when they've got some spare time during the day. They came to some folks relaxing in groups. They selected a spot, and Jamanjug took Otel's flute and breathed into it with his fingers moving alternately up and down on its tiny holes. It released a sweet melody that attracted the attention of the people scattered in the Square. Within a minute, people delighted by his music thronged around him and Jamanjug excelled at playing the flute performed well. He continued playing it, swaying his body with the rise of the flute's sound and Otel put his straw hat in front of the audience and yelled, 'Just give what you can give to this good musician.' In response to his request, people dropped coins into the hat generously.

After Jamanjug had played the flute for a while, Otel decided to change the game. He stepped forward and played his set of two juggle-stones very well, but the crowd who had seen him doing this before clamoured, 'We want the music of the short man.'

Otel, more than happy to do whatever pleasing to his audience to get their money shouted, 'Jamanjug, play the music.' Jamanjug then played the music blending it with acrobatic dance, which made things even better. Once the audience was in the grip of his performance, Gabi, shaking his nipples and his belly, joined him. He danced with him hilariously, and people relished their display more and dropped more coins in the hat.

At the end of the act, Jamanjug shouted, 'My friends, we're going to have lunch. Don't go away. We'll come back and perform another impressive performance for you.'

27

CHAPTER

The three entertainers were thrilled with their performance. Anticipating getting more money next time, they went to a shabby restaurant at the corner of the road. They ate food, and afterwards, they returned to the woodcarver. They came to him already cut the clubs and made the extra juggle-stones they needed. Otel paid him the rest of the agreed amount and then with their things, the trio returned to the Square. They unpacked their stuff at a spot in the Square. After that, Gabi, happy with their new business venture and that he was using his entertainment skills again took the flute from Otel. He played it beautifully to lure the people in the Square to their performance. When the crowd swelled he stepped back to give way to Jamanjug to perform with the juggle-stones.

Jamanjug's display was hilarious. Shifting his small fat feet back and forth, he sent the four stones up in the air, one after another before they glided down to land in his little hands, and the audience marvelled at his performance. The audience couldn't lift their eyes from his marvellous act until he took a break. Immediately after he retreated from the stage, a beautiful woman as short as him and had a gap between her upper front teeth approached him and chirped, 'You're a wonderful juggling player. What's your name, dear?'

Jamanjug, surprised by her sudden appearance, answered sheepishly, 'Jamanjug.'

Smiling at him admiringly, she extended her hand to shake hands with him and added, 'I'm Jawhara. Nice to meet you, Jamanjug.'

He took her hand and answered, 'Nice to meet you, Jawhara.' Then she returned to her position, leaving Jamanjug mesmerized by her beauty.

After the break, Gabi decided it was time for the 'fire-breathing' display. He stepped forward and shouted, 'Ladies and gentlemen, we've something you've never seen before. Make the stage bigger!' We're going to perform a fire-breathing game.'

'A fire-breathing game!?' murmured a group in the front line simultaneously.

'I'm going to breathe fire in front of you. Please make the stage wide and get as far away as possible from the fire I'll spit out soon!'

'Are you a dragon? How can you do that?' shouted a man in the crowd.

'No, I'm a man like you,' said Gabi, turning towards Jamanjug. 'Light the club,' and Jamanjug set light to the club's head in Gabi's hand. Then Gabi, holding the kerosene-soaked burning club in front of his face and dancing breathed out the kerosene vapour in his mouth above the flaming torch, creating red and yellow flames in the air. The sudden flames forced some people to cower back. He kept spitting flame balls into the air, and the spectators stunned by his display watched him in fascination until he finished his fire practice and took a break. Thereafter, Otel strutted onto the stage and shouted, 'Ladies and gentlemen. It is time to give some incentives to this magician who spits fire.' He moved around the audience with his hat to collect more money from the awe-stricken spectators.

There was more to come. After a short break, Jamanjug took to the stage with three kerosene-soaked, flaming club torches, and he juggled them like the juggle-stones. It was another mind-blowing show for the people of Awsa. The spectators wondering how he could manage the burning clubs jumping up and down from his hands without burning himself, gawked at him with breathless excitement. After performing for a while, he took a break, and Jawhara jumped out of the crowd again, put her scarf on his shoulder and screamed, 'You're a great magician, Jamanjug. I like what you do.'

'Thank you,' he said, smiling at her.

While Jawhara and Jamanjug were still talking interestingly, Otel emptied the money he had collected from the spectators into his pouch. Then a giant man carrying a big club joined the crowd, and Otel started to shiver with fear when he saw him. The man walked to Otel and whispered in his ears, 'Carry on collecting the money. We need it.' But Otel was frozen with fear and couldn't move. The giant repeated, 'Stop panicking, imbecile. Keep collecting the money and tell your friends to continue playing the fire stuff.' Otel trying hard to conceal his distress told Jamanjug to perform another fire-juggling display, but Jamanjug understood something was wrong with him and asked, 'What's going on, Otel?'

Unable to tell him about the big man, Otel replied, 'Nothing, Just play the things.'

'We aren't playing anything unless you tell us what's going on,' demanded Jamanjug with Gabi, who sensed something wasn't right too.

Before Otel could say a word, the giant man growled, 'Come with me, Otel.' Together, they walked away from the crowd, and Jamanjug and Gabi followed them.

They stopped at the Square's corner, and the giant took the pouch with the money from Otel. He emptied it into a leather satchel he carried and walked away with it. Gabi and Jamanjug asked Otel, 'Who's this man who took our money?' And Otel lamented, 'His name is Jabal Guhaa. He's a ruthless bully. He always steals my money.'

As soon as those words had come out of his mouth, Gabi ran after Jabal Guhaa and shouted at him, 'Hey, you can't take our money and walk away.'

Gabal Guhaa stopped and turned back to see the person shouting behind him. He saw Gabi approaching him and roared, 'What money?'

Jabal was ten feet tall and had an immense body and elephantine feet. He was a thief who lived outside the city with his wife, who was four times smaller than him. He used to venture into the city and extort money and other valuable things from individuals he'd targeted. Otel was one of his regular targets. Jabal was only afraid of the kingdom's soldiers. So to avoid them when stealing he ducked into the dark alleyways and systematically robbed his victims.

'It's the money you've taken from that man,' Gabi, pointing at Otel roared.

'What I take from that man isn't your business,' he said and walked away.

'You can't walk away with our money,' Gabi moved in front of him.

Jabal Guhaa never thought there was a man who could challenge him in this country. He smiled at him slyly and said, 'Hey man, mind your actions. You can't stop me.'

'Give me the money. After that, you're free to go,' Gabi shouted.

'You're making a big mistake. My freedom isn't in your hands, little man,' Jabal growled. He shoved him forcefully aside and walked away.

Gabi stumbled backwards. He regained his balance and charged at him. Unfortunately, before he reached him, Jabal hit him hard with his club on his left torso. Gabi winced with excruciating pain in seconds then enduring the pain, he jumped at him, and they locked onto each other. They frantically tackled each other. Sadly, Gabi was tossed away within seconds and landed on the ground.

Gabi was bigger than the average man, but he was twice smaller than Jabal Guhaa. He quickly got to his feet and charged at Jabal once more. This time he punched him in the face in quick succession, and Jabal's eyes blurred from the onslaught of Gabi's powerful blows. However, Jabal still managed to catch Gabi's right hand in midair and again brought him under his control.

After their hands had been locked together for a few seconds, Jabal lifted him up and brought him down with a crushing blow. He sat on him and started beating him in the face mercilessly. Gabi shielding his face with his hands from his blows, struggled desperately to free himself from the pressure of the big man. Unfortunately, his attempts were useless. Gabi kept protecting his head with his hands and tried squirming to get himself free from the ruthless opponent. Once it seemed almost hopeless, Gabi dipped his right hand's fingernails into Jabal Guhaa's left eye, and Jabal-Guhaa jerked back. This was a precious moment for Gabi, who quickly got to his feet and fought back viciously. With his fists, he pounded on his face and every other tender spot on his body and in addition to this Jamanjug gave him Jabal's club, which had fallen on the ground earlier, and Gabi using it beat him viciously.

The two men's battle was brutal, but it was entertaining for the spectators in the Square. A large crowd had gathered around to watch Gabi brutally battering Jabal Guhaa with his club. Gabi still beating Jabal Guhaa, now unconscious and bleeding, the mysterious prince, Hanad appeared in the crowd and shouted, 'Stop beating him. The man is going to die. Don't kill him.'

Gabi stopped beating him, and the gruesome battle culminated in Jabal Guhaa without a pulse and sprawled on the ground. And Gabi winced with pain, standing over him with Jabal's club in his right hand. After he had caught his breath, Gabi took the leather satchel with the money and staggered away in the direction of the Citadel. Prince Hanad, Jamanjug, Otel and a group of spectators, including the short woman with the gapped front teeth followed him. As they were inching out of the Square, Hanad moved close to him and said, 'My friend, well done. You've defeated the ogre who menaced those weaker than him.'

Gabi didn't answer his remark. Instead, he kept limping towards the Citadel. Before Gabi and those who followed him got far, the Awsa Security Army got the news of the fight in the Square in a rush. They chained Gabi's hands together and swooped on Jabal Guhaa lying on the ground. They checked his airways and pronounced him dead. Then leaving behind his immense body sprawled in the Square, they hauled Gabi to the Citadel. Otel, Prince Hanad, Jamanjug and some curious spectators, including Jawhara followed them to the Citadel. When they reached the entrance, the guards allowed only the security men, their prisoner and Otel to enter the building. Jamanjug told the guards that he was one of the men with the princess from Zaila, but they refused to admit him. Jamanjug begged for entry. Unfortunately, their answer was the same.

The security men brought Gabi to a dark dungeon in the Citadel, where the Kingdom of Awsa kept the most dangerous criminals. They shackled his hands and legs with heavy chains and locked him up in an iron-gated cell, and they warned other people to stay away from him as he was a dangerous murderer.

Prince Hanad and Jawhara watched Jamanjug from a corner while he was begging for entry. They came to him after he was denied entering the building, and Hanad said, 'My friend, they may allow you in tomorrow. Come with us. You'll stay with me tonight.'

'You're a prince. Can't you convince them to let me in?' Jamajug asked Hanad.

'I'm not the prince you think I am. I'm not a member of the royal family. Let us go home,' Prince Hanad replied. It was true that Hanad wasn't an actual prince. Neither his father was a king nor his mother was a queen. He was just a self-appointed prince. Yet people who knew his background and his family called him a prince. However, Hanad had connections within the Kingdom of Awsa. His cousin was the chief of Awsa border guards, and he was a fresh army cadet waiting for a placement. He could have helped Jamanjug to enter the building, but he wanted to know more about the ailing princess and the men with her, so for this reason, he was taking him to his house to ask questions about them.

'Why are you faking to be a prince when you aren't one?'

'I'm faking nothing. Don't screw up my wish.'

'What wish?' Jamanjug asked surprisingly.

'When I was three, my mother said to me on my birthday, 'Hanad make a wish,' and I told her I wanted to be a prince. Then she said, 'You'll be what you want to be, son.' Since that day, my name has been Prince Hanad.'

'Sorry. I didn't mean to hurt you,' Jamanjug solemnly replied.

'It's okay,' Hanad said, and together they walked away.

28

CHAPTER

Healer Saba's medicine didn't work as expected. Before Gabi and Jamanjug left the Guest House this morning, Marian went to Dhudi's room to administer her morning medicine. After she gave the medicine Dhudi, 'Marian, my limbs are so stiff. Please message me with the black seed oil.' Marian thought telling her that she would have it in the evening as prescribed by Saba. Instead, she started massaging the oil on her body. Rubbing the oil on her legs and hands Marian noticed that her limbs were unusually stiff. Astounded at the strange stiffness, Marian thoroughly examined her legs' movement and realised that something was seriously wrong with them. She reported the adverse condition to Prince Abacha, who afterwards dashed to Healer Saba and explained to her what had happened. Alarmed with the news, Saba came with him in a hurry and examined the princess's body. It didn't take her long to discover that her medicine had made the princess's limbs so stiff. Disappointed with the outcome, she apologised to Abacha for the condition caused by her potion and told him that she had no other medicine that could fix the problem.

The Prince panicked and asked her what else he could do. She advised him to find a healer in Idaleh, a small hamlet in the country's southern corner. Then Prince Abacha determined to find medicine quickly for the princess. Heastened to his house to get the things he needed for his urgent journey. He came home, his mother in the living room. He got into his room and picked up a canteen, a small leather bag he usually carried with him, and a sword. He filled the water in his canteen and marched to the door. Just as he was leaving, his mother came out of the living room and asked him, 'You look in a hurry. Where are you going, son?'

He stopped and replied, 'I'm going to Idaleh to find better medicine for the Princess.'

'What happened to the medicine you gave her?' she asked curiously.

'It made her limbs stiff. I must find a good healer for her.'

'Leave this girl and her problems alone. I'm going to get a good girl for you. Her illness is incurable,' she worryingly said to him.

'I can't leave her like this, Mother,' replied Abacha, heading to the door. Leaving behind his mother staring at him anxiously, he dashed to the stable of the houses. He jumped on his horse and set off for Idaleh. After being on the road for more than half of the day, he arrived at the hamlet in the evening. He stopped near a woman kneading dough by the fence of her house, and from the back of his horse, he shouted, 'Madam, where is the healer's house?' The woman stopped what she was doing. She stood up and pointed at a cottage standing alone between two big trees in the corner of the hamlet and shouted, 'That's Healer Dabib's house.' He thanked her and drove his horse towards the cottage. He came to a small chubby man with bushy grey hair and a goatee beard as grey as his hair and dressed in a messy cloak, sorting through some fresh tree roots in the front yard of his house.

'Good evening, Healer Dabib,' Abacha greeted him, getting down from the horse.

'Good evening, prince,' said Dabib, who stopped sorting things and stood up to receive his royal visitor. He met him at the entrance and said, 'My prince, welcome.'

'Thank you,' Abacha replied.

Dabib put a worn-out wobbly chair, the best one he could find in his house, in the yard and asked, 'My prince, what can I do for you?'

'I'm looking for anti-Rijzi medicine. A princess is suffering in our house. She was poisoned with Rijzi,' Abacha explained.

'Rijzi!' Dabib said, very surprised. 'Only the army uses that poison, and it is for the enemy. How did it get into the princess's body?'

Prince Abacha explained to him how she was given the potion, how it had paralysed her limbs and distorted her speech, and how the medicine given to her by Healer Saba had stiffened her limbs. He further explained that the princess was in a critical condition and requested his urgent help.

After listening to him patiently, Dabib rubbed his grey goatee and said thoughtfully, 'Rijzi is a powerful and dangerous poison, and it doesn't have a known treatment. I don't think I can help you, my prince.'

'I've been told that you're a good healer. Please, save the life of the princess,' the prince begged him.

'I have no medicine to cure Rijzi poisoning, and making one would take time.'

'Whatever it takes, we've no choice. Please do what you can,' Abacha implored him once more.

Dabib thought for a moment and said, ' I'll try to create anti-Rijzi medicine for the princess. Go home and come back after two days.'

'No, I'm not going anywhere without the medicine. I'll stay with you until you create it,' Abacha insisted.

'My Prince, creating the medicine will take two days, and I don't have a suitable place for you to stay. Please come back on Tuesday, ' Healer Dabib repeated.

'Whatever it takes, I'm not leaving without it,' the Prince insisted. Healer Dabib succumbed to his pressure. He gave him a mat to sleep on and some food. After that, he began working on creating the anti-Rijzi potion in a messy laboratory in his house.

On the other hand, Abacha's mother decided to stop him from getting involved with the ailing princess. Immediately after he left home she got dressed and took a horse to Afambiya, where Maya, her young sister lived with her husband, Boukah, and their children. Maya's husband, Mr Boukah, was a well-known landlord in the Afambiya area. He married Maya after his first wife, who had given him two beautiful daughters passed away, and Maya became a good wife and faithful stepmother to his two daughters, Awlio and Samiya. Maya loved the girls and treated them just like her biological daughters, and the girls considered her like their own mother because of the care and respect she gave them.

After having been on the road for hours, Nadia arrived at Maya's house. Then the family wasn't expecting her begins to scramble to sort out a quick meal and a room to rest for her. When she had eaten and had some rest, Maya asked her, 'My sister, what brought you to Afambiya?'

'Maya, I've got a plan for Abacha.' Nadia said.

'What is it, my sister?'

'I want a wife for him, and I choose him to marry Awliyo.'

Maya had always wanted to find suitable suitors for her daughters and believed Abacha was a good lad. She was delighted at her sister's proposal but wasn't sure how it could happen. 'My sister, I thought you had arranged for him to marry King Erek's daughter,' Maya asked.

'King Erek's daughter has many problems. Her stepmother poisoned her. She's paralysed and has been with thieves since she went missing. Prepare Awliyo for him to marry. I'm sure they'll get on well with each other.' It was true that Abacha had a good relationship with his aunt's daughters, but they treated him as a brother.

'Girls like Abacha but think about him as a brother. I'll talk to her. However, I must talk to my husband first. Give me some time,' Maya explained.

'Maya, we don't have much time. I don't want him to get involved with the paralysed girl with the thieves. I'll send him here immediately after he gets back home. Make him and Awliyo get married,' Nadia demanded.

'I'll discuss your proposal with my husband, and I hope he'll agree with us. Abacha is a good guy,' Maya concluded.

'Okay, talk to him tonight. I want your word by tomorrow early morning,' Nadia instructed her younger sister.

That night Maya discussed her sister's proposal with her husband, and they agreed upon it. Then the following morning, they told Nadia they had accepted her proposal.

Nadia was delighted to receive this news. She thanked them, and afterwards, they escorted her to her wagon. Before climbing her horse, Nadia leaned on her sister's shoulder and said quietly, 'Sister, convince Awlio to be womanly. She should show him that she's interested in him and, when he comes never let him return to Awsa. I'll be back when it is shown that they're getting on well with each other, and their wedding will be arranged afterwards.'

'I will, sister,' Maya replied, and then Nadia, happy with the arrangement took the road back to Awsa.

29

CHAPTER

———

Prince Hanad lived east of the city with his mother and three siblings. On their way to his house, he asked Jamanjug, 'Why did your friend fight with Jabal Guhaa?

'I thought you were in the Square when the fighting began,' Jamanjug enquired.

'He came almost at the end of the fight,' Jawhara interjected.

Jamanjug then explained, 'We met that silly entertainer, Otel, and we came to the city centre with him. We've entertained people with our skills to earn some money, and then this big guy came and took our money from Otel.'

'Your friend is a good fighter. No one would normally dare to challenge Giant Jabal. He's the strongest wrestler in Awsa and a brutal bully. Everybody is scared of him.'

'What's going to happen to Gabi?' Jamanjug asked worryingly.

'I'm sorry to say this, but I think the kingdom will hang him for murdering Jabal Guhaa.'

'Is there a way we can save his life?' Jamanjug asked sadly.

'No, I'm afraid,' Hanad replied.

Jamanjug was terrified to hear this. He felt a numbness throughout his body and lamented, 'It was my fault. I coaxed him to come out with me. If I didn't do that, he would never be in this tragedy.'

'Blaming yourself isn't going to change anything,' Hanad suggested.

As they were passing the city centre, Hanad said, 'Let us check if the giant's body is still there.' They turned to the spot where Jabal's body was lying when the security men pronounced him dead half an hour ago. They found nothing. Wondering what had happened to the body, they looked around for it. Strangely there was no sign of it. 'Perhaps his family took him,' Jamanjug speculated.

'I don't think so. Jabal Guhaa has no family to take his body. His only family is his wife, who lives outside the city, ' Hanad explained.

'Isn't it possible that some other people took the body to bury it,' Jamajug asked.

'Possibly,' Prince Hanad said, and they carried on with their journey. Minutes later, Jawhara said goodbye to them and went home, and the two men kept their way. They came to Hanad's home, which was a shack house consisting of three poorly built rooms and an animal shed in the backyard of the building. 'Mum, I brought a guest tonight. This is Jamanjug. He's one of the five men with the suffering princess from Zaila, ' Hanad said to his mother, who was cooking food in the house's front yard.

'Take him to your room and come back. We need to talk,' his mother said.

He showed Jamanjug to a cramped room Hanad shared with his younger brother and said, 'This is your bed for tonight .' Jamanjug sat on the bed, and Hanad returned to his mother. 'Mum, what do you need to talk about?' he asked.

'Prince, listen to me. I'm struggling to feed my children. Stop bringing friends to the house.' His mother was a widow looking after her four children, so what she said was not unusual.

'Mum, he's denied entry to the Citadel where his other friends live. He'll stay with us only for tonight. Besides, don't worry, Mum, I'll help you. I passed all the cadet tests and will join Colonel Rohan's Border Guards very soon.'

'Sorry, son. I didn't know that your friend was desperate. Go back and accompany him. I'll bring some food to you after I feed the young ones,' his mother said, and Hanad went back to join Jamanjug in the bedroom. While waiting for dinner, Hanad asked Jamanjug how he and his friends met Princess Dhudi and what had happened to her. Jamanjug then explained that he and his friends were thieves on an island in the Red Sea and that one day they found her in their house. He further told him how her stepmother had attacked her before they escaped to Awsa. Hanad was mesmerised by his story and asked many more questions, which Jamanjug answered thoroughly.

The next morning after they had eaten a meagre breakfast, they matched back to the Citadel. They approached several guards at the gate. Hanad had greeted them, and he took aside the head of the guards and spoke with him quietly. After that, the head of the guards said audibly, 'Tell him not to go out without permission next time.' Prince Hanad nodded and returned to Jamanjug and said to him, 'Let us go in.' Jamanjug wondering what he had told the guards, followed him. They came to Kalah and Daweel, who shared the same room in the Guesthouse, and then Jamanjug disturbingly cried, 'Have you heard what happened to Gabi?'

'No,' answered Daweel, turning from a game he was playing with Kalah.

'He's been detained by the security men. He's somewhere in the Citadel.'

Kalah looked at him and grunted, 'What are you talking about? Stop playing games with us.'

'I'm not playing games,' Jamanjug bemoaned.

'Kalah, are you crazy? He isn't playing games. Don't you see he's crying? Jamanjug, what happened to Gabi?' Daweel asked.

'He killed a giant man who took our money, and then he got arrested,' Jamanjug added.

'Idiot! Why didn't you stop him before he got into trouble?' Kalah shouted angrily.

'It wasn't his fault. If I hadn't persuaded him to come with me, nothing would have happened to him. I'm sorry.'

'You said he killed a giant who took your money. Where did you get the money?' Kalah asked suspiciously.

'It was money we earned from our performances. We played fireballs, juggling stones and a flute in the City Square.'

'How could you do all those things? How long were you there?' Kalah asked again curiously.

'We went there yesterday morning and were in the town until evening.'

'Why didn't you tell us what happened sooner?'

'Are you crazy? I've been locked out. Prince Hanad took me to his house.'

'Look what you did, Jamanjug. You went out looking for trouble in a city you don't know. You and Gabi committed a crime in a foreign country. You tricked people into paying you, and you killed a local man. You've incriminated all of us. What can we do?' Kalah lamented.

'Guys, stop blaming each other. It isn't a crime to perform entertaining tricks in this city. They only got into trouble with the giant who took their money. Let us find your friend Gabi,' Prince Hanad explained.

'We must tell Shaman what happened before we go,' Daweel said.

They went to tell Shaman, and then together, they started walking to the Citadel's dungeon. They came to two well-armed guards standing at the door, and Hanad said to them, 'Friends, we come to see our friend, who was arrested yesterday by the security men.'

Then one of them enquired surprisingly, 'Are you looking for the dangerous man who killed the giant?'

'Gabi isn't a dangerous man. The giant was a crook who stole our money,' Jamanjug hastened to say.

'He's in a special detention cell. You can't see him,' the guard said. 'You can see him only on his trial day.'

'Please let us see him,' Shaman pleaded.

'Mister, we can't breach the rules,' the guard replied.

'Can I see the man on their behalf?' Hanad enquired.

The guard thought for a moment, then replied, 'No.'

Hanad took the guard aside and said, 'My friend, you know I'm an army cadet, and Colonel Rohan is my cousin. Don't treat me like this. Let me see the man, ' Hanad cajoled, and afterwards, the watchman led him to Gabi's cell. They stopped at a metal door with a large peephole on the top section. The guard then said, 'Talk to him through the peephole.'

Hanad pressed his face to the big peephole and said, 'Gabi, it's me. Prince Hanad. How are you?'

'I'm fine,' Gabi growled from the cell.

'Your friends are outside. They couldn't come in to see you. Did the crime investigators talk to you yet?'

'No one has talked to me since they brought me here.'

'I think the guy didn't die. If the kingdom accuses you of killing him, tell them you didn't kill him.

Gabi felt relief and growled, 'They said he died on the spot. Why do you think he didn't die?'

'I doubt he's dead. Tell them that you didn't kill him. Don't incriminate yourself.'

Gabi happily replied, 'I will.'

Prince Hanad gave him a small bottle of medicine through the window and said, 'This is medicine for wounds. See you in court,' and then he went back to rejoin the men waiting for him outside. Together they marched back to the Guest House.

Immediately after Prince Hanad and the thieves left, two crime investigators came to see Gabi. They found him badly wounded on his head and torso and lying on the floor of his cell. 'What's your name?' The most senior investigator asked.

'Jamaal Goley,' he growled.

'Do you have any other names?' the senior investigator asked again.

'People call me Gabi,' he replied without looking at the interrogator.

'You killed a man. What was the reason?'

He sat up and replied, 'I didn't kill a man. I fought with a thug who tried to steal our money, and we left him alive.'

'Why did he want to take your money?'

'Ask him,' he growled.

'We can't ask questions of a dead man. You've killed him. Answer the question,' said the interrogator.

He looked at the interrogator with fiery eyes and roared angrily, 'I didn't kill anyone.'

'Our officers confirmed that the man you fought with died on the spot. What made you think that you didn't kill him?'

'Because I don't believe that he's dead,' insisted Gabi, believing Hanad's words implicitly true.

'That's interesting,' said the investigator. 'We'll investigate your case and will talk to you later, Mr Gabi.' Then they left him. They went to the office of the Chief Justice, Chief Dangig. They approached him sitting in his office and told him that Gabi bluntly denied killing Jabal Guhaa. The chief firmly believed that Gabi had killed the giant. He ordered the investigators to find the giant's corpse and prepare a full report for the court then they left to look for the body.

30

CHAPTER

Healer Dabib worked hard to make anti-Rijzi medicine for the suffering princess. He brought together the roots and leaves of different plants, grounded them and squeezed from them the medical liquids he believed would cure the princess. It was painstaking work that took long hours. However, in the afternoon of the following day, he put the liquid into a small bottle and took it to Prince Abacha. He presented it to him sitting on a mat under the shade of a tree at the front of his house and confidently screeched, 'Your Highness, I made this medicine for the princess. It will cure the princess's illness. Please give it to her three times a day before meals.'

'Thank you, Healer Dabib,' said the Prince taking the bottle from him. He stood up, stashed the medicine in his pocket and as he started walking to his horse, Healer Dabib said, 'My Prince, the night will fall on you in the middle of your journey. Leave in the morning instead.'

'Thank you for your concern, but I must deliver the medicine as quickly as possible. The princess is suffering,' replied the Prince, turning away to leave.

'Your Highness, it isn't safe for you to travel at night in this lonely land. The bandits of Hamash Ghedi Hamag can be venturing in your path now. Please consider leaving in broad daylight,' said Dabib still worrying about his safety.

'Goodbye, Healer,' said the Prince reaching for his horse. He jumped on the animal's back and urged it forward. Thinking of the suffering princess, he drove the horse as fast as possible. The night fell on him in lonely rocky land, but the Prince, determined to deliver the medicine quickly, kept his horse jogging along slowly. It was uneasy travelling on a horse in a black night. However, the Prince carried on moving through the increasing darkness of the night. He eventually, reached the Citadel at 9:00 pm, when most people had retired to bed. He put the horse in the stable and then hurried to the Guest House. He came to the princess in her room with Marian and asked, 'How are you feeling, princess?'

'I'm sad, my prince,' moaned Dhudi, who was really distraught about Gabi's arrest.

'Don't be sad, princess. I brought a nice medicine for you,' Prince Abacha said. 'You'll be fine after you take it.'

'My Prince, it's not about my health. It's about Gabi, the man who carried me through the deserts and in the raging seas is going to be hanged,' Dhudi managed to moan though she had difficulty talking.

'What happened to him?' The Prince asked surprisingly.

'Gabi's accused of killing Jabal Guhaa, who took his money and attacked him,' Marian said.

'He killed Jabal! How could he kill the strongest wrestler and the giant everyone fears?'

'It happened. Please, will you save his life?' Implored Dhudi.

'Princess, I'm sorry to hear that your friend is going to be hanged. I'm afraid if what you've told me is true; there is nothing I can do. No one can change the rule of law to their liking. Take this medicine three times a day after each meal. You should be fine when you finish it,' he said, putting the medicine on the table next to her bed.

'Please try to save him,' Dhudi, forgetting her own troubles and worrying about Gabi, drawled again.

'Princess, as I said, there's nothing I can do about him. However, I'll do whatever I can. Good night.' He exited the door, heading to his house. Abacha was a big-hearted young man, and genuinely he wanted to help her. Sadly he could do nothing about Gabi's death penalty. In Awsa, as a matter of law, if a person kills another person, that person must be hanged, and nobody can change that. Thinking of the princess's accumulating troubles, he came to his parents, ready to go to bed. He greeted them, and his mother asked him, 'Did you find the healer?'

'Yes, mum. I brought a good medicine for her,' he replied.

'If she's in luck, your medicine will work for her. You'll not be messing with her anymore,' his mother said.

He didn't say anything about his mother's comment. Instead, he enquired, 'Father, what do you know about Jabal Guhaa's killing?'

'He was killed by one of those thieves with King Erek's daughter,' his father answered excitedly.

'How could that thief kill the scary giant? I mean, what sort of weapons did he use to kill him?'

'He killed him with his bare hands in the City Square before the eyes of everyone,' his father explained. 'Witnesses at the scene said the giant was armed with his big club, but this man had nothing when the fight began but still somehow battered him to death.'

'That's amazing. Is the thief another giant?' Abacha, who had never seen Gabi before, asked.

'I saw him on the day they came here. He's a bit big, but he's a normal man.'

'What has Chief Dangig said about the case?'

'I haven't heard from him yet. Why are you asking?' Asked his father staring at him curiously.

'The princess needs my help. She asked me to save his life. She said he's a good man who carried her through the sea and in the deserts.'

'You can't help her in a murder case,' his mother interjected, and his father added, 'Your mother's right, son. The man is a murderer.'

'It was self-defence. Giant Jabal took their money. Besides, Dhudi's a victim of her wicked stepmother, and she came to us for help.'

'Stop talking about things that ain't your business. Leave this girl and her thieves alone,' his mother repeated angrily.

He thought for a moment and said, 'The man who saved the princess is good. Please, father, have mercy on him.'

'My son, we can't change the law. Get some rest. You will be leaving tomorrow morning for Afambiya,' his father explained.

'Why am I going to Afambiya?'

'Your future lies in Afambiya,' his father added.

Prince Abacha wondering what his mother's plan was went to his room.

31

CHAPTER

The following morning, when woke up Abacha decided to do two things before leaving for Afambiya. First, visit Gabi in prison and second, see the Chief of Security, Dangig and check if there was a way he could help Gabi. So after he had his breakfast, Abacha went to the dungeon. He came to two guards standing at the dungeon's entrance. He told them that he had come to see the man whom security forces had arrested for killing the crooked giant. Then one of the two guards surprisingly cried, 'Your Highness, you cannot see him.'

'Why not?' asked Prince Abacha.

'He's a dangerous man. He killed the giant that everybody was afraid of. Please don't go near him,' the guard said in a worried voice.

'Even though he killed a giant, he's a normal man just like you. Don't be afraid of him. Show me where he is,' the Prince demanded.

The guard led him to Gabi's cell. They stopped at the metal door with the peephole, and the guard said, 'My prince, talk to him through this small window.'

The Prince pressed his face to the peephole and said, 'I can see little from here. The room is dark. Open the door and let me in.'

'My Prince, you can't be alone inside with him. He's a dangerous man,' the guard explained.

'Stop talking nonsense, soldier. Open the door,' the Prince snarled at him, and the guard opened the door. He entered the cell and said to Gabi, sitting in the room, 'My name's Prince Abacha. Princess Dhudi asked me to help you. How are you today?'

Gabi slowly lifted his swollen head and growled, 'I'm fine. How's she?'

'She's fine. I brought some medicine to her yesterday,' Prince Abacha turning his head to look at the guard with him, said.

'Go and get a nurse for him. He's badly wounded,' the prince said to the guard.

'My prince, wait outside while I'm bringing the nurse,' the guard answered.

'I'll stay in. Go and get the nurse for him,' the Prince ordered him, and the guard hurried away to a medicine woman working in a health post in the Citadel.

'Gabi, why did you kill Jabal?' The Prince asked when the guard had left.

'I didn't kill him. I left him unconscious.'

'They said you've killed him.'

'They're wrong, I guess.'

'That's interesting,' the Prince said and asked him more questions.

The watchman returned to the cell with the medicine woman, carrying a small medical pouch and as they walked in Prince Abacha ordered the medicine woman to attend to Gabi's wounds. Then she began her work firstly cleaning the wounds with locally made antiseptic medicine, and then she gave him some pain remedies. When she finished nursing him, Abacha instructed the guards to give him good food and to respect him as an ordinary man.

After that, he went to the office of the Chief of Security. He came to him sitting in his office with two of his aides. He greeted them from the doorstep, and the Chief rose from his seat and responded, 'Your Highness, welcome. What can I do for you?'

'Can I talk to you in private, Chief Dangig?' Abacha requested, and the other two men stood up to leave the room. When they stepped out of the room, Abacha spoke again, 'Chief, I'm trying to help the suffering princess in our Guest House. One of her friends is accused of killing Jabal Guhaa, and I think he's innocent.'

'My prince, I don't think you can help her regarding a man waiting for execution.'

'Why are you so pessimistic, Chief? The defendant told me that he didn't kill Jabal. Even if he did kill him, it was self-defence. Jabal took his money and attacked him.'

'Even though Jabal Guhaa was a crook, he's our champion warrior and wrestler. He fought for his country before, and above all, he's a citizen. He must get justice. When we complete our investigation, the man who killed him will be sentenced to death.'

'What then are you investigating if you already know that the poor fellow in the dungeon killed him?'

'The prisoner denied that he'd killed him, despite our officers having confirmed Jabal's death immediately after the fight was over.'

'Chief, can this poor man get justice?'

'My Prince, don't worry. My department will deliver justice.'

'Thank you, Chief. Goodbye, ' said Prince Abacha getting up to leave. He went back to his house to pick up his things. He came to his mother, dusting the furniture in the chamber. 'I thought you'd already gone?' She queried.

'I just went to take care of a few things that needed my attention before I leave.'

'You must go now. Your aunt and her family are expecting you.'

'I don't understand. What makes you think they're expecting me?'

'You'll see when you get there. Go now and behalf well with them.'

He didn't argue with her knowing nothing he could change her plan to end his relationship with Dhudi. He just picked up his things and started walking to the stable for his horse, thinking of the sick princess begging for his help in the Guest House, and about his parents sending him away to stop him from getting involved with her. He jumped on his fast horse and urged it away to Afambiya. After an hour Abacha arrived at his aunt's house and as his mother said, he came to find that the family were expecting him. They received him in a way that was different from the usual way he was treated when visiting his aunt's house. Before, he was like one of the children. Strangely though, this time, they treated him like a person with high social status.

His aunt and Awlio showed him to a well-furnished room to sleep in, and they gave him nice robes to put on. While he was changing, they fixed a hearty meal for him. The formal reception, the particular room that was given to him, and how his food was presented suggested that things had changed. He linked their actions with what his parents had said to him earlier. 'Aunt, why am I honoured as a king tonight?'

'My son, you're a full man now, and above all, you're going to be the Prince of Afambiya,' she said. 'I must treat you as one of our distinguished royal men.

He didn't ask any further questions, and his aunt and Awlio stayed with him until he retired to bed for a nap. When he woke up in the late afternoon, Awlio, in a beautiful outfit, invited him to tea and sat with him while he was drinking it. Her face flushing with unusual happiness, she served him and stayed in his company. When he had finished the tea, she said, 'Abacha, come with me to the farm. There are things I need to do there.' Together they walked to the main gate of the house. Before they left, Maya called Awlio from her bedroom door, and Awlio went to her. 'Handle him properly. Prepare him to be your husband,' she said to her.

Awlio had similar instructions before. She felt uncomfortable with her stepmother's nagging advice and said, 'Mother, I'm not stupid. Stop repeating things you've already told me,' and she walked away briskly to catch up with Abacha, who waited for her outside the house. Prince Abacha and Awlio were like a brother and a sister before, but today at least one of them sees that relationship differently. Awlio, doing what she had been told to do by people she honoured, started telling him jokes and funny stories to lure him into her world on the way. She made him laugh, and Abacha taking his turn, told her some entertaining stories too. Both were laughing and enjoying their conversation until they reached the farm. They spent the rest of the day together on the farm, either doing small jobs on it or rambling around.

In the evening, they returned home, and they were received by her parents, waiting for their return. The parents invited them into the sitting room and gave the region's favourite evening tea and sweets, and then over the tea, Maya shrieked, 'Have you had a good time today?' and Abacha rushed to say, 'Yes, we had a great time,' and Awlio added, 'I hope it wasn't boring for him.'

'No, it wasn't boring at all for me,' Abacha interjected.

'Glad to hear that your day went well,' her father, Boukah, sitting by his wife's side, added. After they exchanged some brief conversation, Boukah left the room and in a minute, he returned with two things separately wrapped in a brown canvas. He handed them over to Abacha and said, 'Prince, it's a great honour for us to give you this present. It's a special present marked for your manhood transition.' Abacha unwrapped them one after another. The first was a sizeable gleaming sword and the second was a royal dress with dazzling coloured patterns.

It wasn't common practice in Awsa for young men to get a special gift when they reached manhood age. Actually, it was a ceremony improvised by Awlio's parents, who decided to make him feel that he was old enough to take leadership responsibilities and marry their daughter. Abacha examined the bright edges of the sword admiringly, and Boukah continued, 'The sword is the symbol of manhood and heroism, and the dress is in honour of your title as the Prince of Afambiya. Now you're a full-fledged man, Prince Abacha. We wish you all the best.' Then his aunt, taking her turn, added, 'It is a day we've been waiting for, my Prince. As my husband said, today, you've emerged out of the childhood era and entered the world of manhood. Accept our presents to celebrate this occasion.'

Prince Abacha, overwhelmed with the present and gazing at the dazzling sword and the colourful dress in front of him, cleared his throat and said, 'My uncle and aunt, thank you for this expensive special present and for commemorating the occasion of my transition period. Whenever I draw this sword out of its sheath and see its blazing blade, I'll remember you. Thank you.' After that, they happily had dinner together and continued chatting until bedtime.

32

CHAPTER

———❦———

The news of the marvellous entertainment performance in Awsa City Square and the man who defeated the mighty giant of Awsa surprised many people. One of those who struggled to grasp what had happened was a merchant from Zaila. This merchant brought merchandise from Zaila and walked into a store in Awsa City. 'Where's Amir?' He asked a shop assistant at the counter. Amir was the owner of the shop. 'He's at the back section of the store. He'll be back in a minute. Have a seat, mister,' said the assistant who knew the merchant from Zaila and put a chair for him by the side of the counter. The merchant, holding the list of merchandise on his wagons, sat on the chair.

While he was waiting for the shop owner, one of two potters in the store said, 'The act of the tricksters with the ailing princess from Zaila was marvellous. Did you see it?'

'No, I didn't. I was at work that day, but I heard about it,' replied the other porter, who had a red bandana on his head.

'I was there. I watched it from the beginning to the end,' the porter bragged, and the one with the bandana on his head asked, 'Have you seen the fight?' The merchant from Zaila was interested in their conversation when he heard about the princess from Zaila and listened to their conversation carefully.

'Yes, the thief with the Princess of Zaila was a good fighter. He knocked down the dangerous giant in minutes,' he explained, and the one with the bandana said, 'I reckon the guy who killed the giant isn't a thief. Probably he's the bodyguard of the princess.'

''No, he isn't a bodyguard. He's one of the thieves with her.'

'How do you know that he isn't her bodyguard?' questioned the porter with the red bandana.

'I've got a buddy who works in the Citadel. I know many things about this princess and the thieves with her.'

The merchant wondered how on earth the princess from Zaila ended up in Awsa and how she got involved with thieves. He interestingly kept eavesdropping on them until his client came.

'Hello, Hout-Hout. Glad to see you back. What have you brought for us today?' Amir asked.

'There're many things on the wagons. Hair oil, clothes, Abu Faz, frankincense, haberdashery, sugar, flour, rice, tea, cinnamon and many more,' replied Hout-Hout, the merchant from Zaila, looking at the list in his hand.

Amir said, 'Bring in frankincense, clothes, sugar, rice, flour, tea, cinnamon and Abu-Faz oil.'

Hout-Hout got on his feet and went to his horse wagons waiting for him outside the shop. He gave the names of the things Amir wanted to his assistant and instructed him to bring them in. Afterwards, he returned to Amir and said, 'Now it's my turn, Amir. What you have got for me?'

'I've for you honey, cow skin, gee, mats, walking sticks and rare gemstones. Just say a name, and I'll bring it to you,' Amir grinning at him, gloated.

'I need all these things,' Hout Hout replied, and Amir ordered his shop assistant to get the things for his client. While waiting for the goods to be exchanged, Hout-Hout asked, 'Amir, have you heard about an ailing princess from Zaila and thieves with her in the palace of your kingdom?'

'Oh yeah. One of the thieves was arrested two days ago after killing a giant everyone was afraid of.'

'Wow! That's interesting. Tell me a bit more about the princess and the thieves with her.'

'I heard the thieves escaped from an island in the Red Sea to help the critically ill princess, who wanted to come to Awsa.'

'What happened to her?' Hout Hout hastened to ask.

Amir replied, 'She was poisoned.'

'Are you sure she's a real princess from Zaila?' Asked Hout-Hout, who couldn't believe what he heard.

'If she ain't a princess from Zaila, our kingdom won't host her with the thieves helped her,' Amir speculated.

'Do you have any idea who poisoned her?'

'I don't know. Why are you so interested in her?'

'She's our princess, and she has been missing for a long time.'

'You're right. The girl's your princess,' Amir said. 'Anyway, I already told you what I knew about her. Let us get back to our business.'

Hout-Hout was a textile and household merchandise trader. He used to bring goods from Zaila to Awsa in exchange for goods needed in his country. His trade business was more imperative than anything else for him, but the unexpected news of the missing princess became more critical today than his trade. He was thrilled that he found the princess the whole nation was looking for alive. He believed the queen would be extremely delighted once she heard where stays her missing stepdaughter and he would be one of those respected in the queen's circles.

So, he decided to return to Zaila as quickly as possible and tell the queen the big news. He left the shop asking himself, 'Why did the princess go missing in the first place? What made her end up on an island in the Red Sea? Who poisoned her? And how did she meet those thieves?' With these many questions rumbling in his head, he hopped on his horse wagon and drove it off to the shops of his other clients in Awsa. He quickly distributed the rest of his merchandise to his clients and straightaway travelled back to Zaila.

33

CHAPTER

Queen Idil didn't doubt that Kirkir had killed Dhudi after seeing the grave on Faay Island, and she was happy from the moment she saw her grave, but she had to take care of one little problem before all her worries would end for good. The only thing left for her to sort out was the servant who had betrayed her. Idil sitting in her private chamber in the White Palace and sipping a morning tea with a pungent smell, finalised a plan she had already devised to eliminate him. She should kill Bedel immediately after discovering that he didn't kill Dhudi, but she had to wait for Kirkir to recover from his injuries and do the job for her. The moment came. She summoned Kirkir into her private chamber and said to him, 'Kirkir, it's almost three weeks since your treatment began. How are your injuries?'

'Your majesty, I'm doing very well,' he replied.

'Do you mean your wounds are completely healed?' She inquired.

'I would say eighty per cent they're healed,' Kirkir replied.

'I'm glad to hear that,' she said. She paused briefly and added, 'I have a small delicate job for you.'

'What's it, my queen?'

'It's about Servant Bedel. I trusted him, and he betrayed me. I want to see him doomed. I hate people who betray me.'

'Your majesty, my wounds didn't heal altogether yet. Please give me one week more. Afterwards, I'm more than happy to end the life of the man who betrayed you,' Kirkir explained.

'Your injuries don't affect your ability to do this job. You don't need to fight physically with him. All you need to do is to sprinkle gasoline on his house at midnight while he and his family are in a deep sleep and set fire to it and let them char in their beds,' said Queen Idil raging with a passion for arson.

Kirkir was thrilled with the simplicity of the work she wanted him to do. Then he asked hastily, 'When should I do it?'

'Do it when you're ready, but make sure nothing goes wrong. The man and his family must be scorched in their beds precisely at midnight.'

'Trust me, my queen. Nothing will go wrong,' he assured her.

'I like your bravery, Kirkir. Let us celebrate after you take care of this little job,' she concluded, and Kirkir convinced his mission was as easy as curling mice in a cage, went to his room and started planning his delicate task. He listed all the items he needed to exterminate Bedel and his family, and then he went to the shops in the city centre to buy them. He purchased fifteen litres of kerosene oil in a jerrycan, matches and a sprinkler and brought these things to a small house he had in the city. After that, Kirkir went to Servant Bedel's house to familiarize the location of the family he was going to massacre. He secretly studied Bedel's house and his neighbours and returned to his place when he gathered all the necessary information.

At night when most people retired into their beds, he walked to the city harbour to check whether Bedel was off fishing that night. He found his boat tied at the pier. So Kirkir decided that Bedel and his family were in their house and returned to his house. At around 12:20 am, once he imagined the city was in a deep sleep, Kirkir picked up the deadly items he bought to burn the family and went to Bedel's House.

He sneaked into the house from the backyard and sprinkled the kerosene all over it and the front part of the fence to ensure there was no way to escape, and afterwards, he set fire to it. Rapid flames suddenly engulfed the structure from corner to corner. Happy with the crackle of the inferno eating the building, he threw the jerrycan on the roof of the burning structure and disappeared in the black night.

Bedel's neighbours, awakened by the crackle of the intense fire and the bleat of terrified goats in the shed, rushed out of their beds to help the burning neighbour. Sadly, it was too late. They came once the ferociously raging fire consumed most of the building made from straws, poles and leaves. Frantically sprinting back and forth with buckets of water, neighbours fought hard to extinguish the sizzling inferno. Some tossing water on the flames and others throwing sand at the edges of the fire, the volunteers finally brought the situation under control.

Then they searched the charred bodies of the family in ruins. Surprisingly they found nothing other than debris and ashes. Neighbours thought the heat melted the family down or they might not be there at all and then discussed what they should do next. They decided to move the terrified animals in the shed to a safe place and meet again in the morning to discuss further what happened to their neighbour.

Luckily that night, Bedel and his family weren't at home. They were at a wedding ceremony for his wife's sister, and Bedel was organizing the wedding. He left his house at 6:15 pm after putting the goats in their shed and chickens in their coops. Again, Bedel came back at 9:30 pm to check if the animals were safe. After that, he went back to the wedding, and again he returned to his house after the party was over at 1:20 am. Sadly, this time Bedel found his house burnt down to ashes and his goats missing. He was shocked by what he had seen. His stomach churning with fear and his legs numb, Bedel looked around, wondering who did this to him.

He had no enemies, and nothing inflammable that could cause a fire was in the house. After his mind wandered a while, thinking how this could happen, Bedel decided that someone had deliberately burned his house. Again he thought about who that person could be, and then he remembered Queen Idil's words 'Bedel, you've children and a wife you love. I bet you don't want trouble for them, don't you?' And the way she looked at him on the day she was climbing her wagon.

Bedel now believed it was an arson attack and it was behind by the queen but couldn't understand the reason she decided to destroy him after he did what she asked him to do. 'Maybe she discovered that I didn't kill Dhudi, but how?' he thought and returned to his wife, who was in her parent's house with the children. He came to her and the children in a room he put them before he left to check the goats and chickens. He woke his wife up and said, 'Darling, something terrible happened to our house while we were here.'

'What happened?' she asked alarmingly.

'Someone burned our house to ashes, and the goats and chickens are missing.'

'Burned! How could this happen?' Asked his wife shocked.

'I think it was a planned arson attack,' he moaned. 'They wanted to kill all of us. We must act before something even worse happens.'

'Why does someone want to kill us?'

'I don't know exactly why. However, we must escape.'

'Bedel, is there anything you didn't tell me?'

He thought for moments and said, 'I'm sorry, darling. I should tell you this at the beginning. I was blackmailed by the queen, who wanted me to do a horrible thing.'

'Why did she blackmail you?'

'It's a long ugly story. We don't have time to talk about it now. We must leave the town before the day breaks.'

'Why we're leaving? Tell me what's going on, Bedel,' she demanded, and Bedel began telling her Dhudi's story, the reward he took from the queen and the cruel way she looked at him in the past. He concluded his speech, 'Darling, I'm extremely sorry about what I did. I had no choice. Whatever I did, I did for you and the children.'

His wife was disgusted with what she heard and understood what he'd gone through as well. 'Why does she still want to kill us after you did what she wanted?' She asked.

'I don't know, but I have no other enemies. It must be her. Let us run away as quickly as possible.' He got out of the room, and his wife followed him. In minutes they put their children on a horse cart and drove it off, heading westward. As they were leaving the city, she asked, 'Bedel, where are we going to?' And he replied, 'I don't know. We'll go to anywhere the queen I can't find us.'

34

CHAPTER

The following morning Kirkir returned to Bedel's house, hoping to find charred bodies sticking out from the ashes. He came to the neighbours gathered in front of the house's burnt enclosure and chattering about the fire. He told them he was one of the royal servants and Bedel's close friend and asked them what had happened to the house. Then the neighbours explained that they were awakened by the crackle of a fire engulfing the building at midnight and rushed out of their homes to save the family burning, but luckily they found no people who died in the blaze. He asked again if they knew where the family was last night, and they told him they didn't know.

Kirkir was disappointed that his mission failed. He decided to look for Bedel and his family in the city. As he turned away to leave, a woman said, 'If you find Bedel and his wife, tell them that we removed their goats and chickens, and they are safe.' 'I will,' he said and walked away from the scene, heading to the harbour to check if Bedel's fishing still moored where he found it last night. He came to the pier and found the boat in the same place. Afterwards, he hurried to the White Palace to ask the servants who work with Bedel if they had seen him. He came to those working in the kitchen and food stores and asked them if they had seen him this morning or if anyone knew where he was last night.

They told him they hadn't seen him in the morning, but he was organizing his sister-in-law's wedding ceremony last night. He ran to where the parents of Bedel's wife lived. He came to them and sympathetically said to them, 'My name's Kirkir. I work in the White Palace with your son-in-law, Bedel. Someone burned his house last night, and he didn't come to work this morning. Do you know where he is?' And Bedel's father-in-law replied, 'He was directing the wedding of my young daughter till after midnight. We haven't seen him since then. He and his wife should have had breakfast with us this morning, but they didn't show up.'

'Where's his wife?' he asked again, and the father answered, 'I don't know. Probably she is with her husband.'

'Thank you,' said Kirkir, convinced that Bedel and his wife were somewhere in the city and determined to find them. He went where the fishermen gathered and other places Bedel used to go and asked everyone he thought knew Bedel and his wife if they'd seen them lately. To his surprise, no one could tell him any helpful information. He kept searching for Bedel and his wife until the evening. When he was exhausted from finding them, he went to the queen. He came to her relaxingly drinking an aromatic tea she used to drink in the evenings in her private chamber and said disappointingly, 'My queen, something strange happened last night.'

'What happened? The queen was alarmed by his speech.

His head down, he explained to her how well he directed the mission and how it failed unexpectedly. When she heard his story, she disappointingly screamed, 'You're a well-trained soldier. How could this happen? Go, get him and his family and eliminate them.' Kirkir then went to his room, collected his best weapons, and set off to find Bedel and his family.

35

CHAPTER

In Awsa the two investigators investigating the murder of Jabal Guhaa began their investigation, starting to visit his house, which was a cottage that stood alone on a hillside outside the city. They came to his wife herding goats near the hill by the house and happily singing for the goats. The investigators greeted her, and she greeted them back. Strangely Jabal's wife didn't look like someone who lost their loved one. One of the investigators wondering why she wasn't sad when her husband was killed, yelled sympathetically, 'We're sorry for the death of your husband, madam.'

'When did he die?' she asked them without flinching at the bad news.

'Don't you know your husband was killed last Friday evening?' The investigator inquired.

'Nope,' she replied nonchalantly.

195

'When was the last time you saw him,' he asked suspiciously.

She thought for moments and said, 'Three days ago.'

'Have you heard anything regarding what happened to him since that time?'

'Nope,' she curtly replied.

'Is there a place where he stays when he isn't at home?'

'Nope. My husband travels often and returns home when he wishes,' the strange wife answered.

'Do you care about your husband?' asked the investigator, who thought the woman might not like her husband.

'Why are you asking me such a question?' she said, a bit flustered with his question.

'Because it seems to me that you don't care about him.'

'If he died, there is nothing I can do about it. Why should I worry?' Replied Jabal's wife, still maintaining her unusual coolness.

The investigator, baffled by her answers and strange coolness, decided not to ask her any further questions. He said, 'Thank you for talking to us, lady. Goodbye,' and they walked away, heading to the city's main graveyard. They came to the new burial section of the cemetery and checked on the recent graves and their sizes. They couldn't find any tomb that matched Jabal's colossal body. Then they walked alongside a valley in the city and checked dumpsites on the banks of the valley in case his body had been dumped there by people who didn't care to bury him properly. Again they found nothing. They extended their search into the city's bushes and alleyways, and then there was no sign of him.

After that, they went to the houses near where the security forces left his body last Friday evening and asked people if they'd seen Jabal's body or if people had come to take it, and the answer they got was no. After they'd been searching the area for a long time, they went back to their commander. They explained to him about their search, and Chief Dangig, visibly stunned by the unexpected outcome of their investigation, screamed, 'The court needs proof of his death. Go and search in the other parts of the city. We must provide accurate information to the court.'

The two investigators had no choice but to take the order of their commander. They extended their search to other parts of the city. They talked to many more people and combed in bushes outside the city. Sadly they found nothing. On the morning of the third day of their investigation, the senior investigator said to the other, 'The man didn't die. I think he's hiding somewhere, and his wife must know it.'

'What makes you think like that? Our officers confirmed his death,' said the other investigator and the senior one repeated, 'His wife wasn't worried about him. Remember, she talked to us as if nothing had happened.'

'I thought her bully husband abused her, so she didn't care for him,' the other officer replied.

'She didn't seem like a wife who her husband abused. I think she's a pathetic liar. She knows where he is,' the senior one explained.

'What can we do now?' asked the junior investigator.

'We'll begin an undercover operation around his house. Let us go,' he answered. They returned to the Jabal's house and took positions behind a cluster of shrubs growing at the back of the house. Then each taking turns, they kept an eye on the house. At dusk, when the darkness of the night almost filled the sky, Jabal Guhaa, carrying his club, emerged out of the woods. Then investigators squinting at his figure looming in the darkening night, he walked towards his house. Jabal Guhaa played dead to avoid criminal charges on that Friday evening when the security men checked his airways. Since then, he has been hiding in the woods and sneaking into his house after sunset when it turns dark.

Jabal entered the house and the senior investigator, glad they'd eventually found him, said to his colleague, 'He's a big and dangerous man. Two of us alone can't arrest him. Go and get reinforcements. I will keep watching him until you come back with more soldiers.'

The junior officer hastened to the Citadel, and before long, he returned with a well-armed group of men. They besieged Jabal's house while he was still inside with his wife, and the army's commander, standing at his house's front entrance, shouted, 'Jabal Guhaa, we know you're in the house. Come out slowly with your hands on your head.'

Jabal didn't answer.

After moments of silence, the commander repeated, 'We're the kingdom's army. Well-armed soldiers are surrounding your house. Come out and don't think about doing anything stupid.'

Jabal opened the back window and saw men in the rear of the house with their weapons. He closed the window, went to the front door, peeped through a crack in the door, and saw a group of men waiting for him at the house's entrance. Unsure what to do next, he remained inside, and the commander repeated, 'Jabal if you don't come out immediately, we will storm in.'

Jamal Guhaa decided there was no way he could challenge so many armed men and desperately roared, 'Who's the idiot shouting my name? What do you want from me?'

'You know what you've done. Come out without trouble, Jabal,' the commander repeated once more, and Jabal opened the door slowly and came out with his hands above his head. Afterwards, the army men swamped on him and chained his hands together, and then they led him away to the Citadel. Happy that their mission was finally successful, they locked him in a dark cell next to the one they had earlier put Gabi.

36

CHAPTER

Despite the fact that Hout-Hout planned to deliver the exciting news of the missing princess he'd found in Awsa as quickly as possible, his journey took longer than he expected. The heavy merchandise on his horses and the adverse weather conditions he experienced on the way had slowed him down. However, after he'd been on the road for five days and five nights, Hout Hout reached Zaila City at midday. He pulled up his horse wagons in the city's biggest market and instructed his assistants to distribute his merchandise to his customers. After that, he hurried to the White Palace rehearsing on the way how he would tell the big news to the Queen. He arrived at the White Palace's main gate, his message ready to deliver. He introduced himself to the guards at the door and told them that he had an important message for the Queen.

One of the guards, who thought he was a phoney and at the same time respected his state of appearance and age, said, 'Mister, you need to make an appointment to see the queen.'

Hout-Hout believed that he had every right to see the Queen, as long as he had crucial information for her, screamed, 'Are you deaf, young man? I have an important message for the Queen. I want to see her immediately.'

'It doesn't work like that, mister,' said the guard, slyly grinning at him. 'You can't show up at high noon and say I want to see the Queen. You need to make an appointment.'

Once Hout Hout felt frustrated and wondered what to do next, another guard asked curiously, 'Mister, what's the message you have for the queen?'

Hout-Hout replied, 'I found the missing princess. Let me go in. I want to tell the Queen where she is.'

The guard stepped close to him and said with surprise, 'Are you sure you've found the missing princess?'

'Yes.'

'Come with me,' said the guard without a second thought. He led him to the chambers of the Queen. He brought him to the Queen's special butler, Hoob and said to Hout-Hout, 'Mister, tell this man what you've told me,' and Hout-Hout happily repeated, 'I found the missing princess, and I came to tell the queen where she is.'

'Come with me,' said Hoob, and Hout-Hout, convinced that the Queen would be delighted when she got the news of her missing stepdaughter, and he would become one of her most highly valued subjects, followed him. They arrived at the main chamber, and the butler instructed him to take a seat, and then he went to the Queen's private chamber upstairs. Butler Hoob approached her, reclining on oversized cushions and sipping sweet Arabian Sherbet. 'My queen, I've big news for you,' he cried from the doorway.

'What's it, Hoob' she asked imperiously.

'Your Highness, we have here a merchant from Awsa. He says he has found your missing stepdaughter, the Princess of Zaila.'

The Queen was frightened at the unexpected news. She sat forward and screamed, 'Impossible! That merchant must be lying.'

'My queen, he doesn't look a liar,' said Hoob.

'I don't think he's telling the truth. Anyway, I'm coming to see him,' added the Queen, unconvinced that Dhudi was alive, as she rose from her seat. She followed the butler to the main chamber.

'Good afternoon, mister. I've been told that you've found the missing princess,' she said before she took a seat.

'Good afternoon, your majesty. I found the princess and a band of thieves with her in Awsa,' Hout Hout explained.

Her heart sank with the disturbing news. She impatiently demanded, 'Did you say she's with thieves? Tell me more about what you know her and don't lie to me.'

Surprised at her warning, Hout-Hout calmly explained, 'Your majesty, my name is Hout-Hout. I'm a respected trader and a good citizen of this country. There's no way that I would lie to you. I'm here only to tell you what I know about your missing stepdaughter and the thieves with her.'

'Sorry if you felt offended. Go on. Tell me what you know,' the Queen, hardly able to control her emotions, mumbled.

Hout-Hout forgot the eloquent words he'd rehearsed on the way. Anyway, he just explained to her how he'd initially heard the story of the missing princess, the investigation he'd later carried on and concluded his speech by saying, 'Your Majesty, the princess is critically ill in Awsa. She needs urgent help.'

The Queen rose from the seat and said, 'Hout-Hout, I doubt my stepdaughter is alive. Besides, I'll investigate whether your story is true or not. Now you can go but don't tell this news to anyone. It's queen's order.'

Hout-Hout gave up his hope of being one of those respected in her chambers got to his feet and returned to his business.

For Queen Idil, this was yet another complication in Dhudi's mysterious sequence of reappearances. Her blood surging with anger she went back to her private chamber. On the way, she pumped into one of her housemaids in the hallway and snarled, 'Call Kirkir for me.' The maid hurried to find Kirkir and told him that the queen wanted him immediately. He came to her and then her heartbroken and tears brimming in her eyes she screamed, 'Kirkir, I assigned you two missions and both failed. What kind of skilled soldier you are? Tell me what you did that night when you went to Dhudi's room. A merchant from Awsa says that she's still alive.'

'My queen I already told you what had happened. I gave her the poison as you instructed and while I was also thinking of breaking her neck a man came rushing into the room, and then I ran away.'

'I think she didn't die that night. The merchant told me that she's with thieves in Awsa. She's alive and Bedel is on the loose. What can we do?' she sadly lamented.

'Impossible, my Queen. That merchant is lying. How can she still be alive when we found her grave on Faay Island? On the other hand, don't worry about Bedel. I'm still looking for him and once get him he's over.'

While they were talking, she made up her mind. 'Get ready. We'll be going to Faay Island tonight to exhume what's in that grave,' she explained.

Shortly after the darkness of the night filled the sky, they sneaked out through the back door of the palace and went to the pier. They took a boat and sailed to Faay Island. When they arrived at the island, they hurried to the grave and dug it out with a shovel. Surprisingly there was no corpse in it. The tomb was a decoy, and the queen realised that Dhudi hadn't died and she'd escaped with the thieves. So with this knowledge, she thought about what to do next on her way back to the city. She decided to bring Dhudi and the thieves home and personally deal with them. So the following day, she wrote the following letter to the Sultan of Awsa:

Dear Sultan Kandhafo,

I hope my message reaches you well. I heard that you are harbouring the thieves who kidnapped my stepdaughter and destroyed her life. I want you to immediately hand over these criminals and my stepdaughter to my envoy, who is coming to you with this letter. I am hoping for your full cooperation.

Idil Gabadah, the Queen of Zaila and Thorny Land

When she'd finished writing the letter, she invited Farah Shalaqbeen, the Commander of her Security Army, to her private chamber and said to him, 'My stepdaughter is alive, but she's critically ill in Awsa. The thieves escaped with her to Awsa. Take this letter to the Sultan of Awsa with you and bring her and the thieves home.'

Shalaqbeen asking himself how the thieves and the girl whose grave they found on Faay Island had ended up in Awsa responded, 'My Queen, I'm a junior officer. General Gaboos is the most appropriate official that should deal with that kingdom on your behalf.'

'I don't want General Gaboos to be involved in this. You'll be my special envoy to Awsa, and you're a full colonel from now on. I promote you. Take the letter with you and bring home the princess and the thieves. I must punish those thieves who destroyed the life of my stepdaughter.'

Farah Shalaqbeen was overwhelmed with the promotion and said, 'My Queen, I accept the task, but I wonder how the young princess is still alive when we've already found her grave on Faay Island.'

'The grave was fake. A reliable merchant from Awsa has confirmed that the princess is now critically ill, and the thieves are in Awsa. Bring them home. The thieves destroyed the health of my stepdaughter. They must pay the price.'

'How did they manage to get there?' Colonel Farah Shalaqbeen asked.

'You'll get the answer from them. Go and bring them home,' the Queen chirped with annoyance.

'Very well, my Queen. I'm going to organise a caravan, and we'll leave tomorrow morning,' said the Colonel, holding her letter and ready to leave.

'Let me know when you're ready. I'm sending with you Kirkir and Beautie, the special carriage for stepdaughter.'

'That would be helpful,' said the Colonel, starting for the door.

After Shalaqbeen had left, she summoned Kirkir to her chamber and said to him, 'Kirkir, you'll take Beautie, and your job is to take care of the princess on the way. I'll give you certain medicines for her before you go. Use your special skills. Please don't disappoint me this time. You have failed me twice before. Make sure she dies on the way. '

'I won't let you down, my queen. How about Bedel and while I'm away who'll take care of your security?' He asked with much concern, as though he was the only one who could protect her.

'There's no one as special as you are, Kirkir. Anyway, don't worry about me and bedel for now. Get ready. Colonel Shalaqbeen will be leaving in the morning.'

37

CHAPTER

Princess Dhudi's hope of getting better with Healer Dabib's medicine shattered after her stomach severely bloated. On Wednesday, the fourth day from the time when she began taking the medicine, her belly had ballooned to an incredible size. The maids saw what had happened and gave her some herbal laxatives, which they thought would have let out whatever was bothering her inside. Unfortunately, nothing had happened, and her stomach continued to balloon, and she found it hard to breathe.

The worst came on Friday evening when the maids were with her in the room, her eyes suddenly rolled back, and she started frantically sucking for breath. The maids were frightened and screamed for help, and then Shaman and Jamanjug, sitting on a bench outside the building came quickly and asked, 'What happened, Marian?'

'The Princess's belly is going to burst. What should we do?' Marian chirped.

The two men shocked by the news looked at each other, and Jamanjug asked Marian, 'Do you know any healer to call?'

Marian replied, 'There's a health post in the south wing of the Citadel.'

'Let us go there. Come and show us where it is,' Jamanjug grunted without a second thought. So, Marian in front they rushed to the Health Post. The health post place was run by two medicine people, the lady who had previously treated Gabi in the dungeon and her husband. They approached the couple sitting on overused broken chairs in a room, and Jamanjug frantically explained the suffering princess's situation to them. The woman picked up a box containing several bottles of different sizes and a few clinical kits and came with them in a hurry.

They came to the princess writhing in her bed in unbearable pain. The woman quickly examined her abdomen and took her temperature. She then gave her some pain relief drops from a bottle in the box and told the maids to open the room's windows to let in some fresh air. When they had opened the windows, she gave them the bottle with the medicine and told them to provide the princess with one spoonful from it whenever she felt pain. Additionally, she explained to them that her health post couldn't fully treat the princess. So they should look for a knowledgeable healer who could cure her.

The medication halted the excruciating pain temporarily. Unfortunately, two hours later, Dhudi groaned again in the grip of severe pain. They gave her the medicine in the bottle and put a wet towel on her body to cool down her rising temperature. Disappointingly, these measures weren't enough to ease the pain. With this,

Jamanjug decided to act before it was too late. He went to Prince Hanad's house. He came to him sitting with his mother in the kitchen and eating some snacks. After exchanging the usual pleasantries, Jamanjug hurried to say, 'My friend, the princess is in critical condition. We need a healer who can help her immediately.'

Prince Hanad quickened to say, 'Healer Saba can treat her.'

'Saba has already tried to treat her, and sadly her medicine failed. Do you know another healer?' Jamanjug said.

Prince Hanad thought about who else they could ask for help. While pondering what to do next, his mother said, 'Shokali could cure her, but I think he's too old to administer medicine now.'

'Mum, Shokali is long since retired. Do you know someone else?' Hanad said.

'No,' his mother replied.

'If there's no other healer. Why don't we check if the old man can do something for her?' Jamanjug desperately enquired. Shokali was a ninety-year-old man who lived in a small hamlet five miles away from Awsa City with his wife, who was as old as he was. He used to treat local people stricken by the venoms of dangerous snakes and scorpions and man-made poisons. However, his useful service had become debilitated as he was physically debilitated. 'Okay, let us go,' replied Prince Hanad, who knew the village Shokali lived.

They took a horse cart Hanad borrowed from a friend and drove off to Arda, where Shokali lived. They reached the hamlet nearly at sunset and asked a group of men, chatting outside of a small tea shop where Healer Shokali lived in the village. The men then directed them to a small cottage in a cluster of similar houses in the corner of the hamlet. Moments later, they approached an age-consumed male feeding softened food to a female as old as him in the cottage's front yard. It was apparent that the woman couldn't look after herself and was entirely dependent on her husband.

'Hi, Healer Shokali, we come for help,' Hanad said from the gate of the cottage's enclosure.

The old man tipped his head up, put his right hand behind his right ear to hear him better and screeched, 'What!'

Prince Hanad understood that the old man had hearing difficulties. She shouted louder, 'Healer Shokali, we need urgent help.'

'What kind of help do you need?' screeched the old man, standing up from his seat with the aid of his long walking cane.

Hanad doubted that this frail ancient man could have the ability to cure people. However, looking at Shokali's body arched as a bow he shouted again, 'I'm Prince Hanad, and this is Jamanjug. We come to you for help to treat a poisoned princess who's suffering in the Citadel. Please can you help us?'

Shokali thought Hanad was an actual prince and replied, 'My Prince, I don't know how to help you. What's the poison that she's had?'

'She's been given Rijzi.'

'How has it affected her body?' Shokali asked. Afterwards, Jamanjug, raising his voice high, explained how the Rijzi poison had paralysed her body, about the failed medicines, about her belly being bloated and that her life was at risk unless she got urgent treatment. The old man shook his head sideways and screeched, 'It's a miracle the princess has survived from the Rijzi has paralysed her limbs and distorted her speech in that way.' He paused to think and moments later continued, 'I'll try to create some medicines for her. Go home and come back tomorrow afternoon.'

'My healer, that's impossible. She's dying. We must act as quickly as possible to save her life. Her stomach is close to bursting,' Jamanjug explained anxiously.

'I'll do whatever I can, but making the medicine will take time, and I don't have a ready one.'

'We shouldn't put pressure on you. Anyway, we have no choice. Can you at least give us something to relieve the princess's stomach upset while you're working on a proper medication?' Prince Hanad asked.

After a few moments of silence, the old man rubbed his forehead and screeched, 'I don't have such a medicine. Anyway, I'll make some anti-Rijzi. Go home and come back tomorrow. I can't provide you with a proper place to sleep.'

' Don't worry about us. Make the medicine and save the princess's life if you can,' said desperately, Hanad still looking at the emaciated body of the century-old man and worrying about his well-being and at the same time wanting to get medication for the suffering princess.

'Wait a minute,' said Shokali, shuffling into his cottage. He came out with two rolled-up light mats for his guest, and as passing his wife munching together her toothless gums by the door he said, 'Ambro, we've some honourable guests tonight. Prince Hanad and his friend are with us.'

'Biscuit is good,' she mumbled, munching more with her toothless gums.

'I didn't say biscuit, Ambro. I said Prince Hanad,' screeched Shokali, embarrassed at his wife's confusion.

She repeated a similar phrase, and then Shokali looked at Hanad and said, 'My Prince, forgive us. Biscuit soaked with milk is her favourite food, and she has hearing difficulties as I do.'

'Don't worry about what she has said,' Hanad replied.

Then Shokali gave them the mats and added, 'These are all we have got for you. Help yourselves.' Hanad and Jamanjug, grateful for his hospitality, thanked him and walked away with the mats to their horse cart, and Shokali shuffled back to his house and began working on the medicine.

38

CHAPTER

———✦———

The following morning Shokali carrying a pot of tea came to Hanad and Jamanjug. He gave them the tea and told them that the medicine was ready. While they were drinking the tea, he returned to his room and came back with three bottles in a small wooden crate. Then the old man holding the box in one hand and the other his cane, screeched, 'My prince, let us take this medicine to the princess.'

'Healer, you don't have to come with us. You're too frail to travel. We will take the treatment to the princess and administer it for her if you teach us how to use it,' Hanad explained.

'No. I must administer it to the princess. It's strong medicine, and it can be harmful if it is misused,' Shokali explained.

'Who would look after your wife if you come with us?' Jamanjug asked, and Shokali replied, 'My daughter will come before she wakes up. Let us go.'

'Are you sure you can travel on a horse cart?' Jamanjug, believing Shokali was too fragile to travel enquired.

'You told me last night that the princess was in a critical condition. Don't waste time. Let us go.'

The two men didn't know what else to say, so they climbed into the wagon and helped him to climb in too. Then Shokali and Jamanjug, sitting side by side, and Prince Hanad driving the horse, the trio took the road. Soon after they left the village, Hanad driving the horse as fast as possible to get to the Citadel quickly saw Shokali dozed off and holding the crate on his lap with his two hands tightly clenched. Wondering how long the sleeping old man could have kept it he cried, 'Jamanjug, the healer has dozed off. Keep an eye on the medicine.'

'I will,' said Jamanjug, who had already seen that the old healer had drifted to sleep and was ready to jump over the crate if it started slithering from his hands. From that moment, Jamanjug and Hanad eyeing the box worryingly continued on their journey. Strangely, even though Shokali was in a deep nap, his grip on the crate remained tight. Whenever his grasp loosens he would clench his hands tight on the box. All the way to Awsa, the two men ready to dive on the crate if it slithered from his hands, and the old healer maintaining his grip whenever the box seemed to be slipping at last, they arrived at the Guest House safely. Prince Hanad quickly climbed down from the wagon and helped Shokali to get down. After that, together, they hurried to the ailing princess's room. They came to her lying on the bed with her belly protruding like a hill and still breathing.

'How is she?' Hanad asked anxiously, and Shaman, who was with her, replied, 'She's in pain, and her stomach is growing bigger and bigger.'

Shokali shuffled towards her bed, squinted at her ballooned belly and murmured, 'Oh God. Her skin is going to crack. She must be suffering a lot.'

He put the crate on a chair and leaned his walking stick between the bed frame and the wall. Then he took the tiniest bottle and a wooden tablespoon with a tiny handle from the crate and asked Marian to open the princess's mouth and firmly hold her head up. When the maid had done what he asked, he counted ten drops from the bottle into the spoon and poured the medicine into Princess Dhudi's mouth. He put the bottle back in the crate and then picked up another medium-sized bottle. He opened the bottle's cap, filled the spoon with the medicine and emptied the medicine into Dhudi's mouth. Shokali returned the bottle to its place, and once more, he pulled out the bigger bottle and gave the princess two full spoons from it. After that, he said to Marian, 'Make sure she swallows the medicine.'

He returned the bottle to the crate and said to the maid, 'She might need the toilet soon. Stay close to her and help her do whatever she needs to do. I'll see her again after three hours.' He picked up the crate then with his cane's support, he shuffled out of the room. Jamanjug followed him and said, 'Come with me. I'll show you to a bed to rest.' He led him to his room and showed him his bed. Shokali had stretched out on the bed, Jamanjug asked, 'Can you tell me how those three different medicines you gave to the princess will work?'

'Based on what you've told me about the princess and her predicament, each medicine has a purpose.' Shokali started to explain the medicines. 'The medicine in the small bottle is to eliminate the Rijzi effects. The medium size bottle contains a body purifier. Its job is to flush out unwanted human waste and the poisonous residues remaining in the patient's body. The third and largest bottle contains energy-restoring treatment. It's called Energy-Hi. The princess needs it because she has been ill for a long time, and the Rijzi poison has weakened her muscles. It'll give strength to her feeble body.'

'It's amazing if your medicine really is going to work that way,' said Jamanjug.

The old healer frowned at his comment and said, 'Make sure the girls are doing what I've told them to do.'

'I will,' said Jamanjug, turning around to leave. He joined Shaman, Kalah and Prince Hanad, sitting on a bench outside the Guest House and waiting for the news of how the medicine would work.

It didn't take long for the medicine to have its effects. Less than an hour had passed when Dhudi squirmed in the bed and asked for the toilet. She was taken to the bathroom and did what she hadn't been able to do for days. After a few more trips to the restroom, her stomach had deflated, and she fell asleep. The maids then notified what happened to the men waiting outside. The men were delighted at the news of the medicine's outcome, and Jamanjug, ecstatic, asked Hanad if they could visit Gabi while the healer and the princess were sleeping. Hanad agreed to go with him, and minutes later, they came to the guards at the dungeon and requested to see their friend. Unluckily the guards wouldn't allow them to see him. However, they did tell them that Jabal Guhaa had been apprehended and he would be on trial the following morning with Gabi. Prince Hanad and Jamanjug were delighted to hear this. They returned to the group and told them about the next day's court hearing, at which everyone cracked a happy smile.

Three hours later, Shokali visited Dhudi, who was still sleeping fast. He asked the maids how she was, and they told him what had happened. Happy to hear that his medicine had worked as he planned, he put the crate on the chair next to the bed, took out the big bottle from it and said, 'I want to give her some more medicine before I go, wake her up.'

The maids forced her to wake up and held her head upright. He gave her two full spoons from the big bottle and five more drops from the tiny bottle. After that, he picked up the little bottle and asked, 'Who administers her medicine?'

'I do,' Marian replied.

'Give her five drops from this bottle every other day for four days.' He put the bottle down, picked up the Energy-Hi bottle, and said, 'She needs to take two spoons from this every day after breakfast for one week.' After that, he pointed at the medium-sized bottle and grunted, 'She doesn't need this one anymore. Its job was to clean her stomach, and that is done now. My prince, I think I should go home now,' Shokali concluded and started picking his things up. At this, the self-styled Prince and Jamanjug, grateful for his service, took him back to his village.

39

CHAPTER

———❦———

Two days later, Gabi and Jabal Guhaa appeared in a court in the Citadel. Their trial was unusual and more dramatic than any other court hearing that had ever taken place in Awsa. Everyone who could have access to the court hurried to secure a spot. Even Sultan Kandhafo, who had other important things to do that day, came with his wife, Nadia, to watch the trial of these two fascinating creatures. The two defendants' families and friends were among those allowed to attend the hearing, but the funny thing was that both defendants had no family members present for their trial. Jabal Guhaa's wife didn't come to the court, and he had no other family members. Gabi had no family in Awsa, but he had friends. His four comrade thieves were allowed to be present, and they all came to his trial.

After everyone had taken a seat, the judge, in a flowing court garb, entered the courtroom overwhelmed with curious people who couldn't wait to see the trial of the unchallenged giant and the man who had beaten him nearly to death from a back door. He sat on his majestic chair, and the prosecuting officer representing the law enforcement agency shouted, 'Honourable judge if I'm given permission, I would like to present the case facing the two defendants before this court today.'

'Permission granted,' The Judge declared, and the officer began presenting the case facing Gabi. He said, 'Your honour, the first defendant, Jamal Goley, known as Gabi, is a dangerous man. He's a member of a group of thieves who escaped from their detention island in the Red Sea. Gabi is a thief and a violent man who risks our public safety. He battered the other defendant in the city centre and caused public disorder. He committed similar crimes in his home country, and that's why the Kingdom of Zaila and the Thorny Land sent him to an island in the Red Sea.'

He paused, turned over a page of his report papers and continued. 'The other man, Giant Jabal Guhaa, is a notorious criminal who secretly robbed and blackmailed our society's members in the city's dark alleyways. On the day he fought with Gabi, he came to Otel, a well-known entertainer and took his money, and when the security forces found him lying in the city square, Jabal played dead to avoid justice. He has a history of robbery, and we have here many witnesses who are willing to testify against him.' He paused again and added, 'Judge if I'm given permission, I would like to ask questions to the defendants and the witnesses in the court to glean more information from them for the benefit of this court and the public.'

Then the judge roared, 'The permission granted.'

After that, the Prosecutor looked at Gabi and said, 'Why do people call you Gabi when your real name is Jamal Goley?'

'It's my nickname,' Gabi bellowed again.

'You're a thief who escaped from a detention centre with other thieves, is that correct?'

'Yes.'

'What did you steal to cause you to be deported to the detention island in the Red Sea?'

'Nothing.'

'What do you mean, nothing?'

'I didn't steal anything. I was an entertainer. My friend and I used to entertain people with our skills. Unluckily, one day we took money from some lousy hordes, who paid us in exchange for our performances, and then they accused us at a court in Zaila of swindling money from them with our tricks.'

'So, you're a swindler. Why did you fight with this man?' The Prosecutor asked, looking across at Jabal.

'He took our money,' Gabi roared.

'You said our money. Who else was with you?'

'Those two men,' he said, pointing at Jamanjug and Otel in the crowd.

'No further questions,' said the Prosecutor, moving on to deal with Giant Jabal. 'What's your name?' The Prosecutor asked.

'Jabal Guhaa,' he bellowed.

'Did you habitually rob people in the city's dark alleyways and blackmail them into giving you their money and possessions?'

'No.'

'Did you take money from Otel and his friends on Friday, 11th of July this year?'

'I didn't take their money.'

'Why did you fight with the other defendant if you didn't take their money?' the Prosecutor, glancing at Gabi, repeated.

'He started it for no reason.'

'Didn't you take the money in this satchel from them?' the Prosecutor asked as he waved the satchel Jabal took from Otel in the air for the court to see.

'I took the money from that little twerp you call Otel.'

'It's our money,' Gabi snarled.

'Quiet. Don't interrupt me,' the Prosecutor screamed before continuing.

'Did you rob people in the dark alleyways?'

'No.'

'Jabal, you lied in response to everything I asked you. Now I'm calling the witnesses who will testify against you and the victims of your robbery.'

'The first witness, Jamanjug, please stand up.' Jamanjug got to his feet.

'Did this man take money from you?'

'N…o...no. He didn't ta….taa….take the money from me.   He took it from my colleague, Otel,' Jamanjug stuttered.

'If he took the money from Otel, it's between him and Otel. Why did your friend want to fight with him?'

'Otel, Gabi and I are entertainers. We performed in City Square together that day, and we earned money, and Jabal came and took the money from Otel,' Jamanjug explained.

'No further questions. Now I'm calling the second witness. Otel, come forward,' the Prosecutor shouted and Otel, waiting for this opportunity and braving himself to testify against Giant Jabal, put himself forward. 'Otel, is this the man who took your money on Friday, 11th of July this year?'

'Yes. This giant used to take my money every time I entertained people and got paid.'

'How did he take your money?'

'Whenever I earned some money through my skills, he would materialise from nowhere at the end of my performance, and then he would take my money. He would drag me into the dark alleyways and squeeze my neck if I refuse giving it to him. He's a horrible blackmailer and bully,' Otel cried.

'That's enough. Now I would like to talk to the other victims of Giant Jabal. Victims stand up,' the Prosecutor shouted, and a group of men stood up in the crowd. 'The court doesn't have enough time to listen to all of you. We'll put some questions to some of you. Talk briefly when asked a question. You go first,' he said, pointing at one of those standing up. The victim then talked about his ordeals at the hands of the giant. When he had finished, the Prosecutor called another man who spoke about what happened to him, and then others narrated how Giant Jabal had ravaged, robbed, blackmailed and shared their earnings with them for many years. The victims unearthed the hidden crimes that Giant Jabal had committed in the dark alleyways. When the Prosecutor had questioned enough victims to show the despicable extent of the giant's crimes, he turned to Jabal and said, 'Are you confessing now to stealing from and blackmailing these people?'

'They're sleazy scoundrels who got the money in the wrong way in the first place.'

'So you confess that you've robbed and blackmailed them, and at the same time, you've no remorse for what you've done to them?'

'They're silly twerps. Why should I feel remorse for them?' Jabal bellowed.

'Your honour,' the Prosecutor said to the judge. 'There are no further questions I need to ask the victims or the defendants. However, I submit that these two men are dangerous criminals and risk our public safety. They must be sent to long-term jail.'

Gabi slowly lifted his head and roared, 'I'm not a danger to the public. I entertain people and make them happy. I want to get my freedom back. The criminal is Giant Jabal.'

'Shut up. It's for the court to decide who is a criminal and who's innocent,' said the judge, who was a grumpy ageing man who never appreciated those who interfered with his court's affairs. 'Now the court is going to reach a verdict.' The judge lifted his head up from the notes he was looking at and spoke again. 'People in the court excuse us while we're deliberating on the sentence for these men. Remain quiet. The court will make a decision soon.' After that, he turned to his court assistants, and they started discussing the two men's sentences in a hushed conversation. After careful deliberation, the judge shouted, 'When we have seen the report of the dangerous fight in the City Square on the 11th of July this year. After the court heard the history of each defendant and the crimes they have committed individually in the past. After listening to Jabal's defence and what his victims have said about him, this court has decided the following sentences:

Defendant Jabal Guhaa, you're a huge, strong, dangerous man who robbed and blackmailed his weak fellow citizens for a long time. You're a perpetrator who knows how to avoid the law enforcement army's attention when you're robbing those who cannot challenge you in the dark alleyways. You disturbed this city's peace and public order when you fought against another man in the city centre, and then you played dead to avoid justice. You must be punished for what you have done to others. So I'm giving you six years of prison,'

The judge paused for a moment and then continued, 'The second defendant, Jamal Goley, known as Gabi. This court has considered your fight with Jabal as an inevitable self-defence type of fight. I don't have any reliable evidence of any crimes you may have committed previously. Therefore this court acquits you of all the charges against you. Now you're free to go.' The judge banged his gavel on his table to indicate that justice was delivered.

Gabi was delighted that he was free. He walked to his friends, huddled in a far corner of the courtroom. Before he reached them, the Prosecutor shouted behind him, 'Hey Gabi, your bag.' Gabi returned to collect the satchel with the money and then hurried to join his friends. He hugged each of them and Marian, who was there too. Afterwards, they went to Princess Dhudi, who was recovering well after she took the old healer's medicine. The group was happy and celebrating in Dhudi's room Prince Hanad came and said, 'Congratulations Gabi. I'm glad you're a free man,' and Gabi, smiling at him, replied, 'Thank you, your highness.'

Hanad walked to Dhudi's bed and asked her, 'My princess, how are you today?'

'I'm very well. Thank you for saving my life, my prince.'

'He isn't a real prince, but he's a good man,' Jamanjug hurried to say.

' He saved my life. He's my prince, and on top of this, I believe a person can be who they want to be. He could be a real prince one day. You never know what will happen next,' Princess Dhudi explained. After that, the group carried on chatting happily.

40

CHAPTER

In Zaila city Colonel Shalaqbeen had put together twelve well-armed men with their transport and two extra horse carriages, one for the prisoners he would bring home soon and another for his army logistics. Afterwards, he went to the queen to inform her that his caravan was ready. He came to her in her chamber and said, 'Good morning, your majesty. We're ready to leave for Awsa. Is there anything you want to advise me of before we depart?'

'Yes, Colonel. Sit down,' said the queen. He sat down, and she gave him a cup of tea. While he was drinking the tea, she left the room to find Kirkir. She found him loitering in the hallway and said to him, 'Kirkir, come with me.' He followed her. She went into her bedroom and picked up two bottles she had already prepared for Dhudi's killing from a chest by her bed. She gave them to him and chirped, 'Colonel Shalaqbeen is ready. Take this medicine and Beautie with you. It's a special medicine for her. Make sure she takes it with her food and drinks. Don't let us down this time. I want her to die on the way.'

'I will, Your Majesty,' he replied obediently.

'One more thing,' she added.

'What is it?' he asked.

'Keep an eye on the Colonel's dealings with Sultan Kandhafo. I need to know everything he discusses with the Sultan and his ministers. Go with him to all meetings,' she added.

'Okay, my queen,' answered Kirkir, delighted that he was the only one trusted by the queen.

After that, she returned to Colonel Shalaqbeen with the letter she'd written to Sultan Kandhafo of Awsa. She came to him as he was still sipping his tea and said, 'Colonel, the special royal carriage for the princess and Kirkir are waiting for you outside. Take this letter with you. It's to Sultan Kandhafo. I wish you a successful journey.'

'Thank you, my queen,' replied the Colonel, rising from his seat to leave. He went to where Beautie was waiting for him and hopped into it with Kirkir, and they drove off to join the caravan waiting for them by the Archery Field. Then Colonel Shalaqbeen thinking about nothing but how he should punish those thieves who had kidnapped the young princess and destroyed her health shouted, 'Let us go' when approached his caravan. He led the army toward the road to the Kingdom of Awsa. The road was rough, and the weather was hot. However, these impediments didn't slow down his caravan, as he had selected the best men and the most potent horses for his mission. On top of these, he passionately wanted to catch the perpetrators who had harmed the young orphan princess.

They kept travelling along the road both days and nights. In the afternoon of the third day of their journey, as they were moving between the mountains in Awsa territory, the Awsa border guards besieged them and ordered them to put down their weapons. Colonel Shalaqbeen shouted from the back of his horse, 'We aren't trespassers. We're a peaceful delegation from the queen of Zaila and Thorny Land. We're bringing a message to the Sultan of Awsa.'

'Whoever you are, put down your weapons,' the group's leader ordered them. After that, the Colonel and his men, who had no choice, complied with his order, and when the guards started collecting their weapons from them, Shalaqbeen retorted, 'As I said earlier, we're a peaceful delegation going to your Kingdom. What's the reason you're mistreating us?'

'If you're a peaceful delegation, why are you so heavily armed?' said the head of the border guards.

'Because we've been sent to bring home a bunch of criminals who escaped from their detention island and a princess they kidnapped,' he explained.

'We can't let such heavily armed foreign men travel in our territory freely. Come with us. We're taking you to our camp,' said the leader.

They were driven towards a chain of hills. They brought them to a small makeshift camp hidden in the hills, and then they were shown to a place in the corner of the base, and the leader said, 'Stay here. You'll receive further instructions when our commander returns later in the evening.'

Colonel Shalaqbeen and his men were upset at the way they were being treated. Nevertheless, nothing they could do about it. At sunset, Shalaqbeen and his men huddled in their spot and, eating a meagre dinner given to them by the guards, the commander of Awsa Border Guards, Colonel Rohan, arrived at the camp. Then a junior officer in charge of the camp hurried to say to him, 'Commander Rohan, we have a Colonel from Zaila and his men here. They're going to Awsa to get back criminals who escaped from the Kingdom of Zaila and a princess they kidnapped.'

Colonel Rohan went to Colonel Shalaqbeen and his men. He introduced himself to them and said to Shalaqbeen, 'Colonel, I've been told that you're going to Awsa to bring home criminals who escaped from your Kingdom and a princess they'd kidnapped. Can you tell me more about the criminals?'

'They're dangerous men who escaped with the princess from their detention island in the Red Sea. We want to bring them home and punish them for what they've done to the princess,' Shalaqbeen explained.

Rohan felt pity for Colonel Shalaqbeen, and his men replied, 'I'll give your weapons back and arrange a guide to show you the way in the morning. Get some rest before then.'

'Thank you, Colonel Rohan. I appreciate your help,' Shalaqbeen responded gratefully. Thereafter, Rohan returned to his camp to arrange a guide for them and return their arms and the following morning they proceeded their journey.

41

CHAPTER

<hr>

The ancient man's medicine got a place in the history books of the Awsa Kingdom after it saved Princess Dhudi's life. On the third day, from when she started taking the medication, the Princess's most paralysed parts of her body began functioning again, and her distorted voice had much improved. Then her two faithful maids, mazed by her quick recovery and wanted her to get even better, massaged her body's stiff areas with oil and helped her exercise daily. On the fifth day, she could walk alone to the toilet and change her dress without help. Happy with the way her body's strength had progressed, she continued exercising, and the maids started walking with her outside the building.

On the evening of the eighth day, Dhudi wearing a beautiful dress and rambling alone around the Citadel grounds, reflected on the changes the old man's medicine had brought to her life. Comparing how she was a week ago with her present state, she sat on a bench and flexed her legs and hands to evaluate their movements. Furthermore, she looked at her withered skin beginning to glow again, sang a song she loved to sing in her childhood to check on the clarity of her voice and realised everything was perfectly normal. Happy with the results, Dhudi began to think about the future ahead of her and what she would do next. While she was thinking about the future, Prince Hanad, in his tight brown jacket and his royally designed hat, approached her from her right side and said, 'Hello, Princess. I'm glad to see you recovered so well and beautiful.'

She stood up and happily greeted him, 'How are you, my prince.'

'I'm very well,' he said.

They sat down together, and he asked curiously, 'You know I'm not a real prince, and you're still calling me a prince. Why is that?'

'Before my father died, one day, he said to me, "You can be what you want to be, Dhudi." So one day, you can be who you want to be. Believe in your dreams.'

'Thank you for encouraging me, but do you think a person's wish can change their social status or fate?'

'Everybody has a choice and an ability to shape their future. Stick with your dream and believe in yourself,' Dhudi advised him.

'I'll take your advice seriously, my Princess. By the way, how is your health progressing?'

'Everything is getting better perfectly, ' she joyfully replied.

'Can you walk faster?' he asked.

'I can run like a stallion,' she joked.

'I'm glad to hear that,' he said, smiling at her beautiful figure admiringly.

'Thank you, my prince. You saved my life,' she said gently in tones of gratitude.

'My pleasure,' he said, gazing at her interestingly.

After they had talked for quite a while on the bench, he said, 'Can I show you around tomorrow?' And Dhudi, more than happy to tour Awsa with him, hurried to say, 'Sure. What time?'

'At 10:30 in the morning, if that's okay with you,' he answered.

'See you then,' she answered. They rose from the bench and walked together to her room. They stopped at the door, and Hanad repeated, 'See you tomorrow morning, at ten-thirty,' and then he made his departure.

42

CHAPTER

That evening after Hanad had left the princess, Colonel Shalaqbeen and his men arrived at the Bulwark in the west of the Citadel, and his guide introduced him to the base commander. Then after the introduction and a brief conversation, the commander said to Shalaqbeen, 'Colonel, I'm going to tell the Chief of Security that you're here, and I hope afterwards he'll arrange your meeting with our Sultan. Get some rest.'

'Thank you,' Colonel Shalaqbeen replied, and the commander left to report the guests from Zaila to Chief Dangig. He came to him in his quarter and explained to him about the Colonel from Zaila and the reason he came to Awsa. The Chief then told him that he would see the Sultan in the morning. So the following morning, Chief Dangig went to the Sultan's court and told him about the Colonel from Zaila. Sultan Kandhafo was keen to know what was going on between the orphan princess and her stepmother, the Queen of Zaila. So he ordered him swiftly to bring him to his chamber. After that, Chief Dangig went to Colonel Shalaqbeen and introducing himself to him said, 'Good morning, Colonel. I'm Chief Dangig, the Chief of Awsa Security Army.'

'Good morning to you, Chief. I've been expecting your visit. The commander of the base told me about you,' The Colonel replied.

'Are you ready? Sultan Kandhafo and his councillors are waiting for you,' Dangig added.

'Yes, Chief,' answered Colonel Shalaqbeen, dressed smartly in his army uniform and prepared to meet the officials of Awsa.

'Let us go then,' Dangig shouted. As the two men started to walk away, Kirkir cried, 'I'm coming too.' Together, they strode to the chamber of the Sultan. They approached Butler Zaman, who showed them to a waiting room and grunted, 'Wait here for me. I'll tell the Sultan that you are here.' Afterwards, Zaman went in and said to the Sultan with five of his councillors in his chamber, 'Your majesty, we have here the Colonel from Zaila and Chief Dangig.'

'Bring them in,' The Sultan replied, and Zaman returned in a hurry and shouted from the doorstep of the waiting room, 'Chief, the Sultan, is waiting for you.'

Chief Dangig and Colonel Shalaqbeen got to their feet, and Kirkir, who wanted to come, did the same. As they walked out of the room, Dangig said to Kirkir, 'You don't need to come with us. The Sultan is expecting Colonel Shalaqbeen only.'

Kirkir argued, 'I'm from the queen too. I must come.'

'No. The Colonel can deliver the message from the queen. You stay,' Chief Dangig repeated.

'No, I'm coming,' Kirkir insisted. Colonel Shalaqbeen wondered what made him so adamantly on coming with them. He looked at Chief Dangig and said, 'Chief, let him come with us.' Together, they entered the chamber, and the Sultan said, 'Colonel, welcome to Awsa. What brought you here?'

'Your majesty, I'm here to deliver a message from the Queen of Zaila,' said the Colonel, walking towards the Sultan to give him the letter from Queen Idil.

The Sultan took the letter from him and began to read it carefully. When he'd finished reading it, he said, 'Colonel, I want to have a private consultation with my councillors. Please go back to the waiting area. We'll call you after we've discussed your queen's letter.'

'Certainly, Sultan,' replied the Colonel, turning back to leave.

When Colonel Shalaqbeen and Kirkir had left the room, the Sultan said, 'Councillors, listen to me carefully. I'm going to read out the letter from the Queen of Zaila for you.' He read the letter out loud, and when he'd finished it, he said, 'You've heard what the queen of Zaila is saying. Advise me what to do about it.'

His Minister of Interior Affairs, who spoke first, cried, 'Your majesty, I think we should return these people. We must comply with the criminals' return agreement we've entered into with the other kingdoms.'

Another councillor with the Sultan the day Dhudi and the thieves arrived at the Citadel took the speech. He said, 'The orphan Princess told us that her stepmother had tried to kill her and that the thieves helped her to escape with her life to Awsa. I don't think we should send them back because they're vulnerable people at risk of unfair prosecution.'

'I think we should send all of them back. We don't need to get involved with the problems of that kingdom and its people,' another councillor declared.

'The girl isn't a thief. We don't have to return her unless she wants that, but the thieves must be sent back,' another councillor explained.

After everyone had their say, the Sultan reached his own decision and declared, 'We'll send the thieves back, but the orphan Princess will stay with us. Someone go and get the Colonel.'

Colonel Shalaqbeen and Kirkir, who insisted on coming with him, returned to the chamber, and the Sultan said, 'Colonel, according to the treaty signed by all the kingdoms, we'll hand over to you the thieves, but the princess will stay with us.'

'Sultan, we must take the princess back too. We can't leave her behind,' Shalaqbeen argued.

'The Princess isn't feeling well now, and I don't think she wants to return to Zaila. Leave her here. She'll be safe with us,' Sultan Kandhafo explained.

The Colonel thought for a moment and said, 'Can I see the princess?'

'No, you can't,' Kandhafo answered.

'Why I can't see her,' Colonel Shalaqbeen, surprised at the Sultan's answer.

The Sultan found it hard to answer his question. He thought for a moment and said, 'Colonel, I would like to talk to you privately.' Then all the other men left the room except Kirkir.

The Sultan looked at Kirkir and said, 'Mister, I want to talk to the Colonel alone,' so Kirkir had no choice but to leave the chamber.

After Kirkir exited the room, Sultan Kandhafo grunted, 'Colonel, the Princess made a serious allegation against her stepmother. She told us that the queen had tried to kill her twice, so I can't send her back with you.'

'Impossible! How could the queen kill her stepdaughter?' The Colonel asked with astonishment.

'Don't ask me a question I can't answer, Colonel. Make your own discreet inquiry when you get back home. For now, take the thieves.'

'Please let me have a word with her. I would like to know what the thieves have done to her.'

'They didn't do anything bad to her, I guess. They saved her life. Please don't insist on seeing her.'

'Sultan, why can't I talk to her?' The Colonel asked.

'If she learns that you came here to take back the men who saved her life, she'll ask me not to send them back. You should take the men and leave quietly,' the Sultan explained.

The Colonel understood the Sultan's reasons and submissively said, 'In that case, I'll take the thieves back as you suggest, Sultan.'

'Good, I'll write a letter to your queen, and someone will bring it to you. Make sure that you leave secretly with the thieves early in the morning,' the Sultan concluded.

After the meeting, Kirkir and Colonel Shalaqbeen thinking about his conversation with the Sultan went back to the Bulwark, and Sultan Kandhafo went to his house. He said to his wife approaching him to help him take off his robes, 'Nadia, we have a Colonel sent by the Queen of

Zaila and thorny Land. He wants to take Dhudi and the thieves back.'

'That's wonderful!' Nadia shouted excitedly. 'I'm glad that girl is going to where she belongs. Return the girl and her thieves.'

'Nadia, that's cruel. The girl is an orphan who lost both of her parents. We can't give her to someone who'd tried to kill her. She'll stay with us,' said the Sultan holding his ground to protect Dhudi.

43

CHAPTER

———❧———

As they agreed yesterday evening, Hanad returned the next morning to Princess Dhudi. He came to her wearing a beautiful dress and waiting for him on the bench outside the building. They happily greeted each other and walked together to the Citadel's main exit, heading to the town. As they approached the gate, Hanad, feeling proud of being with the Princess from Zaila, greeted the guards, and the guards, impressed by how well the feeble young princess had recovered from the devastating illness that had almost crippled her and beautiful, greeted him back. Leaving behind the guards gazing at them admiringly, they exited the door and carried on towards the city centre. The couple talking animatedly about their past times strolled into the City Square, and Hanad said, 'This is where your friends were entertaining the people when Giant Jabal Guhaa came and fought with Gabi. It is the hot spot of the city revellers.'

'It's a beautiful place,' Dhudi replied. Then they continued their journey further into the city centre. They entered the busiest part of the town, and Hanad showed her shops selling many different things, the dairy produce area and the fine clothing boutiques. They carried on touring the most interesting of the city. While wandering in the market, he told her about Jawhara, and then Dhudi, curious about the woman asked him, 'Can we say to her hello while we're in town?'

'Sure,' he replied, and at the same time, he led her to Jawhara's shop. They came to her busy selling wares. 'Good morning Jawhara. This is Princess Dhudi, the Princess of Zaila and the Thorny Land. Princess, this is Jawhara.'

Jawhara was thrilled to meet the Princess from Zaila and said, 'Nice to meet you, princess.'

'Nice to meet you too, Jawhara,' Dhudi replied.

Jawhara looked at Hanad and said, 'How're Jamanjug and his big friend?'

'They're all good. Jamanjug asked me about you. He wants to see you,' answered Hanad.

'Bring him with you next time when you're coming to the town,' she replied, smiling at him happily. Frankly speaking, Jawhara fell in love with Jamanjug at first sight. She wanted to see him and Jamanjug couldn't stop thinking of her since he saw her. Sadly, despite being busy with Dhudi's illness and Gabi's arrest, Jamanjug didn't know where to find her until he asked Hanad where he could find her. Jawhara was the only girl of his size he had ever seen, and she was so beautiful. So she was immensely attracted to him.

'I'll bring him along tomorrow if you're around,' Hanad said, and Jawhara, happy at the thought of meeting Jamanjug, replied, 'I'm looking forward to seeing both of you.'

'Be around. I'll bring him,' Hanad said and walked away with the Princess.

Walking side-by-side with the princess as they left the shop, he said, 'I think they fell in love with each other. Jamanjug kept asking me about her, and she wants eagerly to see him, I guess.'

'It looks like you're right, Hanad. Her face flushed with happiness when you talked about him,' Dhudi replied and then, chatting enthusiastically, they kept touring the city. After visiting most of the city's main parts, they went to his house at noon. They came to his mother and his siblings having lunch in the kitchen. 'Mum, this is Princess Dhudi of Zaila and the Thorny Land,' he shouted as they entered the house's compound. His mother stood up, shook hands with the Princess, and said, 'Welcome, princess.'

'Nice to meet you, madam,' said Dhudi, who still didn't know his mother's name.

Hanad's mother was embarrassed that she had no facilities to entertain a royal member and worried about what to do next. Anyway, she hurriedly said, 'Come with me, princess.' She led her into a shabby room, and as they entered it, the mother decluttered it quickly and added, 'Sorry, Princess, we got only two rooms, one for the boys and one for the young kids and me. This is the one I share with the kids.'

'Your house and your resources may be small, but you have a big heart, as I've already learnt from your son, madam,' Dhudi replied.

With Dhudi's answer ringing in her head, the mother said, 'Thank you, princess.' After she decluttered the room, she unrolled a new embroidered mat in the centre of the room and said again, 'Princess, this is the best we have. Please take a seat.'

Dhudi sat on the mat and murmured, 'It's lovely.'

'I will be back in a minute,' said the mother as she popped out of the room. She came to Hanad in the kitchen and scolded him, 'Look what you did. I don't have a proper place to sit the princess or food to give her. Stop bringing home unexpected guests, especially those with eminence.'

'Mum, don't worry. She'll share with us what we have.'

After that, his mother gave him a meagre lunch, enough for one person, and he took it to Dhudi and shared it with her. After they ate the food, Dhudi and Hanad joined his mother in the kitchen. They chatted with her for a while, and afterwards, they returned to the Citadel. Then they found a hearty meal on the table in Dhudi's room and ate the food together again. Thereafter, they left the room and met Gabi, Jamanjug, Shaman and Kalah, chatting outside the Guest House. Dhudi told them about her exciting visit to the city and that she had met Jawhara. Immediately after she mentioned Jawhara's name, Hanad looked at Jamanjug and said, 'Jawhara is expecting to see you tomorrow. Get ready. I'll take you to her shop.'

Jamanjug smiled and hastened to say, 'Okay.' His answer was short but laden with excitement.

Hanad turned to Gabi and said, 'Gabi, my friend is having a big party tonight. He invited you as well. Would you come with me to his party?'

'Really? Gabi asked.

'Yes, come with me. You'll meet many good people who like you. The city loves you since you've beaten up the bully giant.'

'I like to meet new people, but I'm afraid of going out since the incident at City Square,' Gabi bellowed.

'Come on. You don't have to worry when you're with me,' Hanad explained confidently.

'If we stay late in town, where should I sleep?' Gabi asked.

'Don't worry. You'll sleep with us,' Hanad explained, and Jamanjug shouted, 'I'm coming too.'

'No, Jamanjug. My room is too small for four people. You stay, and I'll come back to collect you tomorrow morning. Afterwards, you'll meet with Jawhara and stay overnight with me if you want.'

'That's fine,' Jamanjug agreed, and then Gabi and Prince Hanad left for the city.

44

CHAPTER

—✺—

Sultan Kandhafo, morally disturbed by sending back the innocent men, began writing a letter to the Queen of Zaila. In his letter, he said:

> *Your Majesty, the Queen of Zaila and the Thorny Land,*
>
> *Thank you for your letter in which you have instructed me to return your stepdaughter and the men with her. As you requested, I am sending the men who accompanied the Princess, but your stepdaughter is not ready to come home at the*

moment. When she gets better and decides to go home, I'll return her to her country.

Best Wishes,

Sultan Kandhafo, the Sultan of Awsa.

When he'd finished writing the letter, he went to his main chamber and called his Butler, Zaman. He asked him to call Chief Dangig for him. It didn't take long for the butler to bring the chief and the Sultan said to him, 'Chief, give this letter to the Colonel from Zaila and help him haul away the thieves covertly. We don't want the ailing young princess to know this.'

'She isn't ill anymore, Sultan,' Chief Dangig interrupted him.

'What do you mean, she isn't ill anymore?' Sultan Kandhafo asked with astonishment.

'I've seen her walking with a local lad this morning. She's totally healed.'

'She's healed!' the Sultan repeated, stunned at this revelation. 'That's amazing. By the way, I don't want her to notice that I'm sending back her friends. Take my letter. Hand it and the thieves over to the Colonel from Zaila, and make sure he leaves before dawn.

'Okay, Sultan, I'll do it as you wish,' replied Chief Dangig, taking the letter and ready to leave. He went to his office and ordered his security army to round up the thieves at midnight while everyone was in a deep sleep and to take them to the West Bulwark and hand them over to Colonel Shalaqbeen. Then the army, following his instructions, swooped into the guest house sometime after midnight and detained the thieves in their beds except for

Gabi, who was fortunately with Prince Hanad in town. Shaman was surprised at the midnight ambush and asked, 'What do you want from us?' And one of the security men answered, 'You're going home, old man.'

Shaman was frightened and felt like he was about to collapse. Anyway, their hands were chained together, and they were taken to the Bulwark. Then Colonel Shalaqbeen and his men loaded them into the caged wagon before Shalaqbeen demanded, 'Where's the fifth one?'

The head of the team that rounded up the thieves replied, 'Colonel, we checked for him everywhere, but we couldn't find him.'

'I'm not leaving without him,' the Colonel said.

'In that case, we have to report this to the Chief of the Security Army,' replied the man and then Awsa security men went to Chief Dangig and told him about the missing. After that, Chief dangig hurried to the Bulwark and said to Shalaqbeen, 'Colonel, We looked for the missing thief everywhere but couldn't find him. However, we're still looking for him and will bring him to you when we find him. Please leave with other thieves while it's dark. The Sultan doesn't want the young princess to know about this."

The Colonel thought momentarily and said, 'We'll leave, Chief, but your kingdom must hand that thief over to us as soon as possible.' And Chief Dangig replied, 'I promise we'll get him soon and send him after you. Please go.' Shalaqbeen nodded at him and turned round to lead his caravan back to Zaila.

This was another cruel twist for the thieves. The kingdom they thought was their safe haven had sent them back to the ruthless Queen of Zaila. Their heads hanging down with despair in the caged carriage, Colonel

Shalaqbeen and his men shipped them away. As they were leaving the Citadel, Daweel asked, 'What's going happen to us?' And Shaman hopelessly replied, 'I guess they'll kill us.'

45

CHAPTER

The next day, Hanad had no clue about what had happened to the thieves in the Guest House, left Gabi sleeping in his room and returned to the Citadel at 09:30 am to take Jamanjug into town. As he approached the main gate, one of the guards mysteriously asked him, 'Hey buddy, where is the big guy who went to the town with you yesterday evening?'

'Why are you asking?' Hanad, curious about his question, retorted.

'I'm asking because the security forces are looking for him, and he was with you when we last saw him,' the guard replied.

'Why they're looking for him?' Hanad demanded.

'The Kingdom of Zaila and Thorny Land came to take back the fugitive thieves and the princess with them,' the guard added.

Hanad moving closer to the guard asked, 'What happened to the other thieves and the princess?'

'I think they were handed over to a Colonel from Zaila except for the one with you,' he replied.

Hanad now understood what was going on and decided to save Gabi. He hurried back to the town. He hastily approached one of his friends who lived on the city's north side and asked him to borrow his horse. The friend gave him the horse, and Hanad rode it away to his house. He came to Gabi, who had had breakfast and was chatting with his mother. He stopped the horse at the house entrance and, shouted, 'Gabi, we have a serious problem. Let us go. Hurry up.'

'What's going on?' Gabi asked, and Hanad replied, 'We have no time for asking questions. Get on the horse.' Gabi jumped on the horse with him, and Hanad drove it away in a southerly direction. After being on the road for two hours, they approached a small village in the woods. They stopped the horse at the side of one of the village's houses, and Hanad climbing down the horse, shouted, 'Uncle Salhan, how's everybody.'

'We're all fine, Hanad. How's your mother and the kids?' Uncle Salhan shouted back under the shade of a tree in the house's compound.

'They're all right, uncle,' replied Hanad walking in with Gabi to join Uncle Salhan and his family just had their lunch and rested under the tree growing in their compound.

'We weren't expecting you. What brought you here, son?' His uncle asked, and Hanad replied, 'Uncle, I need your help. Can I talk to you privately?'

Salhan stood up and walked away with him. When they got out the closure of the house he asked, 'What can

I help you with, son?' And Hanad started to explain to him about the thieves and the princess he had befriended. He told him everything concluding his speech, 'Uncle, Can you take care of my friend here while I'm away? I want to go back to find out exactly what happened to the others last night. '

'You know you can count on me, Hanad, but you're asking something against the law. Son, don't put yourself and us in danger,' Salhan said worryingly.

'Uncle, don't say that. We're helping victims running for their lives. Just look after him until I return. I'll take care of him when I come back.'

His uncle thought for moments and reluctantly said, 'I'll keep him for you until tonight. Please take him away before the security forces find him here.'

That settled their argument. They returned to the house, and Hanad said to Gabi, 'My friend, I'm going back to find out what happened to the others. Take care of yourself. My uncle will help you.'

'Find for me the satchel and Jamanjug's bow and arrows case. They're probably under his bed,' Gabi requested.

'I will,' Hanad answered, and he jumped on the horse and galloped back to the city. He'd arrived at the Citadel late in the afternoon. he left the horse at the horse stable on the building's south side and hurried to the Guest House. He found Dhudi happily chatting with Marian on the bench outside the building. Hanad understood from her mood that she was unaware of what had happened to her friends. He hurried to her and asked, 'Princess, have you seen your friends this morning?'

'No, is something wrong?' she asked alarmingly.

'Princess, let us go,' he said, walking away without answering her question. Dhudi followed him. He led her to the men's section of the Guest House. Dhudi, struggling to keep him up, asked again, 'Hanad, is something wrong?'

'This morning, I came to the Citadel to take Jamanjug to the city, and one of the guards at the gate told me that the thieves were captured last night. He said that they were given to a Colonel from Zaila. He also told me that the security men were looking for Gabi. So I hid him in a small village in the woods.'

'That's impossible,' Dhudi, visibly frightened, uttered.

Before he spoke further, they entered the men's section and hastened to their friends' rooms. No one of them was there. Dhudi now accepted the stark reality confronting them and cried. Tears running down her cheeks, she asked, 'How could this happen?'

Hanad didn't bother to answer her question. He searched for the items Gabi had told him to find. 'Let us go,' he said when he had collected the things.

'Where are we going?'

'We're going to join Gabi.'

Together they walked out of the building heading to the horse stable. As they were getting out of the building they pumped into Marian, waiting for them outside, and Dhudi said, 'Marian, the Kingdom of Zaila and thorny Land took away my friends except Gabi. I'm leaving now to try to save them. Goodbye, and thank you for everything.'

'Where's Gabi now?' Marian asked worryingly.

'He's hiding somewhere Hanad put him,' Dhudi replied.

'Can he come with me? I'll take him to Asab, where my family live. He would be safe there,' Marian explained.

'I'll tell him this. Goodbye now,' Dhudi said in a hurry and then walked away with Hanad. On the way, as they were passing the Sultan's section, she said, 'Hold on, Hanad. Before we leave, I want to see Sultan Kandhafo.' So they turned towards the Sultan's court. They came to him, just finished his work and getting ready to go home. 'Sultan, my friends are missing. I've been told that they were taken away by a Colonel from Zaila. Is that true?' Dhudi asked angrily.

'Princess, sit down and listen to me carefully,' said the Sultan.

She sat down, and the Sultan sat down too and continued, 'My princess, it is true that we've sent them back to Zaila. We had no other choice. We must send the thieves back to their country. It's a rule agreed by the kingdoms of the lands.'

'My father told me before he died that you and several other men would help me when I need help. You shouldn't have given the men who had carried me on the sea and in the deserts to the cruel Queen. They are the only family I have in this world,' she said in anguish before rising from the seat to leave.

'Princess, I can guess your anguish, but there is nothing I can do about what happened. Just you can stay with us.'

Dhudi distraught, walked out of the room, leaving behind Sultan Kandhafo, wondering how well she had recovered and was beautiful, and Hanad followed her. They strode off to the horse stable. They climbed on the horse together and set off to where Gabi was waiting for them. At sunset, they came to Hanad's uncle and his family sitting in their house's compound without Gabi. With much concern, Hanad asked, 'Uncle, where is my friend?'

'Don't be alarmed, son. Your friend's fine. I hid him in the woods,' Uncle Salhan explained.

'Thank you, uncle,' Hanad grunted.

That night Hanad and Dhudi slept in the house's enclosure with mats and blankets given to them by the family because the family had not had enough rooms. Strangely that night, Hanad dreamed of Dhudi in a glamorous red dress and stunningly beautiful standing in front of him and saying, 'Hanad, if you care about me, save my friends. They're the only family I've got in this world, and he was saying, 'Princess, I can't.' 'Hanad, you can. You are a prince, free my friends,' she replied.

He jolted from his sleep. It was like a real conversation between the two of them. Astonished with this fascinating dream, he sat up, sighed, concentrated and looked around him. Then things he'd dreamed, still vivid in his mind he returned to sleep. However, an hour later, the dream returned in a different form. He dreamed Dhudi rode a horse with him, laughing and playing with him joyfully in a lush green valley and saying to him, 'Hanad, I love you.' Unconsciously enjoying his interaction with her he continued his sleep peacefully for the rest of the night.

46

CHAPTER

On the other hand, Colonel Shalaqbeen sometimes in front of his caravan and at other times following it from behind, kept moving for most of the day to narrow the gap of the distance ahead of them. After long hours on the road and they crossed the borderline between the two countries, he stopped the caravan at sunset in a clear area at the side of the road and told his men to prepare food for themselves and get some rest. After supper, Kirkir couldn't restrain his urge to find the man who had fired the shots that had struck him in the buttocks the night he was with Queen Idil on Faay Island. He went to the thieves that manacled in their carriage. He grabbed Shaman's hand and said, 'Get up, old man.' Pulling his hand, Kirkir added, 'Let us go.' He led him to a far corner and asked him, 'Which one of you is good at shooting?'

'Every one of us can shoot. What are you up to?' Shaman asked.

'Answer my question. Which one of you is usually armed with arrows and a bow?'

Shaman understood that he was after something and decided not to give him any information. He repeated, 'I don't know what you're looking for. Every one of us can shoot arrows.'

'I'll deal with you later, old man. Come with me.' He grabbed his hand again and led him back to the carriage. He pushed him in, turned to Daweel and said, 'You stand up and come with me.' Kirkir took him to the same place and said calmly, 'My friend, we don't have enough food to eat on the way. We must go hunting tomorrow. We need someone good at shooting arrows. Does any one of you have a talent for shooting?'

'Yes. Jamanjug is good at shooting arrows and is a good hunter too. He never misses the target,' Daweel naively explained to him.

'Was he the only one who hunted with arrows on Faay Island?'

'Yes, he is very skilful at it,' Daweel answered.

'Thank you. Let us go back to your friends,' Kirkir said. He put Daweel back in the carriage. Then Kirkir was convinced that the man who shot him in the buttocks that night was Jamanjug. He said, 'Jamanjug, get up.' Jamanjug had already learnt from Shaman what Kirkir was asking about. He stood up his legs shaking with fear. 'Come this way,' said Kirkir, leading him away to his interrogation spot. Before they got far, Colonel Shalaqbeen, who was resting in the corner of his caravan, noticed Kirkir's movements and shouted, 'Kirkir, what are you doing?'

'Colonel, I'm asking this criminal some questions.'

Colonel Shalaqbeen, who had disliked Kirkir since the beginning of their meeting with Sultan Kandhafo sat up from his mat and sneered, 'Leave him alone. Our special interrogators will interrogate him when we get home.'

'I'll ask him only a few questions, Colonel. Will bring him back in a minute,' Kirkir shouted.

'No. Take the man back to the carriage and leave him alone,' Colonel Shalaqbeen barked.

Kirkir turned to Jamanjug and whispered in his ears, 'I know who you are. You'll suffer for what you did to me and the queen that night for the rest of your life. Come with me. I'll deal with you later.' He took him back to the carriage, and Jamanjug was relieved at Colonel Shalaqbeen's intervention, but he wondered what would happen next.

47

CHAPTER

Dhudi had devised a plan last night before she fell asleep and woke up in the morning while others were still in bed. She went to the toilet, brushed her teeth and washed her face. After that, she returned to the compound and woke up Hanad. When he opened his eyes, she said to him, 'My friends are in great danger. We must do something, Hanad.'

Hanad, whose head was still foggy, sat up and said, 'What do you have in mind?'

'I need a fast horse. I have to seek help from my uncle, the Governor of Thorny Land and the Cty of Five Gates,' she explained.

'It isn't safe for you to travel to the land between the two countries. Supporters of Queen Idil and freelance outlaw gangs who live between the territories are in your way. Think of something else.'

'Whatever may happen to me on the way, I have no other option,' Dhudi answered.

'Can we see Gabi before you make a decision? He should have his say,' Hanad said thoughtfully.

Dhudi realised that she had made a mistake in making such a crucial decision without sharing her thoughts first with Gabi. She said, 'You're right. Let us see him.'

Hanad went to wash, and afterwards, they went to find Gabi with the help of Hanad's uncle, who showed them the way. They found him ducking behind trees outside the village. They greeted him and sat down with him, and then Hanad said, 'Gabi, the princess wants to go to Thorny Land to get help from her uncle. What do you think?'

Gabi twisted his neck towards Dhudi and bellowed, 'That isn't a good idea, princess. Your plan of seeking help from your uncle isn't bad, but you can't go there. The followers of your stepmother are there on the way. Don't put yourself at risk. I'm going instead,' Gabi explained.

'No, Gabi. I can't let you go. I'll go. Stay with Hanad and his uncle until I come back,' Dhudi insisted.

'Princess, don't worry about my safety. Just write a letter to the Governor of Thorny Land and the City of Five Gates, Harer. I'll take it to him, and I'll be back with his message to you immediately. I promise everything will be fine,' Gabi, who was already planning his journey to Thorny Land in his head, justified himself confidently.

'Gabi, my heart will break if the people of my stepmother get you before you have reached the headquarters of my uncle,' she repeated.

' I'll disguise myself as a religious man, a Mullah spreading the word of God. I just need a Qameez of my size, rosary beads, a turban, a long stick and a horse. They'll never find me with these things, and the mission is accomplished, Princess,' Gabi further explained.

'That's a beautiful idea. How did such a thought come to you?' Asked Hanad, amazed by his plan.

'The princess inspired me.' Gabi replied.

'How did I inspire you,' asked Dhudi, who was also amazed at his idea and wanted to know what she had done.

'You inspired me when you said to us, 'You can be who you want to be', and you showed us how to improvise a boat. You've activated my creativity and my thinking ability. Thank you, princess,' Gabi explained.

'I'll find a fast horse and the other things you need for you and will show you the way,' Hanad hurried to say, and the princess impressed by Gabi's strategy, added, 'I'll write a letter to my uncle.' Then they went together back to the village. They ate breakfast, and an hour later, Gabi put on his disguise of a long black Qameez, a turban, rosary beads and a cane found for him by Hanad's uncle. Afterwards, the trio mounting on two horses, one for Gabi and the other shared by Dhudi and Hanad trotted away towards the border between Awsa and Zaila kingdoms. Their horses galloping as fast as they could they travelled through the terrain of rolling hills, rough rocky grounds and narrow paths. At late noon they emerged into a small village situated near the base of Awsa Border Guards, where Hanad's cousin, Colonel Rohan, the Commander of Awsa Border Guards, lived with his wife and his first baby son. They approached Rohan playing with his baby on his house's patio while his wife was busy in the kitchen. After exchanging quick introductions and drinking some water, Hanad stood up and said to Rohan, 'Brother, can I have a word with you privately?'

'Sure,' Colonel Rohan replied. Together they walked away from Dhudi, Gabi and the baby cooing in his cradle. When they had gone far enough so that no one else could hear them, Hanad grunted, 'Brother, I need your help.'

'What can I do for you?' Rohan asked.

'I need you to help Gabi to cross the border safely. He's going to deliver the princess's message to the Governor of Thorny Land and the City of Five Gates.'

'Is he the missing thief?'

'Yes.'

'Are you insane? How can we help a wanted thief? I must arrest him right now,' Rohan ranted.

'You're not my brother if you would ever think of a such thing. Will you help us or not?' Hanad retorted angrily.

'If I do what you said, I will commit a crime against my kingdom.'

'Colonel, you're wrong. You're just assisting him in crossing the border quietly. After that, it's up to him if he gets himself caught in his country.'

Rohan thought awhile and then said, 'Why are you helping these people anyway?'

'First of all, they're my friends. Furthermore, to tell you the truth, I love the princess.'

'I see. In that case, I'll do what I can.'

As they turned around to go back, they saw men on horses heading towards them. 'I think you've been followed,' said the Colonel. He ran back to his house, and shouted, 'Gabi, get in the house and don't come out.'

A few minutes later, three well-armed security men on their horses had reached them in a hurry, and one of them abruptly climbed down from his horse. He walked Rohan and said, 'Sir, we're looking for a fugitive who escaped from deportation, and we believe he's in this territory.'

'What made you think he's in this territory, officer?' Rohan enquired.

'The last time someone saw him, he was with that young cadet,' the officer said, pointing at Hanad.

Rohan looked at his cousin and said, 'Hanad, did you assist a wanted man?'

'No. I didn't assist anybody,' Prince Hanad protested.

'Hanad, we've been to your house and also, to your uncle's house, where you stayed last night. We believe you know where that man is. Please help us to catch him. Otherwise, we'll charge you with assisting a criminal if we discover later that you've helped him.'

'I told you I didn't help anyone,' Hanad screamed and Rohan added, 'Stop harassing him. He told you that he didn't help. Go and find the man.'

The three security men were unsatisfied with Hanad's answer and they couldn't argue with the colonel. They mounted on their horses and went away. However, before they got far, their leader said to others, 'They're hiding the man somewhere, I guess. Let us keep an eye on them from a close hideout.' They rode away further, pretending that they were going away. When they had disappeared from sight, they turned around and hid themselves and their horses behind trees. Then they spied on Rohan and his guests from there.

On the other hand, after the security men had gone, Dhudi started writing a letter to her uncle, Farah Ebbie, the Governor of Thorny Land and Harer, the city of Five Gates. In the letter, she wrote:

Dear Uncle,

I hope my letter reaches you well. Uncle, maybe you're convinced that I've died, though I am still alive despite my stepmother, the Queen of Zaila, having tried to kill me twice. I'm at the border between Zaila and Awsa with friends assisting me. Uncle, with your help, I want to save my friends, who a Colonel from Zaila captured in Awsa and challenge the wicked Queen who tried to kill me. Please help me to free my friends before the brutal Queen kills them in cold blood. Also, please help me reclaim my parents' kingdom and property. I hope you will stand on my side and allow me to find justice.

Dhudi Erek, the Princess of Zaila and Thorny Land.

48

CHAPTER

—❦—

The following morning at dawn, while people were still in a deep sleep, Rohan quietly woke Gabi up and told him it was time for him to leave. Then Gabi expected such a call, hastily packed his things up and together, they disappeared quietly into the darkness with two horses. Mindful not to attract anyone's attention, they led the horses carefully towards the border. Without hassle, they eventually crossed the valley that divided the two countries, and Colonel Rohan, pointing at mountains in the southerly direction, grunted, 'I can't go beyond this point, my friend. There's a path to Thorny Land between those two mountains. Take it and be careful. Hamish's militia and Zaila Border Guards can be creeping around on your way.'

'I will, Colonel,' Gabi gratefully replied and drove off his horse towards the mountains. After negotiating rough, rocky ground strewn with tangled trees alongside the maintains, he found the path to Thorny Land and galloped away. After traversing several miles, and the sun had fully risen, Gabi saw a village looming in his way. It reminded him of how the people in the desert oasis had tormented him and his friends. So, afraid of a similar experience, he left off the path to the left and continued his journey. When he was almost passing the village and was considering returning to the track, he saw two riders on fast horses catching him up from behind. His heart started beating fast with fear, but he calmly travelled at the same pace. They approached him in a hurry, and one of them veering his horse close to him asked, 'Who are you, Mullah?'

'I would like to ask you the same question, son,' Gabi, concealing his fear, said.

'We're Zaila and Thorny Land Border Guards,' the man answered.

Gabi froze with fear when he heard that they were border guards. However, somehow he maintained his outward calmness and said, 'I'm a preacher spreading the word of God.'

They looked at each other, and the one questioning him asked again, 'Where are you heading to, holy man?'

'I'm heading to Thorny Land. I'm going to save people from disease and hellfire.'

'If you're going to Thorny Land, why did you leave the road to avoid the village on your way?' The man asked again, eyeing him warily.

Gabi thought for a moment and replied, 'I couldn't enter that village, son.'

'Why not?' The man asked.

'Last night, I had been told in a dream that I shouldn't enter the first human settlement I find on my way.'

'So you get divine messages from God in your sleep,' the man enquired.

'That's right. The Almighty guides me to what I should do.'

'Where did you come from?' The man asked him once more.

'I come from Awsa, where I cured people who contracted a strange illness, and now I'm going to help others suffering in Thorny Land,' Gabi bravely lied.

'Mullah, if you can cure people, there're children and elderly folks who need help in the village. Come with us and cure them,' the man repeated.

'I'm afraid I can't. As I said earlier, I was told in my dream not to enter it.'

'What's the reason God would prevent you from entering the village?' The other man asked.

'I don't know. Perhaps some sinful people who disobeyed their creator are in it,' Gabi defended himself.

'If you're a good holy man help these dying people,' the man repeated.

'I can't,' Gabi insisted.

'A man of God would never leave people suffering. Please help them,' the other man, who was convinced that Gabi was a holy man, implored him.

Gabi thought for a moment, and then an idea struck him. He said, 'Son, I told you that God had forbidden me to enter the village. Bring the sick people to me, somewhere outside of it. I'll read the word of God onto them.'

'Okay, come with us,' said the man. Then Gabi followed them. They brought him to a large tree outside the village and told him to wait there while they got the sick people. As they walked away he halted at them, 'My sons, bring a gallon of water with the ailing people.'

The two men hastened to the village, and within a short time, they came back with three emaciated children and a scraggy woman, coughing deep in her chest on hand wagons. They put them in front of Gabi, whose head was bowed down as he pretended to pray, and then one of them said, 'Mullah, They're here.'

He slowly lifted his head up and said, 'Bring them closer to me,' and the men moved the patients close to him. After that, he began mumbling inaudible prayers over them and dry spitting on the water in the container. Whenever he finished a set of his strange prayers he dry-spat either on the water or the sufferers.

After twenty minutes of an agonising inaudible reading, he looked at those who brought the patients and said, 'Give each of them a cup of fresh milk and a spoon of honey with some of this holy water two times a day for one week. Also, give them fruit juice and porridge with goat's milk daily.' Thereafter, he climbed on his horse and continued on his journey. His horse galloped as fast as it could the rest of the day. At sunset, he emerged into a big village sprawling on both sides of the road. He stopped outside the nearest house and asked for water from a woman cooking an evening meal in her front yard. She gave him a large bowl of water. He drank some and gave some to his horse. Then he said, 'Thank you, madam,' and turned away to carry on his journey.

'Where are you heading to, Mullah?' the woman asked.

He stopped and answered, 'I'm going to Thorny Land.'

'Mullah, it's going to be dark soon. Stay with us tonight,' replied the woman, who felt sympathy for the man of God on his long journey.

'I can't,' madam. I'm going to cure people suffering from diseases. I must get there immediately,' said Gabi, who wanted to deliver the princess's message as quickly as he could.

'Mullah, I'm glad to hear that you cure sick people. My husband snores throughout the night, and he has bad nightmares as well. Please stay with us tonight and cure him,' she explained.

He thought for a few seconds and said, 'I'll read the word of God when I return. Now I must go.'

'Mullah, please stay. It's nearly sunset, and the night will fall on you in a lonely land,' she said, and at the same time, she grabbed a mat and put it down for him in the yard. Gabi felt that he had no choice and decided to stay. He faced her and asked, 'Where's your husband?'

'He's in his workshop. He'll come in a few minutes. Please pray for him to God when he comes. I can't rest in our bed with him at night. His snores keep me awake, and these nightmares torment him.'

The two of them talking in the front yard of the house, her husband came, and the woman said to him, 'Shoko, this is Mullah Gabi. He cures people who suffer from diseases. I asked him to stay with us tonight and read the word of God to you.'

'Nice to meet you, Mullah,' said Shoko, who carried on to his bedroom to change his dress. Minutes later Shoko returned and together they sat down to dinner. Over the food, Gabi asked Shoko questions about his snores and nightmares, and Shoko explained how he felt. Through his story, Gabi understood that Shoko had severe nostril congestion and said, 'Shoko get some black seed oil for me.' Then Shoko's wife went inside the house and returned with the oil. After that, Gabi started reading his fake prayers over Shoko and the oil. When he'd completed the reading, he roared, 'Put the oil in your nostrils every night before you go to bed. Your snores and nightmares will vanish afterwards with God's will.'

Shoko did what he was told to do before he and his wife went to bed that night. Surprisingly, sometime before midnight, Gabi began snoring, and he screamed, 'Jamanjug, stop pestering me.' His scream woke up the couple, and they came out of their room with a lamp to check what had happened to their guest. They found him swatting away invisible things with his hand and rolling over and mumbling Jamanjug's name and other things. He was having nightmares, dreaming that Jamanjug was gently stroking his nostrils with a twig. The sensation of the brushing twig increased to an irresistible level, and then Gabi rolled over, sneezed and mumbled audibly, 'Idiot, little man, stop bothering me.'

After they'd listened to him for quite a while, Shoko said to his wife, 'Arfon, if this man can cure nightmares and snore, he would surely cure himself. Let us go to bed,' and his wife whined in agreement, 'I don't know what to say, darling. Let us go.'

In the morning, they gave him breakfast, and before he left he said to the husband, 'Shoko, come closer. I must read the word of God to you before I leave.'

Shoko was in doubt about the prayers and the treatment. He reluctantly asked, 'Mullah, last night you had nightmares. Who's Jamanjug? He bothered you a lot in your sleep.'

Gabi didn't remember his dream and was scared by his host's question. Wondering how much information he'd given out in his sleep he asked, 'What else did I say, Shoko?'

'You were saying, 'idiot little man. Jamanjug, stop pestering me.' Who is Jamanjug anyway?' Shoko repeated.

'Jamanjug is a small devil who pesters holy people. When you're doing the holy work of God, sometimes devils will bother you in a bid to stop you from your good public service.'

'That's true,' whined Arfon, who believed that the little man who'd bothered the preacher was indeed a devil. She encouraged her husband to accept the treatment. So Gabi began mumbling and dry spitting on Shoko. When he'd finished his lousy performance, Gabi stood up and said, 'God bless you, friends. I have to go. Goodbye.' He hopped on his horse and took the road to Thorny Land's capital, Harer. Despite the hot weather of this tropical country, Gabi didn't rest that day until sunset, and the following morning, he was back on the road. At noon once he and his horse were exhausted, Gabi approached Harer, the second city of the Zaila Kingdom from the north. The city had Five Gates, each leading to one of its five districts and it was surrounded by a tall wall. He entered it from the north gate and proceeded to Governor Ebbie's headquarters in the fourth district. He came to a watchman at the entrance of the governor's compound and shouted from the back of his horse, 'I come to see Governor Farah Ebbie. I have an important message for him.'

The watchman respecting him as a revered religious man replied, "Mullah, leave the horse here and come with me. I'll show you where he is." The watchman led him to a conference hall in the compound's east corner. He brought him in front of Governor Ebbie, reclining on a big cushion and chatting with Harer district commissioners and a group of chiefs.

'Governor Ebbie, this holy man has a message for you,' the watchman shouted from the doorway.

The Governor looked respectfully at the religious stranger and said, 'Come in, Mullah,' and Gabi, gazing at him walked in.

Governor Ebbie was a seventy-year-old thin man. His hair was white and patchy, and his beard was long and as white as his hair. Gabi wondered how such an ancient man could help another person. He gave him the letter from Princess Dhudi and said, 'Governor, this is from your niece, the daughter of King Erek. She needs your urgent help.' The Governor flinched at the unexpected news. He took the letter from him and said, 'Mullah, please sit down.' Gabi sat in a corner, and the old man passed the note to an assistant sitting on his right side and screeched, 'Read it loudly for us.'

The assistant read the letter loudly. When he'd finished it, the Governor screeched again with much alarm, 'Mullah, is it true that this letter is from the princess?'

'Yes. She's at the border between Awsa and Thorny Land with friends.'

'Mullah, may I ask you how you got involved with the princess?' Ebbie asked him curiously.

'I'm one of five men who have been helping her since she went missing,' Gabi explained proudly.

'How did you meet her?' The Governor demanded, and Gabi began telling Dhudi's story, starting from the day they found her sleeping in their room and concluding with how she'd recovered from the Rijzi poison that almost killed her.

Governor Ebbie couldn't comprehend what he'd heard. He lamented with confusion, 'I thought the young princess was safe and well off under the care of her stepmother. I neglected the only heiress of my cousin.' He stood up and picked up a long black cane that was leaning on the wall next to him. Then said, 'Mullah, come with me,' and walked with the support of the stick towards the door. Leaving behind the chiefs dumbfounded by what they'd heard, he led Gabi to his residential quarters. He handed him over to a servant in charge of the guest rooms, and said to him, 'Put this Mullah in a nice room and feed him well.' After that, he returned to the commissioners and the chiefs in the meeting hall.

49

CHAPTER

T he old Governor, bursting with burning anger returned to the district commissioners and chiefs in the meeting hall and screeched, 'Commissioners and Chiefs, you have heard what was written in the letter from the Princess. Advise me what to do.'

'Governor, I think we should send a group of armed men to the border to bring the princess home. Afterwards, we'll decide what to do next,' one of the commissioners explained.

'That's a good idea. Let us first bring the princess home,' another chief added.

'Any other ideas?' The Governor asked.

'What else were you expecting from us to say, Governor?' an old chief roared in the corner of the room.

'You didn't say enough. The heiress of the Kingdom of Zaila and Thorny Land is in danger and more importantly, there are questions surrounding her disappearance,' Governor Ebbie screeched. 'We can't just send a few men, who may bungle their mission. I need a large army to come with me to the border early in the morning. I want to pick up the Princess from the border, and then go to Zaila with my army and her to find out what exactly happened in the royal family after the late King's death.'

'Governor, it's hard to put together a large army in such a short time. On top of this, you're too frail to lead a large army on an arduous journey. Appoint a General who can do the job on your behalf,' another chief suggested.

'No, I must confront the queen and ask her why she tried to kill the orphan princess under her care,' the old Governor replied angrily.

'Governor, it's impossible to organize a large army by tomorrow morning. Most of our warriors are in remote villages. Above all, it will look like you're inciting a civil war if you take a large army to Zaila. Let us send a group of well-armed men to the border with that Mullah to bring the princess home,' the chief repeated.

'I'm not inciting a war. Leave this to me. I know a better way to deal with it,' the old Governor rising from his seat, said furiously.

'Governor, hold it. If you go to Zaila with the princess and a large army to challenge the queen, this may lead the country into full-scale civil. If this happens the Oromia and Abbysians will benefit from the mess and will take parts of our land when we get weakened. Don't put our kingdom and our land at risk for the sake of a single person. The nation is greater than your niece, Governor. Let us find another way to resolve the issue.'

Governor irritated by what the chief said screeched angrily, 'Whatever happens, I'll go. I must protect the only daughter of my brother' and walked to a large horn of war hung on the wall. He picked it up and exited the door with it. He stopped in the middle of the forecourt of the building and blew it. The horn emitted an alarming, booming sound that filled the air and men in the compound rushed out from their rooms and gathered around him. He blew it again. Disappointingly the old man, who was too weak to keep blowing the horn, coughed. So, one of the men around him noticed his difficulty took the horn from him and started blowing it. Each time he breathed in it facing in a different direction, the man kept blowing the horn until he was satisfied that all in the surrounding areas had heard the message. Then he returned the horn to him and said, 'Governor, I think that's enough.'

The Governor nodded at him and turned to look at the men who surrounded him. His blurry eyes dancing on their faces he screeched, 'Warriors, we've got a serious situation. I need a large army. Those who can ride take fast horses. Go to the remote villages and towns of Thorny Land, and bring me armed fighters by tomorrow at dawn.' The men obeyed his order. They scrambled on their horses and galloped away in different directions, and Governor Ebbie returned to the conference hall.

People in Harer and its outskirts responding to the horn's alarming call streamed to the Governor's headquarters. Armed warriors, who thought the city was under attack, others eager to help or curious about what was going on, everyone rushed to the compound and demanded to know what had happened as they arrived. Ebbie walked into the centre of the anxious people and shouted, 'People of Thorny Land and the City of Five Gates, thank you for your quick response to my call. We've got a serious situation. The Princess of Zaila and Thorny Land's alive. She's at the border, but she needs our urgent help. I need an army to come with me to the border tomorrow morning. Those who aren't armed, please go back home, but the armed warriors stay with us. We will be leaving tomorrow at dawn.'

'Governor, has the princess been at the border all the time since she disappeared?' A man in the crowd yelled, and a woman asked, 'Governor, what is the reason the princess went missing in the first place?'

'The Princess will answer your questions when we bring her home. Now please do as I said,' the Governor responded, and the citizens of Thorny Land respecting their leader's word, began streaming back to their original locations.

50

CHAPTER

The next morning before sunrise Governor Ebbie, who had slept little last night but was unusually energetic, went to the warriors that gathered in the compound. He came to many of them sleeping, and others were chatting in small groups or welcoming the new arrivals at the gate. He stopped in the centre of the army and screeched, 'Warriors, it's time to go. Get ready.' Thereafter, those already awake hastened to wake up the men sleeping and pick up their weapons. As the army rushed to their horses Governor Ebbie walked to a horse brought to him by one of his assistants. He climbed onto it and shouted, 'Warriors, let us move,' and at the same time he drove off his horse towards the gate. As he exited the gate, he halted the horse by the side of one of the watchmen at the entrance and said to him, 'Tell those who come late to follow us and catch us up on the way.'

After that, the old Governor had on both of his sides Gabi and his two lieutenants, Arays Danan and Ali Salool led the army to the border. They kept moving as fast as they could for the rest of the day. In the evening, they settled in a clearing by the road, and again hit the road the following morning. Nearly at midday on the third day Gabi on the frontline with the Governor and his two lieutenants, the army approached the same village that Gabi had refused to enter two days ago. As they were passing the village, one of those two riders who had stopped him that day among a group of spectators saw him and shouted to his colleagues, 'Look, the big mullah is with them!'

The spectators looking at the horses sending columns of dust into the air with awe, the Governor and his army continued towards the border. Within a short time, they reached the borderline that divided the two countries, and the Governor abruptly halted his horse and gestured for his men to halt too. Then the horses jolted to stop. He instructed his deputy, Arays Danan to keep the army there and Ali Salool, two bodyguards, and Gabi to come with him. Having Salool and Gabi on his sides and the guards following them from behind, he crossed the borderline to the other side. As they stepped into Awsa territory, Colonel Rohan's surveillance men hid behind trees at once jumped out of their hideouts and shouted, 'Stop. Identify yourselves!'

'Relax guys. I'm a friend of Colonel Rohan, and this is the Governor of Thorny Land. We're going to the Colonel's house,' Gabi proudly explained. Then the surveillance men satisfied with his explanation escorted them to Rohan's house. They came to the Colonel playing with his son in the front yard of his house, and Princess Dhudi and Hanad, whose relationship had deepened since she recovered from the Rijzi poison's effects sat under a tree near the house.

Governor Ebbie and Gabi climbed down from their horses in a hurry and walked over to the tree, and Princess Dhudi believing the old man with Gabi was her uncle stood up quickly and started striding towards them. They met in the middle, and she embraced warmly with her uncle. Dhudi was elated to have one of her blood relatives today. She held him tight, and Governor Ebbie holding her in his hands lamented, 'I'm sorry for what happened to you, Princess. I thought you were better off in the care of your stepmother.'

'Thank you for coming to me, uncle. I'm glad you're here with me today,' Dhudi happily chirped.

The old Governor, whose eyes were moist with tears of happiness added, 'Dhudi, I'm so sorry that I didn't help you when you most needed me. Let us go home.'

She went to Rohan's house to pick up her things. As she walked away, Governor Ebbie turned to Rohan, Hanad and Gabi, who joined him while he was hugging his niece and said, 'Gentlemen, thank you indeed for helping the Princess. I'm so grateful for the way you've treated her. I learnt everything from Gabi.'

'Governor, we did what we thought was right. Please take care of her from now on,' said Rohan feeling relief at her uncle's arrival.

'I will,' screeched the Governor turning away to go to his horse. As he started walking, Dhudi returned with her stuff nudged Hanad aside and said to him, 'Hanad, 'I'll come back to you after I free my friends. Wait for me in Awsa.'

'No, Dhudi. I'm coming with you,' he replied.

She looked him in the eyes and said again, 'I don't want to drag you into another trouble. You have already had enough. Stay at home. After I deal with my stepmother, I'll come back to you and afterwards, you'll come with me to Zaila.'

'Sorry that I didn't tell you about my dream. The night we were in my uncle's house, I dreamed of you asking me to free your friends. It was like a real dream and since then I've been thinking about how I can help you to free your friends. I'm coming with you and will fight side by side with you until the end. Please allow me to come,' Hanad explained.

Dhudi thought for a moment and said, 'If I asked you to free my friends in a dream, I'm awake now and asking you to stay. I'll come back to you when I sort out my problems. Please stay.'

He took her hand and said, 'Princess, that was more than a dream. Something real was in it. Please let me come.'

Dhudi saw on his face how passionately he wanted to come with her. She squeezed his hand and said, 'Let us go.' They walked to her uncle, who was waiting for her by the side of his horse. As they approached him, Dhudi said, 'Uncle, Hanad is my good friend, and he's coming with us.'

Governor Ebbie, who had been watching them while she was talking to Hanad, and could guess the bond between them through their body language looked at Rohan and said, 'Colonel, is it okay if this young man comes with us?'

'Yes, Governor, but please take care of him. He's my cousin,' Rohan replied. Governor Ebbie glanced at Dhudi holding Hanad's hand and said, 'Let us go.'

They hopped on the horses and trotted back to the border, where the Governor had left his army. Before long, they joined the army, and Ebbie shouted, 'Warriors, the Princess is with us alive and well now, but many questions about her disappearance need to be answered. Let us rest and eat well before we go to Zaila.'

Dhudi twisted her neck towards him and said, 'Uncle, you're all tired, but the men carrying me in the deserts and the sea when I was ill are in great danger. Please, we must hurry to save them.'

The Governor then called one of his men and said, 'Artan, take a fast horse and go to Zaila. Tell The Chief Minister, Gurey Asseyr, and General Gaboos that I'm on my way with my army and the Princess. I want those men who helped the princess since the queen tried to kill her to be safe. If the Queen and her supporters harm those innocent men, Zaila will face the worst bloodshed.' Artan nodded at him and hastened to his horse. He jumped on the horse and galloped away to deliver his master's message. As Artan started his journey, The Governor glanced at Dhudi and said, 'Princess, your friends would be fine. Let us wait for the army to eat and get some rest. We'll be moving soon.'

51

CHAPTER

Colonel Shalaqbeen had been on the road for five days and five nights with his caravan and was thinking in all these times about what Sultan Kandhafo of Awsa had told him about Princess Dhudi arrived at the White Palace on Friday at high noon. He could not put aside thinking about things the Sultan told him because some of them had seemed unusual, and he felt like he had dragged himself into a dangerous business. Kandhafo's words still disturbingly ringing in his head, he stopped the caravan at the rear of the Palace and went to the carriage that carried the prisoners. He opened the door and ordered the men manacled inside to come down. As soon as they got their feet on the ground, he led them through the back door of the building and locked them up in one of the two cell rooms in the Palace. After that, he put the keys in his pocket and walked away.

'Colonel, give me the keys. I'll take them to the Queen,' Kirkir shouted.

'No, Kirkir. I'll keep them. Go and tell the Queen that I'll come to see her tomorrow morning,' said Shalaqbeen, who had disliked Kirkir from the day they met Sultan Kandhafo.

Kirkir, feeling humiliated, went to the Queen's chamber. He came to her relaxing on her soft cushions. Before he could speak, she sat forward and screamed excitedly, 'Kirkir, I could barely wait for your return. Did everything happen as planned?'

'My Queen, we couldn't bring the princess and one of the thieves home. Just we brought four thieves.'

'Do you mean you've killed her and one of the thieves on the way?' She asked.

'No, my Queen. We weren't allowed to see the princess, and one of the thieves went missing. I think Colonel Shalaqbeen has more to say about them. He had a private meeting with the Sultan.'

'I told you to be with him at all times. What was the reason you couldn't attend the meetings with him?'

'The Sultan didn't want me to know everything.'

'That's interesting,' she said with surprise. 'Where is Colonel Shalaqbeen now?'

'I think he went to his house. He told me that he would come to see you tomorrow morning.'

'Where are the thieves you've brought?' she demanded.

'They're in one of the two cell rooms, but Shalaqbeen took the keys,' he replied with his head down.

'Why didn't you bring the keys with you, Kirkir?' she inquired.

'Shalaqbeen wouldn't let me have them. Please take the keys from him when he comes. We need to glean information from these thieves. They know things we need to know,' answered Kirkir, who couldn't wait to torture Jamanjug to death.

'I will. You look tired. Get some rest. We'll talk later,' said the Queen, and Kirkir went to his room.

Queen Idil was disappointed that her mission had failed again. She started to think about what to do next. Her temperature rising with anger, she thought confusingly. After thinking for a while, she asked herself, 'Why does every plan I make end unsuccessfully?' Then she stood from her seat and went to the toilet to have a shower to cool down her rising temperature.

On Saturday morning, Shalaqbeen came to her reclining on comfy cushions. 'Good morning, my queen,' he roared from the doorway.

The Queen sat forward and replied, 'Good morning, Colonel.'

He gave her the letter from the Sultan of Awsa and added before he sat down, 'Your Majesty, it's from Sultan Kandhafo.'

She read the letter, sighed and said, 'Pieces are missing from the puzzle. Why did the Sultan of Awsa not let you see the princess?'

'My Queen, the princess has made serious allegations about you. That's why I think he didn't allow us to see her.'

'Do you believe what Sultan Kandhafo has told you?' She asked curiously.

'Your majesty, I don't know what to believe anymore. I'm confused,' Shalaqbeen replied, with hints of sadness in his voice.

'Tell me everything about your private conversation with that Sultan,' demanded the Queen, looking him right in the eyes. Then Shalaqbeen began narrating what he'd heard from Sultan Kandhafo. Without missing any vital detail when he'd finished, she asked, 'Do you believe me, or do you believe in what that Sultan has told you?'

'I believe in you, my queen,' he replied dutifully.

'Excellent. Let us get to business. First of all, I'm the leader of the nation. It would be best to do things as I say,' she emphasised.

'Okay, my queen. What should I do?'He asked obediently.

'We're in a serious situation, colonel. So we must make serious decisions. First, eliminate the thieves before anyone knows they're here with us. Take them tonight at midnight and kill them. Second, organize a large army. We'll force that Sultan to hand over the girl and the missing thief.'

Shalaqbeen, struggling with his conscience, thought for a moment and said, 'My Queen, I can't kill these men that way. I never did such a horrendous large execution. Above all, many people have already been involved in their case. We can't keep their execution unnoticed. Let us send them to a secure detention island.'

'You never did things like this before. Don't worry. Kirkir will help you. He knows how to deal with such things.'

'My queen, but we can't keep this secret! We mustn't kill them,' Shalaqbeen hastened to say.

'When we declare our war with Awsa, no one will think about these petty thieves. The attention of the public will be on the war.'

Shalaqbeen was terrified at the enormity of the mess he had gotten himself into. He looked around, thinking about what else to say. After a moment of silence, he replied, 'Okay, my Queen. I'll do whatever I can, but I don't think this will be easy.'

'Shalaqbeen, you aren't doing this because I want it to be done. Remember that you will be the General of my kingdom's army. Be sure they are to be killed tonight.'

'Okay, my queen,' he said, rising from his seat to leave. As he was exiting the room, she halted him. 'Give the keys to Kirkir. We want to find out what these thieves know before they die.'

'Okay, my queen,' he replied and left.

52

CHAPTER

Artan hasn't rested since the beginning of his journey. He arrived at the regular army barracks in Zaila on Saturday at 4:00 pm and said to a sentry at the gate, 'I'm delivering a message from the Governor of Thorny Land and the city of Five Gates. Where's General Gaboos?'

The sentry turned back to face General Gaboos, who was topless and playing a game with his Deputy, Habad Gaas, under the shade of a large tree by the gate and shouted across to him, 'General, this man has a message from Governor Ebbie for you.'

'Let him in,' the General responded unconsciously, as his attention was on the game.

The sentry then gestured to Artan to enter the barracks, and Artan walked in. He approached the General and his deputy, still engrossed in the game and said, 'Good afternoon, gentlemen.'

General Gaboos stopped the game and said, 'Good afternoon. How can we help you?'

'My name's Artan. Governor Ebbie sent me to deliver an important message. Can I talk to you privately, General,' Artan emphasised.

General Gaboos stood up, put on his shirt and walked away with him. When they had gone far enough from the others, the General asked, 'What's the message?'

'The Governor instructed me to tell you and the Chief Minister that he's on his way to Zaila with a huge army and that he wants the men who had helped the princess when the queen tried to kill her to be safe until he's coming,' Artan explained.

General Gaboos was shocked at the message. 'Is the princess alive!' He asked.

'Yes. The princess is with the Governor, and she wants the men captured in Awsa by a colonel sent from Zaila to be released,' Artan answered.

The General then said, 'What you're saying is unbelievable. Please, tell me more about the missing princess and the men you say have helped her.' Artan then explained how they'd found the princess with friends at the border, about the Mullah she'd sent to Harer and what he'd heard about the thieves who were captured in Awsa. When he'd finished, the General said, 'I'll try to find out about those men. Go back to the Governor and tell him not to enter the town with a huge army. I'll meet him outside the city.'

'General, make sure those men are safe. The Governor has threatened that if they're harmed, Zaila will face bloodshed. Bye, General.'

'Eat something before you go. A long journey is waiting for you.'

'No, General. I must see the Chief Minister immediately. I have a similar message for him too,' said Artan, turning away to leave.

'Wait. In that case, I'm coming with you. I must talk to the Chief Minister about this as well.' Gaboos returned to his deputy and told him, 'Habad, you're in charge of the barracks. I'm going to see the Chief Minister.'

Habad Gaas was a tall man with a bushy moustache, had stained teeth and hazel-piercing eyes and usually he chewed tobacco. His eyes rolled up weirdly when he felt uncomfortable about something. He rolled his eyes upward and said, 'General, you look anxious. Is something wrong?'

'Yes, Colonel. Something is surely wrong. Take care of the camp while I'm away. We'll talk later,' Gaboos said and walked away with Artan. Before long, they came to the Chief Minister, sitting in the living room with two chiefs. General Gaboos greeted them from the doorway, and the Chief Minister responded to his greetings and invited them to come inside. After they had sat down, the Chief Minister grumbled, 'General, I wasn't expecting you. What brought you here with this gentleman?'

'This man and I have a delicate matter to discuss with you, Chief Minister. Can we talk to you in private?' General Gaboos replied.

The Chief Minister glanced at the chiefs and said, 'Gentlemen, can we put our meeting on hold?' The two men then hurried to vacate the room. As they stepped out of the room he added, 'General, we can talk now.'

'This is Artan. He's delivering a shocking message from the Governor of Thorny Land. Artan, repeat what you've told me. The Chief shall hear it all,' General Gaboos said, and Artan started to retell the message. As the Chief Minister listened, his eyes grew wider and wider at what he heard.

When Artan had finished the story about the princess, the Chief Minister said, 'I never thought my ears would hear such news. General, what should we do?

'I think Artan should go back to the Governor and tell him that we're working on releasing the men who helped the princess. Afterwards, we'll meet him outside the town.'

The Chief Minister welcomed his idea. He said, 'That's a good idea. Artan, do as the General has said. Tell the Governor not to enter the town. We'll meet him after we see the Queen.'

'I will, Chief Minister,' Artan replied getting up to leave.

Immediately after Artan exited the room, the Chief Minister said, 'General, let us go and see the Queen. We must share the message from Governor Ebbie with her and see what she says about it.' They got to their feet quickly and went to the Palace.

'Who is this colonel, who captured the thieves from Awsa anyway?' the Chief Minister asked as they walked.

'I have no idea. Probably he's a mystical colonel, another part of all the mysterious things we've heard from the messenger from the Governor,' General Gaboos answered vaguely.

The two men kept talking about Governor Ebbie's message until they came to Butler Hoob, who just happened to step out from the main chamber with a kettle and empty cups on a tray. 'Good evening, Butler. Where's the Queen?' The Chief Minister asked.

'Good evening Chief Minister. The Queen's in her private room. She's resting,' the Butler answered.

'We would like to see her. It's urgent,' the Chief Minister emphasised.

'I'll go and check if she can see you. Please have a seat,' Butler said politely and went upstairs. In minutes, he returned with Queen Idil resplendent in her royal garb.

As she walked into the chamber, she said, 'Good evening, gentlemen.'

'Good evening, Your Majesty,' they responded simultaneously.

She sat down and asked, 'My Butler told me you want to see me and it's urgent. What's going on?'

'My Queen, we've been approached by a messenger from the Governor of Thorny Land. He told us that the Governor had picked up the missing princess from the border two days ago, and he was heading to Zaila. He's coming to ask you questions about the disappearance of the princess. The messenger also told us that the Governor wants the men, who a colonel from Zaila captured in Awsa to be safe and released. We come to discuss these matters with you,' the Chief Minister explained.

The unexpected news dumbfounded the Queen. However, she managed to suppress her feelings. Choosing her words carefully, she said denyingly, 'I have nothing to discuss. Let us wait for the Governor to come and hear what he says.'

'Is there a colonel you've sent to Awsa to bring home thieves who absconded from their detention island?'

Queen Idil, embroiled in her horrible secret plots and vile lies, couldn't answer his question. She was confused and didn't know what to say. She rose from her seat and said, 'I'll answer your question and the questions the

Governor of Thorny Land has for me simultaneously. Excuse me, gentlemen. I was in the middle of something when you arrived.'

'My Queen, Governor Farah Ebbie is asking to be released men who helped the princess since she went missing. If those men exist, please tell your security men to transfer them to the courthouse detention centre,' The Chief Minister added with a note of anxious caution in his voice. She walked out of the room without a response. Wondering how things were getting out of her control, Queen Idil went to her bedroom. She lay on her bed, and with her eyes fixed on the ceiling, she started to think about the Governor of Thorny Land and Princess Dhudi. After she'd been on the bed for quite a while, a premature idea struck her. It was a desperate decision and the last resort. However, unsure if it would work, she got up and left the room looking for Kirkir. She found him loitering in the main corridor and told him, 'Kirkir, we must change the plan.'

'What happened, my queen?' he asked anxiously.

'The Chief Minister and General Gaboos know we have the thieves here. Never do anything stupid until we devise another plan. Be ready. Tomorrow morning we'll visit Chief Gabal.' With that said, she went back to her room.

53

CHAPTER

The following Sunday morning, the Queen and Kirkir each on a horse left the Palace quietly to find Chief Gabbal Hassan, the chief of her clan. Gabal lived in a village a few miles away from the city. Their journey didn't take long. They approached him feeding horses in the backyard of his house. He stopped what he was doing when he saw the Queen coming and walked in her direction to receive her. After they exchanged the usual greetings, he led her to his house, leaving Kikir outside with the horses. They sat on stools made of cow skin in a room he used as a sitting room and asked, 'Your Highness, what brought you to my village today?'

'My Kingdom is in danger, Chief. I need your help,' she said.

'That's impossible! Who can endanger your kingdom, my queen? Tell me what's going on,' he demanded.

Then she began explaining to him about the thieves who had escaped from Faay Island with her stepdaughter and how they were found in Awsa. About her request to the Sultan of Awsa to return the thieves and her stepdaughter. The response she'd received from him. She also explained to him Governor Ebbie and his army coming. She concluded her long talk by saying he was the only one she could trust, and she needed his help.

Despite Gabbal being the chief of her clan and it was his duty to protect the members of his clan he found opportunity in her request. Gabbal was an ambitious man. He always wanted to become the governor of a large swathe of the country mainly occupied by his clan and have a say in the kingdom's councils. As part of his plan, he was one of those behind Idil to marry the late King Erek. Unfortunately, before he pushed his agenda forward the king died and later he raised the issue with the queen, but she told him to wait. Today the moment came. Contemplating how he could execute his plan, he casually asked, 'My queen, how did your stepdaughter end up on Faay Island in the first place?'

'Not only you, but many other people are asking this question. We'll know later why she ended up on that island with a bunch of thieves. For now, let us focus on the defence of the kingdom. The brutal Governor of Thorny Land is heading to Zaila with the girl and a large army to overthrow my kingdom. I need a powerful force and a reliable leader who can say no to him, and you're the only one I can trust,' she added.

Gabbal sensed her fear and decided to pull the strings. He lifted his head slowly and said, 'My Queen, don't worry. You're the daughter of the Samo clan and the Queen of the land. Ebbie can't come near your kingdom while I'm alive, but your people must get their rights from your kingdom.'

Queen Idil understood the point he was making. She said, 'I was expecting to hear these reassuring words from you, Chief. When you defend the kingdom from the enemy, you'll be the governor of Samo Land and my close advisor. Is there anything else you need to defend the kingdom?'

'Yes, my Queen, I need weapons to fight with the aggressors and some money to give to some nasty traditional clan leaders who control militias,' he explained.

'I'll give you enough weapons and the money you need. Get your army geared up as quickly as possible. Governor Ebbie may come at any time from this moment,' she added.

'Your majesty, take it easy. The first groups of my men will arrive tomorrow morning and will take their defence positions around the Palace,' Gabbal answered confidently.

'Good. Now I'm going back to tell Shalaqbeen to organise the guards of the Palace and work with you. When you get your men ready come to me. I'll give you the things you need,' she concluded and got on her feet to leave.

'I will, Your Highness,' he replied and escorted her back to her horse.

54

CHAPTER

Yesterday evening, immediately after he and the Chief Minister returned from the Queen's meeting General Gaboos sent two intelligence men to snoop around the Palace and gather information about the Colonel who went to Awsa and the thieves he'd brought back. They gleaned enough facts and returned to him on the following Sunday at midday to report their findings. They told him about the mysterious colonel and the thieves he brought from Awsa. Then the General happy with the information in hand, went to the Chief Minister's house. He came to him having a meeting to discuss the disturbing message from Governor Ebbie with some of his ministers, including the Minister of Justice. He shouted from the doorstep, 'Good afternoon, Chief Minister and ministers.'

'Good afternoon, General' the Chief Minister replied. ' Come in. We were talking about the alarming message from Governor Ebbie and the missing princess he found at the border. Did you get any information on what's happening in the palace? '

General Gaboos sat in a corner and replied, 'Chief Minister and ministers, I'm afraid I've some unpleasant news for you.'

'What's it, General?' The Chief Minister asked with alarm.

'I sent men to the palace to find out the mysterious colonel and the prisoners he brought from awsa. They told me the Colonel the queen sent to Awsa is Farah Shalaqbeen, one of the junior officers of the palace guards, and the thieves he brought from Awsa are four men who are now crammed into one small cell room in the Palace.'

'Impossible! How could the Queen promote one of her guards to the rank of colonel without consulting with the Chief Minister and the General of the regular army?' the Justice Minister asked.

'I think something is seriously wrong with the Queen's leadership. She's overstepped the kingdom's administration rules,' the Interior Affairs Minister added.

'I have the feeling other bad things will happen soon if we don't act now,' the Chief Minister speculated.

'What should we do, Chief Minister?' Another minister asked.

'I don't know. I'm confused,' the Chief Minister lamented.

'Chief, follow your instinct. Say something. You're the leader,' General Gaboos bellowed.

The Chief Minister thought for moments and said, 'General, go to Chief Gabbal. Tell him to convince the Queen to transfer the thieves to the courthouse's detention centre and arrange an appointment with her. The kingdom's councils shall discuss with her what's happening in the kingdom.'

'Chief Minister, do you think she'll listen to Chief Gabbal?' General Gaboos enquired.

'Gabbal is the main Chief of her clan, and he was the one who convinced us to allow her to marry the king. I think she'll listen to him,' the Chief Minister explained.

'I now understand your reasons, Chief. I'll go to him tomorrow morning,' Gaboos said.

'No, General. It's urgent. Please go to him right now, and then both of you go to the Queen today,' the Chief Minister anxiously explained.

'Ok, Chief. However, I think it'll take some time to find him. He's a farmer and lives outside the city,' Gaboos said.

'Do your best, General,' the Chief Minister repeated.

General Gaboos hurried to his army's barracks. He took a horse and went to Gabbal's village. Unfortunately, when he arrived at the chief's house, he was told that Chief Gabbal was away. Unable to proceed with his mission further he had returned to the camp, planning to get back to him whenever possible.

55

CHAPTER

Immediately after the Queen left him, Chief Gabbal thinking nothing, but how he would mobilise his people towards a war he believed was right and what he would gain from it, started to bring together his clan's influential elders. He dashed to one of the elders who lived several yards away from his house. He explained to him what the Queen wanted, and together they went to find the other chiefs. Within two hours, Gabbal and his friend had brought together the most influential Samo leaders in a meadow just outside his village. After that, he shouted, 'My brethren, our daughter, the Queen of Zaila and Thorny Land, has come to me this morning and told me that her kingdom is under attack. The Governor of Thorny Land is coming to Zaila to remove her from power. I promised on your behalf that we'll protect her and her kingdom.'

'What's the reason the Governor of Thorny Land wants to remove her from power?' one of the chiefs interrupted him, and Gabbal answered, 'I guess he decided to take the kingdom from the queen.'

'That's against the law. Did he make any excuse to do so?' An older man asked.

'He's accusing her of trying to kill the late king's daughter. His allegation is false, and he is saying it to justify his wicked plan. We have to stop him,' Gabbal emphasised.

'Impossible! How could that man dare to make such horrible accusations against our Queen?' Another yelled, and Gabbal shouted, 'They think our daughter is a soft touch, and she cannot be a queen. We must show them that she has strong supporters.'

'The regular army should defend the kingdom. Why us?' A short man in a corner yelled.

'The regular army will play their role when necessary. However, this war is between the Queen and that renegade governor. He's coming with the warriors of his Reer Madoobe clan. So the Queen should have her clan's men on her side. We must fight for her. She's giving us weapons and money to defend the kingdom. On top of these, after we defend her kingdom, she'll grant us our own administration similar to the one Thorny Land has,' Gabbal explained. Sometimes raising his voice and other times speaking in a severe low tone he went on talking emotionally until the elders shouted angrily, 'Chief, we must teach a lesson to the Governor of Thorny Land and his clan.'

After he wowed them to war he instructed every Chief to go to his sub-clan and bring all the men who could fight even if they weren't armed, as the Queen would arm those unarmed. Furthermore, he reminded them that the Governor of Thorny Land could come sooner than expected, so the army should be ready by midnight.

Then the chiefs took the road to gather warriors, and Gabbal, happy with the results of his performance, went to the Queen to collect the fortune she'd promised to give him. In the evening he came to her in her chamber and said, 'My Queen, my army is almost ready. I come to collect the expenses and weapons you promised to give us.'

'Well done, chief,' said the Queen, who got on her feet without question. She went to the treasure room upstairs. Within minutes she returned with a full pouch. She gave it to him and shrieked, 'It contains the expenses for the chiefs. Come back tomorrow morning to collect the arms.'

Rising from his seat he said, 'My queen, I'll bring the army tonight,' and walked away with the pouch in his right hand. He came to his house and loosened the pouch's strap to see what was inside. Amazingly, he found many glittering pieces of rare gold and a lot of money. The beautiful fortune increased his urge to fight for the Queen and her kingdom. He stashed the pouch in a box and began fine-tuning his war plan. With his plan well-formulated, he went to the meeting place and found the first group of militiamen, some armed and others unarmed already gathered there.

The militia groups continued coming after the nightfall, and Chief Gabbal kept organising them into small battalions. When the last group came, he led them to the town. Within an hour he brought them to a spot near the Archery Field on the west side of the White Palace. After that, he went to find the Commander of the Palace Guards. He approached guards at the main gate and asked them where he could find Shalaqbeen. They told him that he had gone home. He walked to his house, which was not far from the Palace. He knocked on the door, and there was no immediate answer. He banged on it a bit harder, and this time Shalaqbeen, wrapped in a loose tatty night garment opened the door for him and asked with surprise, 'Chief Gabbal, what brought you to my house at this time of the night?'

'Why are you sleeping when you should be organising your men to war? Put on some better clothes and let us go. Governor Ebbie and his men can come at any time,' grumbled Gabbal, gazing at his nightgown disapprovingly.

Shalaqbeen went back to his room and returned in minutes in better attire. Then they walked away together. As they took to the road, Shalaqbeen asked him again, 'Perhaps I can know now what brought you to my house at this odd time, Chief?'

'Sergeant, I have put a large army behind the Palace. I want to know from you how your men and my men will work together to protect Her Majesty,' said Chief Gabbal.

'The Queen told me that she had spoken with you, but I wasn't expecting you to deploy your men so soon. Anyway, I'm not a sergeant anymore. The Queen has elevated me to a full colonel,' Shalaqbeen explained.

'I didn't know that you were promoted. My apologies, Colonel,' replied Gabbal asking himself how the queen could make him a full colonel.

'Apology accepted. Where should we begin, chief?'

'We need to coordinate the two forces. Make them work together smoothly,' Gabbal said.

'That isn't a problem but I'm worrying about General Gaboos. I don't know if he's on our side,' Colonel Shalaqbeen said anxiously.

'He must work with us. He's the Queen's General,' Gabbal grunted optimistically.

'The Queen can't trust him and the Chief Minister. So I'm not sure if he's going to be on our side,' Shalaqbeen said.

'In that case, the queen needs to get rid of him,' Chief Gabbal said as they were close to the Palace's main gate, and Shalaqbeen added, 'I agree with you.'

They approached the guards at the entrance, and Shalaqbeen shouted, 'Guys, we have Chief Gabbal and his men with us. They come to help us to protect the kingdom. The Governor of Thorny Land is coming with a huge army to overthrow the kingdom. Get ready to defend the queen and the kingdom.'

After that, they went to Gabbal's men. As they came Gabbal picked two men and instructed them to keep an eye on the main road to Awsa, and another two he sent to watch the road go to Thorny Land. Then he organised his militia into three battalions. One battalion he placed on the west side of the Palace. Another company he put on the north side of the building, and the third battalion he sent to the south corner of the Palace. When he directed his men he told Shalaqbeen it was his turn to prepare his army and then they returned to the Palace. They sat in Shalaqbeen's small office and discussed further the best possible ways to protect the Queen and the kingdom from Governor Ebbie.

56

CHAPTER

At around 9:00 am, Chief Gabbal and Colonel Shalaqbeen, happy with their war strategies and preparing to see the Queen saw the two surveillance men that Gabbal had sent on the road to Awsa, returning with their horses galloping as fast as possible. The speeding riders abruptly stopped in front of them, and one of them shouted from the back of his horse, 'Chief, Governor Ebbie and his huge army are coming!'

'How far away are they?' Gabbal asked, and the man replied, 'They're about two miles away. They've just descended from the west hills behind the flat land.'

Without asking more questions, Gabbal twisted his neck towards Shalaqbeen and said, 'Let us go, Colonel.' Together they hastened to the Queen's chambers. Shortly afterwards, they approached her sitting in her private chamber. 'Your Majesty, Governor Ebbie and his army are approaching the city. We need the weapons quickly,' Gabbal shouted alarmingly from the doorstep,

The Queen was panicked at the urgency in his voice. She stood up and said, 'Let's go.' She led them to the arms stores in the west wing of the White Palace. They came to Yussuf Saeem, the keeper of the stores, and she ordered him to open the stores for Chief Gabbal and Colonel Shalaqbeen. Puzzling at her instructions, Yusuf said, 'My Queen, the weapons in these stores are only for the specially trained regular army. Did you consult about this with your councils and the regular army General?'

'We don't have time to consult with those people. The country is at war. Open the doors for the Chief and his men. They're defending the kingdom from a renegade governor,' she screamed.

The storekeeper, who had no choice other than to obey her order, opened the doors one after another, and Gabbal and Shalaqbeen began to arm their men with new guns, ammunition, poisonous arrows, strong bows, lances, spears and other lethal weapons. After they armed their men and put them into their positions, Gabbal asked Shalaqbeen, 'Colonel, do you think General Gaboos would be with us?'

'I don't know. The queen can't trust him. Anyway, he's the Commander of her regular army. He must do what she tells him to do,' Shalaqbeen answered.

'We have to find out whether he's with us or not before the war begins. Let us go back to the Queen,' Gabbal said anxiously.

They hastened back to the Queen's chambers. They came to her in the main chamber with Kirkir. As they entered the room, the Queen surprised at their quick return asked, 'Chief, is everything alright?'

'Yes, my Queen. Our men are in their positions but I wonder if General Gaboos and his army will join us,' Gabbal explained.

'I can't trust the General. However, I'll instruct him to work with you,' said the Queen.

'My Queen, talk to him as quickly as possible. We must know whether he's a foe or a friend,' Gabbal repeated.

'Chief, can you defeat Governor Ebbie without the regular army?' The Queen curiously asked.

'Definitely, we'll defeat him,' he replied.

'In that case, we'll get rid of him if he refuses to join you,' she added. She looked at Kirkir and added, 'Kirkir, go to the barracks of the regular army and get General Gaboos for me.' Before Kirkir stood up to leave, Butler Hoob entered the room and said, 'My Queen, General Gaboos wants to see you.'

'What a coincidence! Bring him in,' the Queen said with surprise.

Hoob brought the General in. As he entered the room, General Gaboos saw Chief Gabbal, who he'd been looking for since yesterday with the Queen. 'Chief Gabbal, I'm glad to find you with Her Majesty. I've been looking for you since yesterday,' he exclaimed.

Before Gabbal could respond to him, the Queen chirped, 'General, sit down. We need to talk.'

He took a seat, and she repeated, 'General, Governor Ebbie is coming to blame me for attempting to kill his niece. He devised this horrible slander to enable him to take over the kingdom. He either wants to be a king, or he's planning to make his niece a queen. Bring in your army and defend the kingdom with the help of Chief Gabbal and Colonel Shalaqbeen.'

'My Queen, that's impossible. Governor Ebbie can't take over the kingdom that way. Instead of going to an unnecessary war with him, please summon your ministers and councillors and advise them to talk to him,' General Gaboos said.

'General, Governor Ebbie's intention is clear. He has made these false allegations with his niece to cause trouble. Deploy the regular army to defend the kingdom. Ebbie and his militia must be crushed,' she ordered him.

'My queen, give the Chief Minister and the councillors of your kingdom a chance to intervene in the situation,' Gaboos added.

The Queen didn't want to discuss her war with Ebbie with anyone. She screamed, 'General, as the queen of the nation, I'm ordering you to work with Chief Gabbal and stop that traitor who wants to overthrow my kingdom.'

'My Queen, we can't solve the problem with war at this stage. We need to understand what's going on. Give me a chance to talk to him first,' General Gaboos explained, but the Queen decided that what he meant was that he wasn't willing to fight for her. 'General, you're under arrest. Colonel Shalaqbeen, take him to the cells,' she screamed.

Shalaqbeen led the General to the cell, locked him up and returned to the chamber. Then the Queen chirped, 'Shalaqbeen, you're promoted to the rank of General. Go to the barracks of the regular army and take over the army's command.'

'But my queen.....' Shalaqbeen, unsure if he could be a General, attempted to say something, but the Queen cut him short. She shouted, 'Don't question my decision. Take the leadership of the regular army. You and Chief Gabbal must destroy the traitor.'

'Shalaqbeen, the Queen has taken the right decision. We can finish Ebbie and his militia within minutes when we have the regular army with us. Do as she said,' Gabbal interjected.

'That's right. Get the regular army ready and crush him,' The Queen said.

'We will do that, my Queen. Weed out all those who don't want to be loyal to you as you did to General Gaboos and reshape your kingdom. We'll win this war easily,' explained Gabbal, who envisaged a victory within his grasp.

'I'll reshuffle my councils, and you two will be the most powerful men in my kingdom. Go and eliminate the enemy,' she concluded. After that, Gabbal returned to his militia, and Shalaqbeen went to the regular army barracks. He came to Colonel Gaas Habbad and said, 'Colonel, I'm the regular army commander. The Queen has promoted me to the rank of General. Bring the army out on parade. I want to introduce myself to them.'

Colonel Habbad was surprised at his claim and asked, 'Where's General Gaboos?'

'He defied the Queen's order. Therefore, he's in prison,' Shalaqbeen answered calmly and relaxedly.

Habbad's blood surged with fury when he heard that the Queen had arrested General Gaboos. Thinking confusingly about what he should do about the General's unexpected arrest, he stuffed tobacco leaves in his mouth and rolled his eyes up as he used to do when he felt uncomfortable about something. After his mind wandered for moments, he said, 'Commander, come with me. I'll show you your office.' Shalaqbeen followed him. He brought him in front of a detention room that the army used to imprison those who misbehaved. He pushed him inside, locked up the door and snarled, 'Commander, we'll have you here while the Queen has General Gaboos in her cell. Have a good day.'

57

CHAPTER

The horses of Governor Ebbie's large army sending columns of dust into the air and the spears of his warriors sparkling under the sunlight, approached Zaila city from the west. His army continued towards the White Palace, and Gabbal's fighters saw the army coming, scrambled to pick up their weapons and took defensive positions. Ebbie was on the front line with Princess Dhudi, Hanad, Gabi, and his two senior lieutenants thinking about where to position his army. As they advanced towards the city, they reached a cluster of trees behind the Horse Riding and Archery Field.

He suddenly stopped his horse by the trees and shouted, 'Warriors, let us settle here.' Then their horses halted quickly, and the warriors began dismounting from them.He had chosen the place for two reasons. First, it was a place where his army could get trees to shelter, and second, it was a good spot where he could attack the Palace if things turned ugly.

The old Governor, exhausted and weak, also dismounted from his horse and ordered one of his men to climb up one of the trees and check what was happening around the Place. The man went up the tree and squinted in the direction of the Palace. With alarm, he came down in a hurry and screamed, 'Governor, there's a large army moving frantically around the Palace.'

'I think they're getting ready to engage in war with us,' said the Governor, turning his head to face a group of his men on his right side. 'Dhulkhas and Artan,' he called the names of two of the group. Then the men he named quickly moved towards him, and the Governor added, 'The two of you first go to the Chief Minister and tell him where we are and that I want to see him. Second, go to the regular army's barracks and tell General Gaboos that I want to see him too. Be careful. Don't get caught.'

Dhulkhas and Artan avoiding the army at the Palace ran in the direction of the Chief Minister's house. Before long, they came to a guard at the entrance of the Chief's house. They saluted him and told him they came to deliver a message to the Chief Minister. The guard then went to the Chief Minister, who was having a meeting with ministers and chiefs in his sitting room. He came close to him quietly and whispered in his ears, 'Chief Minister, there are two men from the Governor of Thorny Land. They want to see you. What should I do?' At this, the Chief Minister roared, 'Gentlemen, we have here two men from Governor Ebbie. They came to see me. Shall we invite them in?' And several men in the room murmured at once, 'Yes, Chief Minister. Let us have them in and hear what they would say.'

The guard ushered the two men into the room. Afterwards, the Chief Minister who recognized Artan sat forward and grunted, 'Artan, what brought you here again.'

'Chief Minister, we've been sent here by Governor Ebbie. He's waiting for you behind the Horse Riding and Archery Field with his army,' Artan responded.

'Did you tell him my message? Why did he come to the town?' The Chief Minister asked.

'Your Excellency, yes, but the Governor has his own plans. Please go and see him. It's urgent,' Artan emphasized.

'Go back and tell him I'm coming to him soon with a large delegation,' the Chief Minister instructed the messengers.

'We'll tell him your message, Chief Minister,' said Artan, turning to leave.

After that, the two messengers went to the barracks of the regular army. They came to the men in the barracks in an intense situation. Wondering what was going on, they told a guard at the gate that they had come to see General Gaboos. The guard who recognized Artan then led them to Colonel Habbad Gaas, who was in the centre of a group of men chattering around him and said, 'Commander, they come from the Governor of Thorny Land.'

Habad looked at Artan and asked, 'What can I do for you, fellas?'

'We're messengers came to see General Gaboos,' Artan explained.

'Fellas, you cannot see General Gaboos. What does the Governor want from him?'

'The Governor and his army are at the Horse Riding and Archery Field, and he wants to see the General immediately,' Artan repeated.

'The General isn't available. Tell him I'm coming instead of him.'

'We will, Colonel,' Artan replied, and the two messengers started jogging back to their leader. Before long, they'd reached Governor Ebbie waiting for their return, and Artan shouted, 'Governor, the Chief Minister and his large delegation are on their way to see you. Also, Colonel Habbad's coming to see you on behalf of General Gaboos.'

'What's the reason the General isn't coming? I asked for General Gaboos to see me,' the Governor asked.

Artan then answered, 'We don't know, Governor. However, Colonel Habbad said that the General wasn't available.'

'I see,' said the Governor, turning away to face his two senior lieutenants, Arays Danan and Ali Salool. 'Gentlemen, prepare the army. We don't want to be ambushed,' he said and then Danan and Salool strode away to the army resting under the trees. Governor Ebbie sketching a war plan under the shade of a tree, and his lieutenants organising the army in categories, Colonel Habbad arrived on a fast horse. The Governor stood up to receive him, and Habad hastily dismounted from the horse and said, 'Good day, Governor. I've been told that you want to see General Gaboos. I'm here on his behalf. What can I do for you?'

'Good day, Colonel. Is the General busy?' The Governor asked.

'No. The General is in jail,' Habbad answered.

'In jail! How did that happen?' The Governor demanded.

'After receiving your message, he went to the Queen with the Chief Minister, and the outcome of their visit wasn't pleasant, as the General later told me. This morning he went back to the Queen after he saw the large army surrounding the Palace, and she detained him afterwards. Additionally, a young General who the Queen appointed to take over the regular army confirmed his detention to us,' Habbad explained. He paused, stuffed a morsel of dry tobacco into his mouth and continued, 'I'm repeating my question. What can I do for you, Governor?'

'Who's in charge of the regular army now?' The Governor asked.

'I am in charge. I've arrested the man sent by the Queen.'

'In that case, I guess we're in the same boat. Where did the army surrounding the Palace come from?' The Governor asked.

'They're Chief Gabbal's fighters, and they're well-armed. The Queen gave them new rifles and poisonous arrows,' he paused again. He rolled his hazel, piercing eyes upward, spat out brown saliva and added, 'As you said, we're in the same boat. What are you suggesting, Governor?'

'Let us sit down and discuss what we can do together,' said Governor Ebbie. They sat together and engaged in a plan of how they could cooperate in their fight against the Queen's army if she started war. After they'd set out their war strategies, Habbad trotted back to his barracks, and Governor Ebbie went to his lieutenants. He shared the information that he had heard from Habbad with them and told them that the war was imminent. Together they went to the army, and the Governor shouted, 'Warriors, come together.' His army gathered around him, and he repeated, 'The Queen's supporters are well prepared to strike us, and they are armed with new guns and poisoned arrows. Get ready and keep your shields up at all times.'

After that, he split his men into three groups. He instructed a group armed with rifles to take defence before the Archery Field. He ordered Salool to take a group armed with arrows and bows to crouch secretly in the left far-end corner of the field and strike the enemy from the flank when it moves in. He instructed Danan to lead the third group to the field's far-right side, take cover there, and hit the enemy when it entered the field.

Furthermore, the Governor ordered the rest of the army to get ready to help those three groups whenever they needed help. Thereafter, he walked to the group with the rifles and Dhudi, wearing a red bandana on the head and armed with Jamanjug's bow and arrows, joined him with Hanad. Ebbie stopped, looked at her and said, 'What are you doing with arrows and the bow?'

'I want to fight for my friends' freedom and the honour of my family,' she replied.

'Princess, this is not your war. You and your friends must remain behind the army.'

'No, uncle, I don't want to use your army as a shield. I'm going to fight for the men that carried me on the sea and through the hot deserts.'

'No, princess. I came to Zaila to restore your status as the princess of Zaila and Thorny Land. Don't put your life at risk. Do as I say.'

'Uncle, everybody has a day to die. I must fight for my friends' freedom and my parents' legacy.'

'This isn't negotiable. Stay behind the army,' her uncle angrily shouted, and Hanad added, 'Princess, uncle's right.' From that moment, Dhudi and her friends stayed behind the army line.

CHAPTER

At the meeting in his house, the Chief Minister shouted, 'Ministers and chiefs, the Governor of Thorny Land is waiting for us. He wants to know why the Queen tried to kill the orphan Princess under her care, and of course, we want to know how the Queen could do such a horrific thing. Besides, I've received reports confirming that there is a clan militia surrounding the Palace to defend the Queen from Governor Ebbie and that the Queen elevated a junior officer to the rank of full colonel without first consulting her General of the regular army. We must find out what's going on.' Then the Interior Affairs Minister took the speech. His voice full of dismay, he yelled, 'In addition to what the Chief Minister has said, the militia surrounding the Palace belongs to her clan. Chief Gabal gathered them yesterday evening from different areas in his clan's territory. The Queen is acting as a faction leader. We need to defuse the tension before civil war breaks out.'

When he finished, a tall brown-skinned man with a well-trimmed black beard and dressed in two white sheets, one draped on his shoulders and another wrapped around his waist with a large pocket belt, stood up. He cleared his throat and roared, 'The Queen took the kingdom in the wrong direction. She's violating the monarch's code of conduct. We must stop her before things fall apart.' After he finished, the Chief Minister took the speech again. He said, 'Colleagues, the clock is ticking. Let us tell General Gaboos to deploy the regular army between the two warring sides and, subsequently, bring the Queen and Governor Ebbie together to discuss the Princess's attempted murder allegations. Let us go.'

The Chief Minister leading, they trudged to the Regular Army's barracks. They came to Colonel Habbad, whose army had already taken positions between the barracks and the White Palace. The Chief Minister wondering what was going on, said, 'Habbad, where's General Gaboos? We have come to talk to him.'

Habbad stuffed a morsel of dry tobacco leaves into his mouth, rolled his eyes up with fury and replied, 'General Gaboos is in prison, Chief Minister. The Queen had him detained this morning.'

'What happened? Why was the General arrested?' The chief minister asked with surprise.

'I don't know what exactly had happened, but I think the General has refused to fight against Governor Ebbie. A man who she sent to us this morning to take over the regular army's command told us that the General is being arrested.'

Another shocking incident unfolded in the kingdom of Zaila and Thorny Land. Astonished with the news, the Chief Minister stammered, 'Habbad, we're going to see the Governor and the Queen ourselves in person to stop the war. We'll make them talk over the issues between them. Don't engage in any battle with any side until we come back to you.'

'Chief, the General's arrest is unlawful. Only his release can deter us from going to war,' Habad demanded.

'We'll do whatever we can. Do as I said, Colonel,' said the Chief Minister, turning around to go. Leaving behind Habbad unsatisfied with his instructions, the Chief Minister and his entourage hurried off to Governor Ebbie. On the way, they saw the men the Governor placed on the southeast side of the field, and he said to his colleagues, 'It seems that all sides are already prepared for war. Hurry up, brothers. We must stop them before the situation gets out of hand.' The group reached Governor Ebbie having a private conversation with Princess Dhudi under the shade of a tree. They greeted them, and Ebbie and his niece greeted them back. After that, they all sat down under the tree, and the Chief Minister said, 'Governor, I've received your message. However, we need more information on what happened to the Princess. Tell us what you know.'

'The Princess can speak to herself. Ask her what had happened,' Governor Ebbie replied with a hint of sadness in his voice.

'That's fair to say. Princess, tell us what happened to you. The whole country wants to know what's going on between you and your stepmother. How did you end up on the island in the Red Sea,' the Chief Minister said.

Then Dhudi recounted how her stepmother had tormented her before she decided to kill her. She narrated about the night Bedel took her to the sea to kill her, the other murderous attacks she'd narrowly survived and her escape to Awsa with the thieves. She eventually finished her dark story with how she found her uncle. After that, the Chief Minister grunted sadly, 'Princess, you've had a terrifying experience. You're very lucky to survive all these events. Stay with your uncle. You'll get the justice you deserve soon.' He gazed at Governor Ebbie and added, 'Governor, don't engage in any avoidable war with the Queen's supporters. We want to find a peaceful way to solve the crisis.'

'If they attack us, we'll defend ourselves,' Governor Ebbie responded.

'Do whatever you can to avoid bloodshed,' the Chief Minister concluded, and he stood up to leave.

As he and his delegation started walking away, Dhudi halted at him, 'Chief Minister, please also get justice for the men who saved my life.'

'Don't worry, Princess. They'll get justice if we find them alive,' the Chief Minister replied and walked away with his ministers, heading towards the Palace. They crossed the Archery and Horse-riding Field and emerged into Chief Gabbal's heavily armed militia milling around the Palace. The Chief Minister and his delegation were shocked to see the clan militia had the best kingdom's military arsenal. They hurried up to the Palace and soon approached Butler Hoob, standing with another man by the main chamber's door, and the Chief Minister yelled, 'Butler, we have come to see the queen immediately.'

The butler then invited them into the chamber, and as they walked in, he said, 'Chief Minister and councillors have a seat. I'll check if the Queen is available to meet you.'

'Thank you,' said the Chief Minister, passing him to enter the room, and Butler Hoob dashed upstairs to get the

Queen. He came to her as she was sitting with Kirkir in her private chamber. 'My queen, the Chief Minister and a large group of ministers and councillors with him are waiting for you in the main chamber,' he announced from the doorstep.

Without a second thought, she replied,' I don't have time to listen to their nonsense. Tell them that I'm not at home and advise them to come back tomorrow morning.

As the butler took the stairs back to the main chamber, she twisted her neck to Kirkir and said, 'Go to Chief Gabbal and Colonel Shalaqbeen. Tell them to attack Governor Ebbie right now and crush him immediately.'

'My Queen, why didn't you want to see the Chief Minister and those with him?' Kirkir curiously asked her before he left.

'Kirkir, do you think it is a good idea to discuss what we've done with the Chief Minister, the councillors and Governor Ebbie?' she asked.

He replied, 'No, my queen, I'm only asking to satisfy my curiosity.'

'Kirkir, the solution to our problem lies in crushing Governor Ebbie and changing the Chief Minister. Go and tell Chief Gabbal and Shalaqbeen to attack the Governor and destroy him,' Queen Idil, determined to destroy her opponents, emphasised. In response to her order, Kirkir ran downstairs in a hurry. He passed by the Chief Minister and those with him, leaving the main chamber disappointingly and hastened on to Chief Gabbal. He found him with a group of his militia outside the Palace parameter, and he explained to him about the Chief Minister's visit to the Palace and the Queen's decision to wage an immediate war. Gabbal looked in the direction of the sun on the western horizon and said, 'My friend, it's too late to launch a war. It will be dark soon.'

'Chief, it's ordered. You must do it.'

Gabbal looked in the sun's direction again and murmured, 'It isn't a good time to start a war. However, it looks like we have no choice.'

Leaving behind Gabbal about to sprint into action, Kirkir dashed to the Regular Army's barracks to tell Shalaqbeen the Queen's decision for the immediate war. To his surprise, he came to find the regular army already ready for action between the Palace and their camp. He came to Colonel Habbad and said, 'Colonel, where is Commander Shalaqbeen?'

Habbad looked at him slyly and said, 'Do you want to see him?' And Kirkir replied, 'yes.'

'Follow me,' he said, and Kirkir followed him. He led him to the barracks. In minutes he brought him to the room where he'd already imprisoned Colonel Shalaqbeen. He said to two guards at the door, 'open the door,' and they opened it. Then he pushed Kirkir inside and said, 'Join your friend. He needs company.' After that, he walked back to his army, leaving the guards locking the door.

59

CHAPTER

In response to the Queen's order, Chief Gabbal organised his fighters for a full-scale assault on Ebbie's warriors. Unaware of the men Governor Ebbie had planted on both sides of the field, he sent a battalion armed with new guns to strike Ebbie's army behind the field. While he was organising the second wave of his attack, the battalion with the latest firearms dashed into the open lot and opened fire on Ebbie's men and Ebbie's army fired back a few guns they had. The crackle of the sudden gunfire forced birds to fly away and people in the city to come out of their homes and ask each other about the unexpected gunfire. The Gabbal's battalion, still shooting their rifles, kept moving forward until they were deep in the field. Then Ebbie's men on the sides of the field attacked them unexpectedly with flying arrows and catapulted slingshots from different directions. Then the

Gabbal's gunmen now trapped in their enemy, fought hard and at the same time started retreating. Gabbal saw his army being besieged retreating and leaving behind guns and corpses scattered in the field. He sent a brigade armed with poisonous arrows and guns as reinforcements. They rushed onto the battleground, firing their deadly arrows and bullets at Ebbie's men on the sides of the field, and others attempted to grab guns from the corpses scattered on the ground. Ebbie also saw his rival's arrows and bullets taking out his men randomly and sent backup men armed with lances, bows, arrows, and spears to help them. Hanad and Gabi were among this group.

The two armies kept fighting hard. However, Ebbie's men almost succumbed to the pressure of Gabbal's mighty army Colonel Habbad's regular brigade struck Gabbal's men from the east side. It was a big blow to Gabbal, but the Chief and his men fought ferociously to defend themselves and the palace. Sadly, the regular army's power and fighting skills were irresistible, and Ebbie's army benefitting from this opportunity fought back robustly. This was so much so that Gabbal's army was forced to retreat to their positions near the Palace.

Queen Idil was watching the war from the balcony of her house. She didn't lift her eyes from the direction of the battle from the moment it erupted, and she was frightened when she saw the regular army helping Ebbie and Gabbal's militia move back to the Palace. Wondering what on earth was going on, she came out of the building and saw men carrying bodies dangled on their shoulders and others limping with injuries returning from the war zone. Her gaze shifting from corner to corner of the Palace's compound, she spotted Chief Gabbal in the middle of a bunch of his militia, entering the building from the west wing. She waited for him to come, eager to ask what had happened, and Gabbal saw her and walked briskly towards her. He approached her hastily and said, 'My Queen, you should have been sitting in your chamber. What brought you out?'

'Chief, why is the regular army helping Ebbie? What happened?' She asked anxiously.

'My Queen, we saw them turning against us. However, don't worry. We've enough men and new reinforcements will arrive soon.'

'Where's Shalaqbeen?' She asked worryingly.

'I don't know where he is. All I can see is the Regular Army attacking us with Ebbie,' he emphasised.

'Have you seen Kirkir,' she asked, and Gabbal replied, 'No. The last time I saw him, he was on his way to the barracks to deliver your message.'

She looked around to check if someone was eavesdropping on them, and when she confirmed that they were alone, she chirped, 'Chief, I've got the feeling that Shalaqbeen and Kirkir are in trouble and the regular army is against us. What can we do?'

'My Queen, don't worry. We belong to the largest clan of the kingdom. Our countless warriors will come, and we'll strike them while they're still sleeping. We'll crush the enemies at dawn. Go back to your chamber and relax.'

'Please do your best. We can't afford failure,' the Queen emphasised and walked back to her private chamber. On the way, she met Butler Hoob and asked him, 'Are the Chief Minister and those with him coming back tomorrow?'

'Yes, Your Majesty. He said that they would be back at nine,' Hoob explained and then she walked to her private chamber, thinking about her increasing enemies.

60

CHAPTER

A night of uncertainty followed the bitter war. Those who intellectually could understand the peril of the armed conflict gathered in the enclosures of their houses or in public places and talked about nothing but the ferocious battle that raged unexpectedly on the west side of the palace. The ministers and councillors of the kingdom and the traditional leaders gathered again in the Chief Minister's house, and they debated over what they could do their kingdom split up into factions killing each other. Queen Idil, disturbed by the regular army turning against her and worrying about the absence of Shalaqbeen and Kirkir, was restless throughout the night. Governor Ebbie and Colonel Habbad needed each other to have a midnight meeting to discuss new war strategies to maim Gabbal's military power. Gabbal sensed his opponents' increasing pressure was either preparing his militia for tomorrow's mighty offensive or recruiting fresh fighters from his clan. The city had an edgy night.

Sadly, the worst came at the dawn of the following day when Governor Ebbie and Colonel Habbad struck Gabbal and his men from different directions. Then the sudden gunfire woke up the city, and the ordinary citizens, traditional leaders, councillors and ministers of the kingdom all rushed out of their homes.

Councillors and chiefs gathered at the Chief Minister's house yet again, and after a brief meeting to discuss the war, they flocked to the White Palace to tell the queen to stop the war. On their way to the palace, they meet crowds of people gathered already in the main streets. Together they streamed towards the Palace, shouting slogans demanding that the battle be stopped. The Chief Minister leading the councillors and people demonstrating against the war, continued marching towards the Palace. As they came closer to the Palace, the battle intensified further, and stray bullets hit two demonstrators, forcing others to dodge behind buildings. From that moment, the leaders and the demonstrators couldn't go any further because of the flying bullets. The Chief Minister and the councillors wondering what they should do next and dodging bullets behind the Palace wall with demonstrators, Gabbal and his militia running for their lives, came in a rush and passed by them in a hurry, heading eastward.

This was followed by the White Palace falling to the regular army and Governor Ebbie. Colonel Habbad and the Governor with Dhudi, Gabi and Hanad, were among those who first entered the building from the back door, and straightaway, they went to the palace cell rooms. They found the four thieves in terrible shape and crammed in one room and General Gaboos in the other cell. They'd freed them. Then Dhudi, ecstatic to see the house where she had grown up and couldn't suppress her urge to take vengeance on her stepmother, walked to the monarchy's section.

'Princess, don't go there,' said her uncle, who understood her intention. She stopped, and he added, 'Let us go.' Her heart still inclining to the house, they followed General Gaboos, Colonel Habbad and the prisoners who had just started walking towards the forecourt of the building. General Gaboos and Colonel Habbad were talking over the security of the palace in front and others following them, the Chief Minister with the kingdom's councillors, and a massive crowd of demonstrators entered the building from the main gate and flooded inside.

General Gaboos walked briskly towards them. He met the Chief Minister and those with him in the middle of the forecourt and said, 'Chief Minister and councillors, sorry I couldn't come back to you. I guess you know what has happened.'

'I know what happened to you. Colonel Habbad told me that the queen arrested you. Is the Palace secure and safe?' The Chief Minister asked.

'The regular army took over the control of the building. I guess everything should be fine,' the General explained.

'Where's the queen?' asked the Chief Minister.

'I think she's in her chambers,' General Gaboos replied.

The Chief Minister turned round to face the demonstrators, and then with his voice as loud as he could, he shouted, 'People of Zaila and Thorny Land, we've had days and nights of uncertainty in this week. Nonetheless, our torments are almost over now. Go home. We'll address the public when we get enough information from the sides who fought.'

As the words trailed off from his lips, a woman shrieked in the crowd, 'Chief Minister, is it true that the queen had tried to kill the orphan princess under her care? Before she got an answer, a man yelled from the far corner of the crowd, 'Chief Minister, why did the queen give the sophisticated weapons for the regular army to her clan's militia?'

The Chief Minister replied, 'We can't answer your questions now. Go home. We'll come back to you with the answers to your questions.' Thereafter, the folks started returning to the town, and the Chief Minister and a large group of officials hastened to the Queen's chambers. They came to her walking up and down confusingly in the building hallway, and the Chief Minister said, 'Your Majesty, the councils of your kingdom want to talk to you.'

Without uttering a word, she walked to her private chamber, and they followed her. She sat down on her cushions and chirped, 'What do you want to talk to me about?'

'Your Highness, your people have many questions you need to answer. Our citizens are craving to know what's happening within this kingdom.'

'What are the questions they have for me?' She asked.

'They want to know why you gave the weapons for the regular army to the militia of your clan and what you've done to the orphan princess. In addition to these, we want to know the reason you've promoted one of your security men to the rank of colonel before arresting General Gaboos,' answered Chief Minister.

'Some of these are silly questions. However, I'll tell the truth to my people. When do you want me to address the nation, Chief Minister?' She said, trying hard to show that she was a decent queen.

'Your Majesty, there's suspicion of a crime. It would be best if you answered the questions put to you by your people before the court of justice,' the Chief Minister explained.

'Am I a criminal? Why is the congregation going to take place in the courthouse?' She demanded.

The Chief Minister couldn't rush to answer her question. He thought for a moment and said, 'Your Majesty, the congregation is taking place in court because the public wants to know the truth, and there could be witnesses and victims willing to challenge you. You must come to the Justice House on Wednesday morning at 9:00 am.'

The queen couldn't find the right words to say and remained silent. The Chief Minister waited for her response for a while, but Queen Idil trapped in her wicked deeds, didn't say anything. Then the Chief Minister stood up and said, 'Your Majesty, see you at the Justice House.' He then led his delegation back to Governor Ebbie with the Princess and her friend chatting on the Palace's forecourt. He told them that the court hearing would occur on Friday morning and that the venue would be the Zaila courthouse. He also told General Gaboos to bring to the court Shalaqbeen and Kirkir. Lastly, the chief Minister looked at Governor Ebbie and said, 'Governor, you and the Princess would stay with me until the court hearing. You're my guests. Let us go.' Thereafter, the Chief Minister led his delegation, including Dhudi, Hanad and her uncle, to his house.

On Tuesday evening Yussuf Saeem, the keeper of the kingdom's stores carrying a red chest decorated with glittering golden dots, came to Princess Dhudi, Hanad, her uncle, General Gaboos and a group of councillors in the Chief Minister's living room. He stopped at the door and shouted from there, 'I apologize for the intrusion. Princess, may I talk to you privately?'

'Sure,' she said, and at the same time, she rose from her seat.

'Hold it. Please talk to the princess here,' said her uncle, eyeing the box Yusuf was carrying and understanding why he wanted to talk to her privately.

'If the princess wishes me to do so, I will, Governor,' Yusuf responded, and Dhudi wondering what was going on, added, 'You can talk to me here, Yusuf.'

He sat down and said, 'Your Highness, do you know my name?'

'Yes. You're Yussuf Saeem, the keeper of the kingdom's stores,' she answered.

'I've got another name. Did your father ever tell you my other name?'

'What do you mean by your other name?' She asked with surprise.

'Before he passed away, did he mention to you a man with the name Wiseman?'

'Yes, he did, but he never told me exactly who he was and how I could find him.'

'I'm Wiseman and the scroll keeper that I believe your father told you about. Today I came to give you this box. Your parents advised me to give it to you when you turn fifteen, and now you've reached that age. It contains the scroll your father mentioned to you and your other personal properties. Please receive it with my utmost respect.'

He gave her the box, and Dhudi taking it, said, 'I never suspected that this person my father told me about was you. Why did my father make you such a mysterious person?' asked Dhudi taking the box from him.

'It's the kingdom's rule that young inheritors should not have access to their assets and the public responsibilities until they become fifteen. Now is the time. Good luck, princess,' he concluded and stood up to leave.

She opened the box and examined the things in it. There was a yellow scroll, dazzling gold pieces, money, and sparkling pearl beads. One side of the scroll was written on how to run a kingdom and good leadership principles and the song her parents sang for her when she was a baby. The other side explained the family's assets and hoards, the names of their friends and foes, and how her ancestors had ruled the country for many generations. 'These are amazing things,' she said under her breath. She closed the box, and her uncle said, 'This box will help us at tomorrow's court hearing. Bring it with you.

61

CHAPTER

—❧—

Wednesday morning came. Regrettably, it was an unusual Wednesday morning for the people of Zaila City and Thorny Land because their queen was on trial for crimes against humanity. People from all walks of life wanted to know what the queen would say about the disappearance of the young princess and the reason behind the ferocious war that had divided the kingdom streamed to the Zaila Justice Centre. Those who came early had crammed into the court hall and the less fortunate others who came late clustered outside the building. As agreed, Queen Idil, dressed in her royal attire and travelling on Beautie, the special royal horse wagon, emerged onto the forecourt of the courthouse at 9:15 am. Looking at her sides alternately, smiling at the spectators, and waving her right hand in the air to greet the people waiting for her trial, she continued towards the court hall.

Bizarrely no one smiled back or waved a hand at her in response to her queenly gesture. Instead, the country's citizens, convinced she was a wicked queen, looked down to show their dissatisfaction with her. *'They're idiots without respect,'* she thought and carried on her journey. The wagon stopped at the courtroom entrance, the queen and the citizens accusing each other silently. She climbed down from it and walked into the court hall. Then one of the court ushers directed her to a bejewelled chair that waited for her in the court.

Immediately after she sat down, an usher opened a back door to the court. Then The judge of Zaila Court, Hoosh Sandool, dressed in his court black robes, entered, and the usher shouted, 'All rise.' Everyone jumped on their feet, and the Judge walked in. He took his majestic seat, and then wriggling his thin rump on the chair to sit appropriately, he shouted, 'People in Zaila, today we have here an unusual case. The public has questions the queen has to answer. In the hearing, there would be witnesses and victims giving evidence. "Now, I'm calling Queen Idil Gabadah to answer the questions I'm going to ask her on behalf of the public. Your majesty, get in the witness box," the Judge commanded.

Queen Idil walked into the witness box, and those in the front rows in the court gallery frenziedly chattered, 'Our queen's disgraced. She's in the witness box.' The Judge heard the chatter of the people in the hall and yelled furiously, 'Everyone, silence. The court is to begin.' In response to his call, everyone at once stopped their chatter.

Judge Sandool never had in his court any advisors at his side when judging a case. Neither did his court ever have attorneys to defend plaintiffs, nor did a prosecutor accuse people of crimes they might have committed. He only needed a clerk to write down his verdicts, an usher to show the defendants the witness box, and security men to haul away those he had sentenced to a detention centre in the Red Sea. 'Queen Idil Gabadah, you're accused of inciting civil war and causing the death of many soldiers, attempted murders, humiliating and enslaving a member of the royal family, abuse of power and misuse of the public money, incompetence in leadership and promoting a junior officer to high ranks for your advantage. Are you guilty of these charges or not guilty?' The Judge shouted.

'I'm pleading not guilty, your honour,' she snarled.

'The usher of this court gave me the names of your victims and a list of witnesses willing to testify against you. Are you still denying committing these crimes?'

'Yes, I still deny all of them,' she repeated.

'In that case, I must ask you this question. Did you try to kill your stepdaughter, Dhudi, descendent of King Erek, your late husband?' The judge asked.

'That's a ridiculous accusation,' she responded.

'Your Highness, Princess Dhudi, stand up,' Judge Sandool cried. 'Tell us what happened to you before and after you went missing.'

Dhudi, who had yearned to get such an opportunity for a long time, got on her feet and began narrating her painful experience. '*After my father died, Queen Idil made me an enslaved person who scrubs the floors for her and her two children. Then she tried to kill me twice when I was nearly fifteen. Her first attempt was one night when she sent Beddel Subagleh, one of the servants working for the kingdom. He came to my room at midnight with a sack.*' Dhudi, in the middle of her sad story, and the audience mesmerized by her story, gawking at her, a tall thin man as dark as charcoal pushed himself through the crowd in the courtroom. The man dressed in a ragged gown and a tattered shirt continued towards the bench, and the guards hurried to stop him. He struggled with them, shouting, 'Let me reach the princess! I must talk to her.'

The guards grappling with him, The Judge shouted, 'Let him in if he is unarmed.'

The guards then checked if he was armed and then set him free. He hurried to Princess Dhudi. He prostrated in front of her and sobbed, 'My princess, please forgive me or take your vengeance on me. I can't carry the burden of my sins anymore.'

Dhudi couldn't cognize him immediately. 'Who are you? Tell me what you have done to me before I forgive you,' She asked.

'Don't you recognize me?' He said, lifting his head. 'I'm a servant Bedel, the man who almost killed you in the sea. I want justice to be done in this court, regardless of whatever you want to do to me.'

'You're unrecognizable, Bedel. I couldn't recognize you until I looked at your face closely. What happened to you?' Asked the princess, feeling pity for him.

'It's a long story, and I can't tell it in this court. Can I explain it to you later?' he moaned.

'Bedel, sit properly and tell us your long story. We all want to hear it now,' screeched the Judge, who was interested in his story.

Servant Bedel sat up properly and bellowed, 'Princess after you'd swam away in the dark sea that night, I returned to the city. I went to my house, spilt chicken blood on the machete with which I was supposed to kill you, and took it to the queen. I told her that I had killed you, and then she gave me a fortune. I shouldn't have agreed to take your life in exchange for receiving a fortune. I don't know what came over me. Anyway, I didn't use her fortune. I buried it in my house's backyard, and sometime later, an arsonist burned my house down. Then I escaped with my family to a forest in Thorny Land. Since then, we have lived in a lonely forest between the City of Five Gates and Jigjiga to avoid the authorities. I was thrilled when I heard that you're alive, and I've been looking for you from the moment your uncle found you at the border and your news spread in Thorny Land. I'm glad we're here together today.'

People in the courtroom were astonished at the queen's brutality and were mesmerized by his story. When he had finished, Dhudi, saddened by what had happened to him, said, 'Bedel, you're skinny and unrecognizable. I guess your family is in terrible shape as well. I forgive you. Remember, you didn't kill me. You did the right thing when you let me swim away, and that's why I'm still alive.'

'Thank you, my princess, but I must confess I missed the point. I should have run away with you and my family, but I fell into the devil's trap.'

Judge Sandool was shocked by what he had heard. He looked at the list of the witnesses and cried, 'Jamanjug Falahfalah rise. Tell us how you met the princess and ended up with her in Awsa.'

Jamanjug stood up quickly. 'Y...your ha...honour, we found the princess sleeping in our house on Faay Island, and later the queen came to the island at midnight with that man,' he stammered, pointing at Kirkir. 'He gave the princess a poison that almost killed her, and I shot him in the buttocks,' added Jamanjug, pointing his forefinger at his right buttock. The people in the hall then laughed at his action from corner to corner of the room.

'Silence,' cried Judge Sandool, grinning with amusement at Jamanjug, showing his teeth that pointed forward like those of the mole rat. 'Carry on, Jamanjug. How do you know that the attackers were the queen and Kirkir and that you shot him in the buttocks?'

'After they captured us from Awsa, he told me that he would punish me for the pain inflicted on him by the arrows that I put in his bottom that night, and we found the queen's bag after the attack.'

Judge Sandool then said, 'Sit down, Jamanjug. Your evidence is overwhelmingly important. Kirkir, did you threaten Jamanjug in Awsa because he shot you in the buttocks on Faay Island that night when you and the queen went there to kill the princess.'

'Your honour, this little thief shot us when the queen and I tried to bring the princess home. He's a criminal.'

Judge Sandool had reached his verdict now and shouted, 'Kirkir, you were a trusted assistant of the queen, and you helped her to commit heinous crimes.' He paused, glanced at Queen Idil, and shouted again, 'Our queen, we trusted you as our leader, but you're a killer and a blackmailer. You've organized widespread killings, enslaved a little princess in your care, and misused our kingdom's property and power. I am sending you and your assistants, Kirkir, Chief Gabbal, and Farah Shalaqbeen, where there are no people to kill or to mislead. You'll go to Faay Island to replace the good thieves who saved the young princess's life. You'll stay there for the rest of your lives. Take off the kingdom's crown from your head and give it to the Chief Minister, who will officially pass it to the rightful bearer.'

The people in the hall cheered loudly at his decision.

Queen Idil's reign didn't fizzle down gradually, but it plummeted from its heights all at once. Her unwitting evil plans and her greedy personality got her to lose everything she had, including the wealth and the kingdom she'd inherited from her late husband. The loyal army she surrounded herself with and the assets she'd given away to cover her dark secrets couldn't keep her in power. She slowly removed the crown from her head and gave it to the Chief Minister. After that, with her head down, she was hauled out with her assistants by the court guards, and the judge screamed, 'Citizens, that is the end of today's court hearing. Go home,' and then one of the audience in the court gallery shouted, 'Judge Sandool, when will the kingdom councils announce the successor?

'The councillors will have a session to discuss the successor immediately after the ordinary citizens vacate the courtroom,' the judge explained. At this point, the people began streaming out of the court hall. When the vast audience exited the door, the Chief Minister holding the golden crown in his right hand, twisted his neck towards the judge and said, 'Judge Sandool, we need to appoint the successor. I want to invite councils of the kingdom to discuss who will lead the country.'

'Chief Minister, I agree with you. Let us do it right away,' Judge Sandool cried.

'I think the selection of the successor is straightforward. The late king's daughter is the heiress of the crown,' the Governor of Thorny Land and the City of Five Gates said.

'Governor, I disagree. The children of the disgraced queen are part of the monarchy and have the right to seek the throne. More importantly, Princess Dhudi is a minor. She can't be the bearer of the crown yet,' one of the councillors explained.

'Princess Dhudi is the only rightful heiress, and she's mature enough to take the lead according to the rules of our kingdom. She has turned fifteen already, and she received her red box yesterday. She must be crowned right away,' the Governor of Thorny Land and the City of Five Gates repeated.

'Councillors, you heard what the Governor said. Does anyone disagree with what he said?' The Chief Minister yelled.

'Before we anoint the princess as the queen of the country, we must decide the role of the children of the disgraced queen,' the minister of justice yelled, and another councillor hollered, 'The children of that queen have no right to challenge Princess Dhudi. She's the rightful heiress and the nation's favourite princess. She must have the coronation.'

Thereafter, they unanimously agreed that Princess Dhudi would be the country's queen and the Chief Minister put the crown on her head and said, 'Let us introduce the new queen to the citizens waiting for us outside.'

Queen Dhudi had the golden crown on her head and had the kingdom's councils on her sides, followed the Chief Minister, who led them out of the courtroom. The procession taking graceful steps, marched towards the Zaila citizens chatting in groups on the forecourt of the courthouse and waiting for the councillors' decision. As they reached the centre of the open lot, they stopped, and people started swarming around them. When the crowd had grown huge, the Chief Minister shouted, 'Ladies and Gentlemen, people of Zaila and Thorny Land, on your behalf, the kingdom's councils have discussed the rightful bearer of the crown. We've chosen Princess Dhudi, the late king's daughter, as the queen of Zaila and Thorny Land.' As these words came out of his mouth, the people cheered from corner to corner and started singing the following song:

Our beautiful queen, welcome home

Hoobeey yaahoo

We're celebrating your coronation

Hoobeey yahoo

It is a big day for all of us

Hoobeey yaahoo

We'll fight for you, queen

Hoobeey yahoo

And the glory will be on our side

Hoobeey yaahoo

Folks will dance days and nights for you

Hoobeey yahoo

God Save the Queen of Zaila and Thorny Land

Hoobeey yahoo

The new queen's celebration hit the air in full force. Amazingly, it took an exciting twist after Jamanjug and Gabi danced with the crowd and played juggling stones. The crowd still dancing and singing, the Chief Minister said, 'Let us go, my queen.' Dhudi held Hanad's hand affectionately, and the councillors followed him towards the White Palace. As they started their journey, Jamanjug and Gabi hastened to Dhudi, and Gabi said, 'Your Majesty, are we free now?'

'You're free as the wind, Gabi. We're all free,' Dhudi explained.

'In that case, Jamanjug and I are going back to Awsa. Goodbye, your Majesty,' Gabi repeated.

'You're my family. Why are you leaving me?' Said Dhudi

'My Queen, I always wanted to be a father. I'm going to marry Marian,' Gabi replied, and Jamajug quickened to say, 'I want to be a father too. I'm going to Jawhara.' Dhudi smiled at them and said, 'You can be who you want to be, my brothers. Say hello to your future wives for me and come back with them,' and Jamanjug said, 'We will, your majesty.'

As Gabi and Jamanjug turned away to leave, Hanad said, 'Say hello to my mum for me too and tell her that I'm with Dhudi, the queen of Zaila and Thorny Land and that I'm going to be a real prince.'

Dhudi looked at the other thieves huddled next to Gabi and Jamanjug and said, 'Kalah, you're going to be my court jester. Shaman, you'll be my fortuneteller and Daweel, you'll be the messenger of the queen of Zaila and Thorny Land. Let us go.' After that, Queen Dhudi, Daweel, Kalah, Hanad and Shaman followed the Chief Minister and his delegation to the Royal Palace.

– END –

www.ingramcontent.com/pod-product-compliance
Lightning Source LLC
Chambersburg PA
CBHW030556170726
48283CB00002B/356